Raves for Stephen Blackmoore's Eric Carter novels

"For a book all about dead things, this novel is alive with great characters and a twisty, scary-funny story that teaches you not to tango with too much necromancy. My favorite book this year, bar none."
— Chuck Wendig, author of the Miriam Black series

"Breathtaking . . . Carter's wry voice is amusing as ever, but the grief he carries is palpable, adding depth and a sense of desperation to this action-packed adventure. Readers will be eager for more after this thrilling, emotionally fraught installment." — *Publishers Weekly* (starred)

"Not only met, but exceeded, my expectations. . . . Plenty of action and magic-slinging rounds out this excellent second novel from one of my favorite authors." — My Bookish Ways

"In *Dead Things*, Stephen Blackmoore expands upon the Los Angeles supernatural world he first conjured in *City of the Lost*. Blackmoore is going places in urban fantasy, and readers fond of dark tales should keep their eyes on him. Highly recommended." — SFRevu

"Blackmoore can't write these books fast enough to suit me. *Broken Souls* is hyper-caffeinated, turbo-bloody, face-stomping fun. This is the L.A.-noir urban fantasy you've been looking for."
— Kevin Hearne, author of The Iron Druid Chronicles

"Eric Carter's adventures are bleak, witty, and as twisty as a fire-blasted madrone, told in prose as sharp as a razor. Blackmoore is the rising star of pitch-black paranormal noir. A must-read series."
— Kat Richardson, author of the Greywalker series

"Fans will find plenty to enjoy in the long-awaited third outing of necromancer Eric Carter. Blackmoore infuses his increasingly detailed and dangerous urban fantasy landscape with grim yet fascinating characters, and ensures that every step of Carter's epic journey is a perilously fascinating one." — *RT Reviews*

*Novels by Stephen Blackmoore
available from DAW Books:*

CITY OF THE LOST
DEAD THINGS
BROKEN SOULS
HUNGRY GHOSTS
FIRE SEASON
GHOST MONEY
BOTTLE DEMON
SUICIDE KINGS
HATE MACHINE*

*Coming soon from DAW Books

SUICIDE KINGS

STEPHEN BLACKMOORE

DAW BOOKS, INC.
DONALD A. WOLLHEIM, FOUNDER
1745 Broadway, New York, NY 10019
ELIZABETH R. WOLLHEIM
SHEILA E. GILBERT
PUBLISHERS
www.dawbooks.com

First Printing, April 2021
1st Printing

ACKNOWLEDGMENTS

There are four questions that keep me up at night. 1. Why do we park on a driveway but drive on a parkway? 2. Did they realize what it sounded like when they called it a "manhole"? 3. How do you solve a problem like Maria? and 4. The fuck do I write in the acknowledgments?

Those first three questions above I fear will remain unanswered. But what about the fourth?

As I write this, it's just a few days into 2022, which I still have trouble believing isn't 2019 or Year 227 of The Plague. It has been, put mildly, an absolute clusterfuck. We've got a new variant of COVID cramming people into hospitals, idiots making it worse by indulging in that most American of pastimes, "Fuck everybody else who isn't me," and a dreadful misunderstanding of the difference between tapeworms and viruses.

We have lost friends. We have lost family. We have had our lives turned upside down and changed forever. We have become connoisseurs of grief.

I don't think I would have been able to survive it without the friends and family who cheered me on and kept me going.

And so, with the caveat that I know I will forget whole scads of people because that's what I do, here are only a tiny handful of the people who helped make this possible.

My wife Kari, my agent Lisa Rodgers, Betsy Wollheim, Josh Starr, and the entire gang at DAW, dear friends Peter Clines, Chuck Wendig, Kevin Hearne, Jaye Wells, Lish McBride, ML Brennan, Kristi Charish, Jaime Lee Moyer, Lili Saintcrow, Jeff Macfee, Elsa Sjunneson, Meghan Ball, Enfys Book, Brian White, Nathan Long, and most importantly, you.

YES, YOU! THE ONE READING THIS. This is the seventh
Eric Carter book. There is a lot going on, I know. And there are a lot
of other things you could be doing.

Thank you. I appreciate you taking time to sit down with it, and I
hope it is worthy of your attention.

Chapter 1

Wizard fights. They're a thing.

Here's what they're not: Ancient, long-bearded men casting lightning at each other from distant mountaintops. Teenage children waving around wands while everyone around them ignores the phallic implications. They don't happen in a boarding school, an enchanted forest, or far underground where the dwarves dug too deep.

Think a lot less Gandalf and a lot more Thunderdome. They are brutal, bloody affairs of magic and MMA in a no-holds-barred battle mixing fireballs with double collar ties. Even in a "respectable" fight—we've got our own league and everything—people still lose limbs, get disfigured, die.

"I remember a time you were down there," Alice says. We're watching a fight in the Pit between two mages who are kicking the living shit out of each other. One of them has mastered the art of pushing air with his punches so by the time he slams his opponent in the face his fist is really more of an afterthought.

"That was, literally, a lifetime ago," I say. "I was young and stupid. Now I'm just stupid."

Alice doesn't really care who comes to fight or how they fight. Or in my case, how old they happen to be when they fight. I was seventeen.

Alice lets the fighters sort it out themselves for the most part. Before anyone goes in the Pit, the fighters fill out a card saying what they are or aren't okay with. Standard league rules? No fighter leaves until one of them's unconscious? No fireballs, lightning storms, or summoning dead rats? That last one wasn't a thing until I came around.

The cards get sorted to the closest match and that's who you fight. No match? Then you get the leftovers and hope you walk away at the end of the evening. And if a few mages die, well, that's not Alice's problem.

Animate a couple thousand dead cockroaches to go running up the other guy's legs and pretty soon most people don't want to fight you. The ones who do are the meanest, ugliest, hardest motherfuckers around.

More often than not they'd use their fists, not their magic. I learned a lot fighting those guys. Mostly how to get my ass kicked, but after a while, how to *not* get my ass kicked.

Alice and I are in their office overlooking the Pit, the bleachers, the money booths. There's nowhere they can't see when they watch the fights.

"You could have gone pro," they say. I have to laugh at that.

"One, I wasn't that good," I say. "And two, nobody would have let me into the league." There are certain knacks, the type of magic a mage is really good at, that are banned from fighting professionally.

Necromancers creep people out and everybody thinks we can do all sorts of shit we can't, like summon their greatest fears: spiders, clowns, third-grade schoolteachers, alcoholic fathers. Mesmerists get the other guys to punch themselves in the face too often—it's pretty funny to watch. Erotimancers . . . those fights tend to turn into something entirely different, though equally entertaining, on the mat.

They're all fair points, though why anybody has a problem with the erotimancers I honestly don't know.

Necromancy has a stigma, and why wouldn't it? Dealing with death is confronting and when you're in the middle of doing something where you might actually wind up dead, people get weird.

Also, everybody seems to think we've all got huge armies of the dead. Like we've got that much freezer space lying around.

"Still," they say. Alice, or Quick Change Alice as they're known to most, is currently a tall Persian woman with glowing golden eyes. "I could have made a lot of money off of you."

"You say the nicest things. By the way," I say, "I like the look."

"Thank you," they say. They look down at their body and run their hands down their skirt, smoothing out a couple wrinkles. "I only have it for a few more days. I think I've got a Taiwanese stockbroker next. I have to check my schedule. A man this time. I don't like him much, but you work with what you've got."

Alice, in case you haven't guessed, isn't human. I'm not sure what they are. They don't actually have a corporeal form, or if they do, I've never seen it. Instead, they borrow other people's skins.

The skins are from those who've lost too much at the fights, or at one of Alice's casinos over in Hawaiian Gardens. It's their IOU. If you can't pay your debts, Alice will take your marker; for a few days every year for the rest of your life, you're going to black out and Alice gets your skin. I hear it hurts a lot.

"Well, this one suits you," I say. "That our guy?"

One fight has just ended and another is about to start in five minutes. The Pit is in a converted airplane hangar at Long Beach Airport. It's moved around a bit since the airport opened in the twenties, but it's been there in one form or another as long as the airport has.

Alice has put wards and protections on the place that not only keep it invisible from prying eyes, but fold the space around it. A normal, or someone with insufficient magical ability, won't see it, and the space that it exists in simply isn't there for them. It's impressive work.

Mages see it fine. The fold covers the hangar and a sizable chunk of parking space to accommodate at least as many people as she has seats.

Every one of which is filled right now. The place isn't huge. Stadium seating to hold five hundred tops. Usually you'd see fifty, maybe sixty people here on a good night. But right now the place is packed.

In the middle of the ring stands an illusion of Quick Change Alice, a persona they've developed over the years that builds on their primary skill. It changes every few seconds, an old Asian woman, a young black man, boys, girls, men, women, announcing the next fight.

To hear Alice tell it, they can't do anything like that. They take a skin, and yeah, they can do it fast, but not that fast. And once they're in it, they're stuck until the time runs out.

But over the years they've shown up to enough people in different guises to make capitalizing off the lie easy. Everyone assumes Alice could be anyone, which technically is true, but practically doesn't really work that way. It's a useful story they go out of their way to promote.

It's helped keep the rabble away as well as helping Alice maintain some sort of public identity, something they need if they're going to run an operation like this.

"Yeah, that's him on the left." Two fighters are getting ready in their respective spots, stretching, getting hydrated, whatever. The one Alice is pointing out is young, early twenties, got a physique you can only buy from the right sorts of mages. He moves like he's still trying to figure out how his modified body works.

An airhorn blows and a countdown begins. When it hits zero, gates in the cage slide open, letting the fighters in and then closing up behind them.

The Pit's different from when I was fighting. Used to be just dirt blocked off with sandbags. With all that magic flying around, if you sat in the splash zone you deserved what you got.

Now it's an octagon with chain link fencing like you'd see at any

MMA style fight, only more so. The entire thing is encased in a sphere of ensorcelled and warded chain link that keeps any magic from going out or coming in. More or less. It's got some gaps.

The last thing the audience wants is to get flash-roasted from an errant fireball. The last thing the fighters want is the audience tossing random spells in to help their favorite.

The fighters come out onto the mat and it's obvious that the guy who recently bulked up doesn't know how to fight worth a damn. He's running away from his opponent, blocking with weak shield spells, but he's not engaging.

Then he gets close and throws out a palm strike that connects with his opponent's chest, who immediately falls down limp onto the mat. Fight's called, guy goes out on a stretcher.

At least, that's what everybody else sees.

"Huh," I say.

"You know what he did?" Alice says.

"Oh, yeah," I say. "This happens every time?"

"One shot, guy goes down, doesn't get back up again."

"Yeah, they won't. They're all in comas now, right?"

"That's been kept kinda quiet."

"So, nobody's connected them all together and looked at the one thing they had in common yet."

"I'm not stupid," Alice says, annoyed. "That's why I asked you to come take a look. I think I know what he's doing, but I need a professional opinion."

"How long's he been at it?"

"A month now? Maybe two. Noticed it the first week he was in the ring. I mean everybody else has, too, but all it's done has shifted his odds."

"And now his opponents' odds are so bad that if a fighter bets on himself, he makes a fuck-ton of cash if he wins. Only he never does. You're raking in cash on the backs of the desperate, ya know?"

"Well, duh," Alice says. "Been my business model for a hundred years. Or it was. He was a hell of a draw. Still is. But he's too good. He's fucking with my bottom line. His odds are so high the payout sucks and nobody wants to bet on his opponents because everybody thinks they're gonna lose."

"Sounds like they're right," I say.

"They are. That's the problem. I need him gone."

"Ban him."

"Tried it. The minute word got out that I might do that, everybody went all batshit. A lot of the folks down there watching, they're getting off on this."

"They don't even know what he's doing," I say.

"They don't care. They just like blood sports without all that messy blood."

People are fucking weird, mages more so. I understand the thrill of watching a fight. It's exciting, the energy's infectious. But none of the people watching are aware that a murder is happening right before their eyes. If they did, they'd pay double to get in.

"I'll go have a chat," I say. "Don't let him out of the building, and if any of your people see him, have them shoot him if he gets within twenty feet."

"My people don't carry guns," she says.

"Might be time they did."

The hangar has been partitioned into separate sections. The arena and seats, a set of locker rooms, showers, rudimentary medical—which is really just a closet with a bunch of first aid kits and a foldable stretcher.

The Pit has corridors made of the same ensorcelled chain link fencing leading to individual locker rooms. Each opens onto an octagonal corridor that rings the Pit and leads to a wide doorway that lets out next to the betting booth.

It doesn't take long for me to find the right room. The fighter goes by the name Lightning Johnny. No idea what that's all about. I didn't see any lightning. Maybe Cold-Blooded Murderer Johnny was taken.

He's standing at the sink staring into the mirror. I can see his lips moving in the reflection. Whatever he's saying, they're not his words.

From the door I can tell he's definitely been enhanced through magic. It looks almost like one of those Halloween muscle suits but not as severe. There are bulges in unusual places that give it away, and he hasn't gotten used to walking yet. Other than that, there's nothing particularly noteworthy about him. Not quite six feet tall, red hair, light freckled skin. His skin is bright red from the fight, slick with sweat. For all that he's shivering.

I go in and close the door behind me. The noise grabs his attention. He jerks around to face me but doesn't say anything. He has prison tats, a couple of . . . I don't know what the fuck they're supposed to be. Really screwed up swastikas or Nazi SS symbols? One on each pec. The ensemble is completed with an 88 on his belly that looks like the artist was on too much meth at the time. Tats like that should get him into all the right parties.

But the thing that sticks out is his eyes. They can't decide what color they're supposed to be. Brown, blue, brown again. Shapes in his irises flow like clouds blown about by stormy winds.

"Nice fight out there tonight," I say.

"Thanks," he says. Distant, but at least he's acknowledging me. The high must be wearing off.

"How many are you up to a week now?"

"Fights? Two, three. Hey, if you're, like, a promoter, or something, I'm not interested." He turns back to the mirror and ignores me.

"I get that," I say. "You go pro, you're gonna get a lot more scrutiny. Folks might start to put some things together. Maybe figure out what you're really doing. Can't have that."

He turns back to me, startled as if seeing me there for the first time. "The fuck are you still doing here?"

"Having a conversation," I say. "That's all." I don't stop moving, just slowly walking toward him, hands at my sides, empty.

"Yeah, well, go fuck off. I'm not—"

"They're like potato chips, aren't they? Can't eat just one. And the best part? Nobody knows what you're doing." He glances from me to the door and back. I can almost see the wheels turning in his head. "I don't think you want to do that," I say.

"What?"

"You think you can get through me and out of here. You won't."

"Who the fuck are you?" He starts to pull power in from the local pool of magic, but he's not very good at it. He might not even realize he's doing it. It's like he's an engine that can't quite start.

"Nobody important," I say. "Where'd you do your time? Corcoran?"

"If you don't get the fuck out of here in ten seconds I'm gonna kick your ass."

"That where it started? Prison? Stress can bring out latent talents."

"I'm countin', man. Ten."

"Must have been easy there. You walk by, bump into somebody in the yard, and down he goes."

"I ain't killed nobody," he says. "Nine."

"Horseshit and you know it. They're more dead than if you put a bullet in their brain."

"Eight."

"Bodies are just meat," I say. "But souls are where the flavor's at."

I'm about five feet away from him and he's getting really nervous. He looks like he should be able to take me, but that'll never happen.

"Seven, motherfucker."

"How long have you been seeing the ghosts?"

Silence. "How do you know about that?" he says, his voice a terrified whisper.

"You thought you were going crazy. Nobody else could see them. And they're everywhere. Fuck, a prison yard must be crawling with them. You saw them and they could see you. So you keep your head down, do your time, and when you get out it's all phone psychics, carnival card readers, some weird guy in a dark room with a crystal ball. Not a one of them knew what the fuck they were talking about. That about right?"

"The fuck am I?"

"You're a necromancer," I say. "A really bad one. Not your fault, really. Your knack showed up too late and you only figured out one trick. But it's a whopper. And stealing souls feels pretty fucking awesome, doesn't it?"

"Shit, dude. It's the best high I've ever had," he says.

"Can't stomach them myself. It's like swallowing razorblades and puking up grenades. Kind of an acquired taste, I've heard. But see, once you got it, you want more and more and then I'm the guy who gets called to solve your problem."

I see what he's doing long before he tries it. He telegraphs too much. He throws himself at me as I step out of the way and he hits the floor. He scrambles to his feet. I put my hands in my pockets.

"Come on," I say. "You can do better than that."

He puts his arms out wide and tries to tackle me, but he's too cumbersome and I'm out of his way before he can get close enough.

"Dude, I'm right here. I'm not even trying to fight you."

"I'm gonna fuckin' kill you."

"Tell you what," I say, stepping close. "Free shot. Go for it." He gets his hand around my throat and does what he's been doing in the ring for weeks. I can feel him going after my soul. I let him take hold of it.

Like a fish taking bait. Suddenly the energy reverses as I reel him in. I get under the spots where his soul attaches to his body and go through them like a crowbar through a windshield.

If he were much more powerful or knew more about his own magic, I wouldn't be able to do this. But he's young, untrained and stupid. His grip slackens and he tries to pull away, but now I've got my hands on him and I'm not letting go. He'd been pulling out souls in one quick yank. Messy. Left a lot of shreds behind. Just enough so the body keeps breathing.

This way's cleaner, if you can call ripping a man's soul out of his body like pulling off a sheet of toilet paper clean. I get the whole thing. His eyes roll up in the back of his head and his body hits the floor.

It's always weird to me how souls, no matter who they belong to, look like thin gold and silver lace. They're beautiful things even when they're owned by monsters. I hold Johnny's in my hand, feeling it struggle to move on.

Normally, it would drift off to wherever it's supposed to go, and if I release it, that's exactly what it'll do. But who knows where that will be. I doubt any kind of Hell is waiting for him. Justice doesn't exist in this universe.

The first few bars of NWA's "Fuck tha Police" plays from my pocket. I don't give my number to too many people and that ringtone is re-served for Letitia, a friend . . . -ish? Anyway, she's a mage who stabbed me in high school. I don't remember why, but I'm pretty sure I deserved it. I fish the phone out of my pocket and accept the call.

"Hey," I say. "What's up?"

"Got a situation could use your expertise," she says.

"Messy?"

"Very," she says. "You busy?" I close my hand into a fist, squeezing Lightning Johnny's soul into a burst of heat that fades away to nothing.

"Nothing important," I say. "Text me the address."

Chapter 2

Who are you? Not your name, not your title, not your gender. All those are things *about* you, no matter how much you identify with them. But what makes you *you*?

Your memories. Everything you remember is a building block of your identity. They're what sets you apart from everyone else. You can witness the same event with a thousand other people, but your experience of it isn't going to be like anyone else's.

Memory gives us context, meaning. Yesterday builds the foundation for today, which builds the foundation for tomorrow. Take away your memories and you stop being you.

What happens when you add some? What happens when you add a lot?

I am Eric Carter, necromancer, smart ass, maker of poor life choices. I looked into a god's eyes as I murdered him.

I am Mictlantecuhtli, Aztec god of the dead, guardian of Mictlan, thousands of years old in one incarnation or another. I looked into a man's eyes as he murdered me.

Eric Carter died about five years ago and took on the role of a god as part of a deal he . . . I? I can't tell, anymore, struck with Mictecacihuatl, Santa Muerte, goddess of Mictlan.

Then somebody wanted Eric Carter back and performed a ritual to chip off a human-sized chunk of Mictlantecuhtli and dump it into a corpse.

I feel like I'm driving a badly abused but well-restored used car. A family heirloom, if you will. It's my grandfather's body. He's one of the few people in my family tree who wasn't cremated.

I'm a man, a god, my own grandfather. Who am I? *What* am I? It's hard to deny my own humanity considering that I am, for all intents and purposes, human. But that's just meat.

At the moment I'm some guy standing outside a small, five-story Art Deco building in the Downtown L.A. Broadway District wondering why I'm bothering doing people things: walking, breathing, existing.

The building's been gutted and turned into lofts that'll only set you

back about fifteen thousand a month. Too close to Skid Row to be
bougie, too close to Bunker Hill to be lowlife. Open plan, exposed
pipes, beams, cement floor, walls that don't meet the ceiling. It has its
own parking lot on the first floor and a private elevator. Nice place if
you can afford it.

I take the elevator up and get off on the penthouse floor. Door's
open. I let myself in. The décor's different than you'd expect in a hip-
ster hovel like this. Instead of paintings from some little art gallery in
Silver Lake you've never heard of, the walls are covered in posters for
a mage fighter named Fireball Freddy. A distant memory of the guy
floats to the surface. Saw him fight once. Quite the asskicker.

It's been a weird month since I've been back. Teasing out Eric Carter's memories from Mictlantecuhtli's. Considering Mictlantecuhtli
spent the last five hundred years trapped in jade, you'd think it
wouldn't be that hard. Just pull out the last forty or so and you're
golden. But when all you can do is think, you do a lot of thinking.

Like, I have this irrational, to my mind, at least, hatred of the Span-
ish. The most I remember about Spain is a week I spent in Ibiza, and
most of that is a drunken blur.

Mictlantecuhtli, however, saw his people enslaved and almost his
entire pantheon wiped out. Those are clearly Mictlantecuhtli's feelings. Still, I find myself feeling weirdly enraged anytime the subject
comes up. Don't even get me started on colonialism.

"Eric?" Letitia calls from one of the rooms.

All the Fireball Freddy memorabilia gives me an idea whose loft
I'm in. I don't know if Freddy ever fought at Quick Change Alice's,
though it's a pretty good bet. A lot of good fighters cut their teeth in
the Pit.

Freddy went professional and stayed at the top of his game for a
good long while. He retired before he started losing. Living the rest of
your life as an unbeatable legend is better than becoming an old man
who got his ass kicked by some up-and-comer.

Being a pro, Freddy never killed anybody. Intentionally, at least.
You really have to hold back. Even some amateur pit fights have that
rule. Not Alice's, of course.

It's hard for a manager to build up somebody's career if they're just
going to get ganked three fights in. You start murdering your opponents, you get dropped fast.

As I'm sure you can guess, Fireball Freddy's signature move was
the fireball. Turned them into an art form. He'd shoot these rapid fire,
four-alarm nightmares that make the opening of *Apocalypse Now*

look like a grease fire. Amazing he never cooked himself in the process.

But he sure as shit cooked his opponents. He didn't kill, but if you went up against him it was a pretty good bet your career was over. He was big on disfiguring other fighters. Real bastard, that Freddy.

Folks knowing they might get their face melted off worked out pretty well for him. Guys would get in the ring and throw in the towel after he burned all the hair off the top of their heads.

So yeah, this is a nice place. With Letitia saying things were messy, I wasn't really expecting a nice place.

"Yeah, it's me," I say, stepping into an equally nice bedroom with a walk-in closet, king-sized bed. The gutted corpse leaning against the corner wall, nailed upside down to a cross and wrapped in vines and duct tape is an interesting design choice.

"Bold statement," I say. "Clashes a bit, but still makes it work. I'd love to talk to his decorator."

He's held in place with honest-to-god real thorn-covered vines. I didn't think you could find them out here, but no, there they are. Wrapping around his forehead in a crown, around his waist as a belt, and around his ankles. I always use barbed wire myself. Easier to get hold of.

He's been gutted from crotch to jaw, his insides pulled out, intestines hanging in front of his face like rope. From the way the blood is spread on the floor, bed, walls and ceiling, I'd say dude here was trussed up first and killed after. Big guy. Fully clothed. So he didn't get hit in his sleep.

Funnily enough there's blood spatter on the walls, which I would expect, but there are no gaps in it. No footprints, either. If a normal did this, they'd be soaked in the stuff. But that's just an interesting detail. Simply the fact that somebody took this guy out tells me it was a mage.

If this is Fireball Freddy, likely, but hard to tell with his guts hanging in front of his face, he would not have been easy to take down in a fight. And if it is him, he never got a shot off with his signature move. There's no charring on the wall.

"Yeah," Letitia says. "We're trying to get hold of them now. Dude, you look like hell."

"I'm not sleeping great," I say. Or at all. At least not for the last four days, or maybe it's five. I'm running on caffeine, Adderall, and occasionally some cocaine just to mix it up.

Besides being a mage, Letitia's an LAPD detective, but don't hold that against her. It's really more of a cover for what she spends most of her time doing. She's part of a group called the Cleanup Crew. Sounds like what it is. They clean up magical shit to, hopefully, keep all the normals from realizing that there really is more to Heaven and Earth than is dreamt of in their philosophy.

These days that's a tall order. There's a toxic fog of poisonous gas in South L.A. that hasn't moved in over five years, for example, kept in place with magic so it doesn't spread further and kill more people.

To say folks are suspicious is an understatement. But the Cleanup Crew does what it can with mage scientists and studies and conspiracy theories and a whole lot of feasible-sounding bullshit that nobody really buys, but nobody really knows how to explain otherwise, either. The Crew has been trying to figure out how to get rid of the fog without killing everyone left in Los Angeles ever since the god Quetzalcoatl blew up the industrial city of Vernon to send me a message.

"You doing all right?" she says.

"Peachy," I say. "I don't see any black-and-whites outside," I say.

"This is Crew business," she says. "At least for me it is." She tilts her head toward the corner where I have totally missed a young blonde woman standing with her arms crossed and a grim face.

"For me it's personal." Amanda Werther. Letitia I was expecting. She's the one who called me. Asked me to swing by to give her my professional opinion as a necromancer.

I know Amanda, but I don't know much about her. We met last month under not-exactly-ideal circumstances. She's the daughter of the man many think is the most powerful mage in Los Angeles. From what I hear she's no slouch herself.

Pieces start connecting and though I don't know why this has happened, I think I know why I'm here, and it's not to give my professional opinion on necromancy.

"What exactly are you looking for from me?" I say.

"I wanted—" Letitia starts but Amanda cuts her off.

"Do you recognize him?" she blurts out. I can feel her drawing in power from the local pool of magic. Add that to what she's probably already packing and somebody's looking to be in a world of hurt. Possibly me.

I may not know Amanda well, but I do know she's cool under fire. If she's reacting like this, she's off her game, which might sound like a 'yeah, no shit,' sort of observation, but any mage with her background has seen her share of dead bodies.

"Hard to say with his intestines in his face," I say, ignoring her tapping the pool. I'm not sure she realizes she's doing it. "But I'm guessing this is Fireball Freddy. Never met the guy. Saw him in New York once. Hell of a fighter. I don't see any footprints in the blood so neither of you has actually gone over and looked, have you?"

"It's pretty obvious how he died," Amanda snaps. She is pissed.

"Yeah, but there's a lot more than that going on here," I say, turning to Letitia. "Kind of surprised you don't have this one already zipped up."

Mages kill each other all the time. We tend not to poke our heads into each other's business unless it becomes a big enough issue for a large enough number of us. Otherwise the law of the land is pretty much whatever you can get away with.

"Tried to tell her, but she wanted to wait for you," Letitia says. She doesn't sound thrilled about it, and I can guess why. As the scion of the most powerful man in L.A., I'm thinking Amanda's used to getting her way. Snapping out orders goes with the territory.

I gesture at the blood on the floor and the walls. "You got everything you need from all this?"

"Yeah," she says. "Whatever you want to do, knock yourself out."

"You might want to stand back," I say. "I've been practicing, but this one's kinda new." This spell isn't necromancy per se. Let's call it necromancy-adjacent.

"Old dogs learning new tricks?" Letitia says.

"Give me a break," I say. "I've only been alive for a month. Everything's fucking new."

I should have just been one more soul going to, well, wherever it is I would have gone to. But like I was saying, I'd made a deal with the Aztec goddess of death, Mictecacihuatl in her guise as Santa Muerte, to take the place of her dead husband and help rebuild Mictlan. We had a complicated relationship.

I went and did the death-god thing. And over time I sort of grew into the role. Literally. I was kind of a seed for the god. It was a good gig. I liked it. I was happy.

But nothing good lasts forever.

I step to the edge of the blood, put my hand out, and concentrate, shaping the spell in my mind. It's something from Mictlantecuhtli's memories. I know everything he did and how he did it. More or less. Thus my occasional existential issues.

The blood, dried and coagulated, suddenly turns liquid, the pool pulling in on itself like quicksilver bouncing across a table. The blood is drawn off the walls, the ceiling. Framed posters and lampshades jerk when the blood is yanked off of them.

Same for ol' Fireball here. Every drop of blood, on his clothes, covering his face, even whatever he's still got inside shoots toward me into a swirling mass about the size of a soccer ball. Soon it's all spinning, clouds and eddies forming and breaking up.

Now this is the tough part. I've done manipulations like this, but they weren't all liquid. This is the part where either I have it or the Cleanup Crew is going to have a lot more to clean up.

I squeeze my hand and the ball begins to shrink. Displaced water pours out as steam and the room begins to warm as the ball gets smaller and smaller. Over the space of a couple heartbeats, the loft feels like a sauna and I have a marble of compressed blood floating in front of me. I release the spell and the marble falls to the floor with a heavy thunk. I pick it up. Not bad. I put it in my pocket.

"When the hell did you learn how to do that?" Letitia says, opening a window. "Smells like burning metal."

"Either last week or sometime in the third century," I say. "Take your pick."

That spell took a lot out of me and vertigo makes the room sway. I shake it off. It wasn't that it was too much magic, it's that it was something only a god should be doing.

I'm not sure how to explain it. The spells I'm remembering from Mictlantecuhtli aren't for humans. They taste different. Metaphors for magic don't really hold up. It has a taste, or a smell, or just a feeling, and it will be different everywhere you go. New York tastes like hammers and metal girders, Mexico City tastes of blood and dust, ancient and new.

Los Angeles is all over the place, all the different cultures and identities running through it like colored fabric through a braided rug, though it's changed since I was here last, changed since the fires.

Mictlantecuhtli's magic compared to human magic is like cooking with the same ingredients, but using a different recipe. Or, hell, maybe it's like music. I don't fucking know. Like I said, metaphors for magic don't really hold up.

See, resurrecting me without Mictlantecuhtli would be like trying to unmix paint. Eric Carter and Mictlantecuhtli were all one big, swirling mass. So instead Mictlantecuhtli was summoned and shoved into a human corpse. A human body isn't going to contain a god for very long. There's just not enough room for the power.

When the body filled up, it got capped off, and the rest of Mictlantecuhtli went on its merry way, leaving me behind. I'm whatever parts of Eric Carter–Mictlantecuhtli will fit inside a human body.

And voila. A necromancer is born. Or reborn. With an extra helping of god sauce.

"Somebody wasn't happy with this guy," I say, "but I don't think it was personal." I walk across the floor to the grisly crucifix, bend down to get a closer look at the corpse. I pull a pen from my pocket and use it to lift the loop of now-desiccated intestines covering his face.

"Yeah, that's Freddy, all right." There's that flare of magic again coming off of Amanda. See, with mages there are only a couple of ways we can tell there's another one nearby: when we cast a spell, and when we pull in power from the local pool. Magic's everywhere there are people, and a lot of places there aren't, and a mage can tap it like a keg. Thing is, any other mage in the area will feel it.

"How about I answer the question you're not asking?" I say. "No, I didn't kill him." Amanda looks at Letitia, who nods to her. She knows I'm telling the truth. "Also, you need to learn how to not show your hand, princess."

"Excuse me?" Amanda says. Not just anger, but indignation.

"He's right," Letitia says. "You're lit up like a fucking bonfire. If you're really thinking of doing something with all that power, everybody in the surrounding dozen blocks will be ready for it."

"I—Shit. Sorry. I'm not—Never mind." I can feel the energy drop. "I'm sorry for thinking it was you."

"Why? I'd be your first pick. If you didn't hit me up thinking I'd done it, I'd have thought you were an idiot, and we all know you're not an idiot."

"Why are you saying it isn't personal?" Amanda says.

"Not for him, it wasn't," I say. "This is all for your benefit." Amanda turns a little green as she gets what I'm saying.

"It was staged," Letitia says. She joins me over by the corpse looking it over. "Something immobilized him, and then he was tied up and gutted. This was for show."

"Oh, fuck," Amanda says.

"Tell me how close I get," I say to Amanda. "You walk in here, see him like this, recognize that he's been strung up for a necromantic ritual. You don't know what kind. Since I'm the only necromancer in town that you know of, it stands to reason I might have done it. So, you call up Letitia and tell her there's a mess the Crew needs to clean up and use her to bring me here so you can find out if I killed him. That about right?"

"Yes," Amanda says, voice quiet. I can see where her brain is going. This is her fault. He'd be alive if it wasn't for her. The first isn't true,

but the second one is. He would be alive if it weren't for her, just like
my sister, or my friend Alex, would be alive if it weren't for me. Or the
hundred-thousand people who died when Quetzalcoatl lit the fires
that burned down Los Angeles. Doesn't matter that we're not the
ones who pulled the trigger.

"Now I'm insulted," Letitia says. "You used me to get to him."

"I wasn't lying," Amanda says, suddenly defensive. To her credit,
she doesn't deny it.

"I know," she says. "That just makes it worse. I didn't catch it."

"What'd she tell you?" I say.

"That there was a ritual you might know about and a mage corpse
the Cleanup Crew should probably do something about. She didn't lie."

That's where Letitia's knack falls down. A skilled liar can get past
her simply by not giving her all the information. It really works better
with yes-or-no questions.

"Not like you had a reason to think she was," I say.

"I'm right here," Amanda says.

"Yeah, I'll get to you in a minute." The more I think about it, the
more pissed I am. "What do you want to do?"

"Take her over my goddamn knee." She turns to Amanda. "You
don't fucking do that. I don't care who you are. You want my help, you
fucking ask for my help. Don't ever try to manipulate me. I barely
know you other than your daddy's a scary motherfucker. If you want
to know how few fucks I give about that, go ask him about the time I
ran him over with an F-150."

Amanda is speechless. She's processing all this and it looks like
some of it is getting through. Mostly, though, she looks like a deer in
the headlights.

"I . . . I am so sorry," she says. "I didn't think. I found the body
and—no, there's no excuse."

"Damn right there isn't," Letitia says. She points at me. "You want
to talk to him, just call him. I am not your go-between. I'll have some
people come to collect the body. It'll take a few hours. I don't want to
see your overprivileged white ass here when I get back."

We follow Letitia into the main room. She gets into the elevator,
stabs a button, and glares at Amanda as the doors close.

"I am such an asshole," Amanda says.

"You kinda are."

"Gee, thanks."

"What, you want me to lie to you?"

"No," Amanda says.

"To be fair, she's being kind of an asshole, too."

"And you?" she says.

"I'm always an asshole."

She flops into a leather club chair. She's exhausted. She hid it pretty well, but now she's letting it out. Probably doesn't have the energy to hold it in anymore. Tears in her eyes are threatening to spill over and she's holding them back by a supreme force of will.

"Is there another necromancer in L.A.?" she says.

"If there is, they didn't do it," I say. "That stunt back there wasn't necromancy. It was more like a toddler drawing dinosaurs."

"I don't know necromancy," she says. "But I know what some of the rituals look like. That looks like a necromantic ritual."

"It was supposed to," I say. "And it kinda is one. This one is to make the dead speak the truth. The thorny vines are okay, but they're expensive and hard to get hold of. Barbed wire is easier. Duct tape's definitely a thing I would use."

"It sounds like they got everything right."

"Except one big thing. Spell grabs whatever residual life energy is still in the body. You ask a question it knows the answer to and it tells you, provided there's enough brain that hasn't rotted."

Amanda cocks her head. Now it's a puzzle. She gets up and goes back into the bedroom. Whatever feelings she has on the situation have been shunted aside like she threw a switch.

"It wouldn't work," she says, pointing to the crotch-to-throat tear all his guts are hanging out of. "This wound tore through his diaphragm. His lungs couldn't inflate, so there'd be no air to push past the vocal cords. He wouldn't be able to talk. The entire ritual would be wasted."

"Right. Though I suppose if you were a good upside-down lip reader it might kinda work."

"Goddammit, Freddy," she says. "I am so sorry."

"Who would go to all this trouble to make you think I did this? And what was Freddy to you? Whoever did it wanted to get him off the board and tried to keep me from coming on. This thing stinks of politics. I don't like politics."

Mage politics. They're like normal politics only with more assassinations and curses, and even bigger assholes. I hate it. I've tried to stay out of it. I knew it wasn't going to last. I'm too visible. Have too much of a reputation. But I would have liked to be alive again for more than a month before getting roped into this shit.

Somebody's trying to force my hand, or Amanda's, or, fuck, I don't know whose. Whatever's going on, I don't like it. I've been used as a pawn too many times already and it's left friends and family dead.

"Otto," she says. She stands up and faces me. The weariness is still there, but there's a determination that she clearly gets from her old man. This woman's made of iron. I'd feel sorry for whoever has pissed her off, but they're at the top of my shit list now, too.

"Otto?"

"My cousin. Otto Werther. He's trying to box me in. And he will unless—fuck, I don't know why I'm even trying to fight this."

"He seems to think I can do something to break you out of that box," I say. "What's this special help he thinks I can give you?"

"I need you to kill him for me."

Chapter 3

The Nickel Diner is one of the holdovers from a bygone era. At least, the building's been there a long time. It's named not because anything on the menu's a nickel, and by the way try the maple bacon donuts, they're to die for, but because it's on Fifth Street. Like that Tom Waits song about Skid Row, "On the Nickel." A few blocks east is Skid Row proper, or what used to be. That whole area was the hardest hit when the firestorm ravaged the city. Too many dead to count. Too many ghosts.

We're sitting in a corner booth at the back of the diner. Good sight lines and neither of our backs to a window. I can see the living walking the street, or driving by. They are heavily outnumbered by the dead.

I don't put my back to windows because I've been shot through them enough times to be sick of plucking glass splinters out of bullet wounds.

Amanda's excuse I can only guess at, but despite her social standing and her father's power, or maybe because of it, it's clear she's walking around with a target on her back.

I don't recall how old she is, but right now she's wearing an over-sized sweater, eating French fries dipped in a chocolate shake, and she looks impossibly young.

Outside the world is flooded with ghosts: Echoes, Haunts, and Wanderers. So many that the barrier between the dead side and the living gets thin in spots. In here there's light and warmth and French fries and chocolate shakes. The world is a very strange place.

"When you got shot in that warehouse party," I say. "How old were you?"

She stops, a fry halfway to her mouth. "Seventeen," she says. "I'm twenty-three now." When Quetzalcoatl set out to burn down L.A., he had a psychotic sicaria from Mexico with him to sow as much chaos as she could. Killed a lot of people. Got folks looking at me for the murders. That was fun.

She started with Amanda. Walked up to her in the middle of a warehouse party and blew her brains across the dance floor. At least that's what everybody thought. But if you're the scion of the most powerful mage in the city, you make damn sure you have some safeguards built in.

The ghost situation Downtown is better than it was, but I can still see some areas where ghosts might break through. And if that happens it'll be a complete shitshow. Ghosts eat life. When I want something out of a ghost, I'll bribe them with some fresh blood. A few drops is all it takes and it drains the life in nothing flat. Imagine what just one ghost can do if it slipped through.

Fortunately, that's not too likely after I sealed a bunch of the holes about five years ago. Stay on this side of the veil and you're fine. Slide over to the dead side, though, you better have your running shoes on. The Echoes aren't a problem, they're just recordings, the dead's last moments played over and over again on a loop. Even Haunts aren't too bad. They're aware, more or less, but they're stuck in one location. They're pretty easy to outmaneuver.

But the Wanderers will fuck you up. You know that scene from every zombie movie ever where the horde runs at the camera? Yeah, that's Wanderers. They'll sense life from miles away and come running.

And there are a *lot* of Wanderers in Downtown.

"Was it actually you who got shot?" I say.

"Sort of? I can't really go into detail. Not the first time it's happened."

"Fair enough. So, Cousin Otto. Seriously? Otto?"

"My father's name is Attila," she says. "Trust me, in my family Otto's downright pedestrian. How much do you know about my family?"

"As little as I possibly can," I say. "I try to stay out of the politics. Your dad tried to kill me once. He and my grandfather ran together back in the day. Oh, and he's over two hundred years old. And I thought you and he were the only Werthers in the States."

"We are. Otto's based in Germany. He manages the family businesses in Western Europe with his brother Hans and my aunt Helga. Uncle Liam covers Scotland, Northern Ireland, and England down to Leeds. Ireland and Wales are under my aunt Siobhan."

"Ambitious. What about the other mages in those areas?"

"Most of them leave us alone, but every couple weeks someone will try to move in on one of our territories. Sometimes they succeed, but not often. We're really more likely to kill each other. We're very good at that."

"How many people are in your family?"

"Immediate family? A dozen or so, though only a handful are

actually important. Overall, hundreds. Only the immediate family have any real ability, but even that's pretty garden variety. Magic thins out the further out on the family tree you get."

Something's not adding up. "You and your dad are the only ones in North America," I say.

"Americas in general," she says. "It's complicated. Like everything else about us isn't. The rest of them aren't allowed to set foot here without permission. After the fires when everyone thought I was dead a few decided to do exactly that. It wasn't pretty."

That's one thing about her father I have to respect. He doesn't fuck around. I'm still amazed how I managed to survive his coming after me a few years back.

"Yeah, I can believe that. But why?"

She's thinking about how to answer that, chewing her lip and tapping the table with a finger. "Fuck it," she says. "Dad's a couple hundred years old. Every fifty, sixty years or so he figures, 'hey, maybe I can have something resembling a normal life,' like that's ever been an option." Things are starting to click into place.

"He's had other kids," I say. "They were all killed?"

"He's been married twice before and had three other children," she says. "I'm all that's left. Not for lack of trying."

"Jesus. And this is all because of your relatives?"

"Isn't family great?"

"What about the other mage families? The Rochambeaus, the 'Aumākuas? They haven't had a hand in any of it? I know you've all been fighting."

"Fighting is a strong word for it. Mostly we're just moving against each other's businesses, taking out lesser mages tied to each other's families, that sort of thing. They have an incentive to keep us alive. They've had to deal with our family before. The mage war in 1917 would have gone differently if my dad and Aunt Helga hadn't sided against my uncles.

"After the war they pushed everyone who was still standing out of the country. Helga and he had a falling out in the fifties and she took her kids and moved back to Europe."

"You have a very fucked up family," I say.

"No shit," she says. "A lot of the power bases of the different families in the states have fragmented. There's too much infighting for them to really band together."

"You and your dad are the only ones keeping the rest of your family at bay."

"Right. Look at L.A. It's the nexus for the five major players in Southern California, the whole Southwest and down past Mexico, really. The most powerful are the Werthers, my dad. Followed by the 'Aumākuas and the Rochambeaus, who are both in the middle of dealing with their own schisms. Most mages out here have some connection through different alliances to one power or the other, and one schism or the other."

"The Magical Mafia," I say.

"We've been called worse."

"Now I'm really glad I've stayed out of mage politics."

"What makes you think you have?" she says.

"I'm a free agent. I don't like anybody. And nobody likes me. Half the mages out there are convinced I'm some sort of demon and the other half think I have an undead army waiting to march down Wilshire."

"Are you listening to yourself? People are fucking terrified of you."

"Which is exactly what keeps me out of this shit."

"No. It is exactly what pulls you in. When you were twenty you created a huge power vacuum by murdering, the fuck was his name?"

"Jean Boudreau," I say.

"Right. A man who had been untouchable until you—What did you do anyway?"

"Packed a car with a bunch of propane cannisters and a brick on the accelerator. Ran it into him and set off the propane. Then I dragged him to the dead side and fed him to ghosts."

Amanda stares at me and then finally remembers to blink. "My dad's right about you. You're fucking psychotic."

"Can't really argue that one. So I killed Jean Boudreau. So what? I also got run outta town on a rail for it."

"And then you came back and did it again when his spirit somehow survived that and showed up for vengeance. Then you go and make an even bigger power hole by taking out his old lieutenant who'd stepped into his shoes."

"Technically, I didn't kill him. And how do you know all this shit?"

"Because knowing it is what keeps me alive," she says. "You get in bed with an Aztec death goddess, go to Mictlan—a place most mages don't even realize exists—and kill her and her husband, then put some girl you barely know and yourself on the throne."

"It was a little more complicated than that."

"Then you die. Spend a few years as a fucking god, and to the horror of pretty much everybody, come back to life."

"Okay, yes. That did happen. But it's not like I brought myself back to life. If you can call it that. I didn't even want it. I'm not even sure I'm me."

She's not listening. She's on a roll. "For an encore you destroy one of the most powerful entities ever to walk the fucking planet, who's existed for the last eight-thousand years."

"Counterpoint," I say, ticking off on my fingers. "Did you miss the part about me burning down most of Los Angeles? Blowing up an entire city? That toxic cloud you and your buddies at USC you've been helping keep in place? Quetzalcoatl?"

"When we met on campus last month, do you know how many people came up to me looking for anything about you they could put into thesis papers?" she says. "One guy wanted to write your biography. You've been at the center of some of the most momentous events in the history of mages in America. All that does is make you even scarier. Quetzalcoatl. Another god. You have conclusively proven that there's an afterlife."

"Any necromancer worth a good goddamn knows there's an afterlife. I just have a little more direct experience with it than most of them."

"That shit you did with the blood tonight."

"That was nothing. I can think of at least twenty people who could pull that off without a hitch."

"Except that you remember that spell from your time being. A. Fucking. God."

Amanda is standing on the booth seat now, yelling at me, and people are starting to stare. I start to worry they think this creepy old guy is doing something horrible to this sweet young thing and then remember that this is a new body and I look in my early thirties at most. So they probably just think I'm an abusive boyfriend. Either way I lose.

"We're doing lines," I say to a concerned looking couple two booths down. "She has an audition tomorrow." I cast a silence spell around our booth so at least they won't hear her having a meltdown.

"Will you sit the fuck down? Fine, I get it. Some people think I'm special. They also think I murder puppies and eat babies."

She slides down back into the booth seat. "No, you do not get it. The thing everybody is terrified of is that you're not with any of the factions. You're a wild card. Everyone knows about you. Everyone has heard stories. There are mages out there right now who know we're here talking and they are shitting their pants."

"Oh, please."

"Let me put this into perspective for you. You are talked about by a lot of people as being equal to the Werthers, the 'Aumākuas, or the Rochambeaus. Families. Groups of mages. You're one guy." Something's not adding up.

"You said there are five major players. Say I buy this bullshit about me being one of them. I'm counting four." And then I get it. "Gabriela."

Gabriela Cortez, La Bruja, is a mage who runs a shelter for the homeless, human and otherwise. She's a five-foot tall Latina sorority girl who looks as imposing as you would guess. She's one of the most powerful, ruthless, and terrifying mages I've ever met.

She's a sociology grad with a soft spot for addicts, convicts, the mentally ill, ghouls, vampires, aswang, bakemono. Hard to build up a safe place for them with legitimate funding. Banks aren't exactly falling over themselves to build a shelter for monsters.

So she did what most mages do, turned to crime. Less-than-legitimate businesses are easier to run when you're a mage, and they make a fuck-ton of money. But she got too successful with her miniature criminal empire and caught the attention of a whole bunch of unsavory types. Even when she was delivering cartel sicario heads back to their employers in plastic shopping bags, they didn't take her seriously.

So she created La Bruja, a terrifying old crone who commanded an army of gang members who had flocked to her as some kind of Downtown saint.

She kept skinning people and cutting off heads, but this time she did it as a horrifying, cackling witch. Only then were they all scared of her enough to leave her alone. Until they didn't.

"Another wild card who's just as powerful as anybody else we're talking about," Amanda says. "More than some, and she's got a fucking army of followers. They don't follow her because of blood ties, or agreements, or contracts. They do it because they love her. And most of them aren't even human. People might be shitting their pants that you and I are talking, but they go buy one-way tickets to anywhere else when the two of you are in the same room together."

"I fucking hate politics."

"Welcome to my life," she says.

"Let's get back to Otto and why you think I'm going to kill him for you."

"I don't think you will," she says. "I hope you will. But I doubt you'd be up for it." She looks down at her empty plate of fries. She waves over at the waitress who comes up to the table and stops dead.

Oops. I forgot the silence spell. It's quick and dirty and just makes a barrier to sound. Outside the bubble no one can hear us, but we can't hear them, either. As far as the waitress knows, she's just gone deaf. I untie the spell, dropping the bubble. Sound rushes in like a freight train. She shakes her head, snaps her fingers at each ear.

"You all right?" I say.

"Oh, yeah. Need to get my ears checked. What can I get ya?"

"Another plate of fries and a chocolate shake," Amanda says.

"You?"

"You got a bottle of ridiculously overpriced single malt back there?"

"If I did, I'd have already drunk it," she says.

"Coffee, then. Thanks."

She takes the order and walks off, still unsure about her hearing. Mages managed to go centuries without most normals figuring out that magic really exists and I've always wondered how. Little shit like the spell I just cast won't tip a normal off, but experiences like this can stack up. And then you get something like the entire city burning or the South L.A. Toxic Zone. Even with mages in positions of power covering things up as best they can, pulling off shit like that is mind-boggling.

Sure, there are conspiracy theories, but they're buried underneath other conspiracy theories. There's no way to deny there's something wrong with a toxic cloud that doesn't move, but as long as people keep thinking it's anything but magic, great.

That's gonna bite us in the ass someday. Redirecting people's attention from magic to some other crackpot idea sounds good, but in the long term we'll be dealing with whatever one sticks the most in people's minds. I just hope it's something that doesn't get too many people killed.

"All right, fries are on their way. Tell me about Otto."

"First I gotta explain the family curse."

"A family curse? You seem to be doing pretty well for a cursed family."

"Not everybody sees it as a curse. It's one as far as I'm concerned," she says. "Sometime in the fifth or sixth century some of my great-great-whatevers decided that they needed to keep us all from killing each other and ending the bloodline."

"Yeah? How's that working out for you."

"Funny. And fuck you. The curse goes down through generations. They wrote up a bunch of 'Thou shalt not' commandments. Like 'Thou shalt not kill the shit out of each other.'"

"And people listened to them?"

"Not even. Half the family was lost to the curse in the first few years. They took it seriously once the bodies started stacking up and they realized it wasn't all plague. After a while they started looking for loopholes in what they could and couldn't do."

The waitress brings the food and Amanda starts stress-eating the fries. She doesn't even acknowledge the woman other than to watch her put the plate down and nod at her. I take my coffee and thank her. Man, I thought my manners were bad.

"Sounds like a lot of trial and error."

"Probably more error than trial. Eventually, nobody was sure which prohibited behaviors would make their heads pop," she says, "and which ones wouldn't. It was safer to assume they all would, and our family's been living by that code ever since. It's cut down on the infighting. At least publicly."

"I bet. And you want me to kill Otto because you can't."

"Yeah," she says. "But not how you think. There are few circumstances where we can move directly against each other. Usually we use assassin proxies hired through cut-outs to do it. Get enough middlemen in there and the curse doesn't trigger."

"Congratulations, you just won the Most Dysfunctional Family Award," I say. She laughs, but there's a hint of panic in it. "How many times have your relatives gone after you?"

"Nine that I know of. Ten others are strong maybes. This latest move might be the one that takes me out, though. Otto's found a previously unknown piece of family lore in an art collection in France. It's been independently verified by so many experts you couldn't possibly buy them all off."

"New rules?"

"Newly discovered loopholes none of us knew about. It boils down to this. Once a century, anyone in the family can challenge the validity of the reigning leader's heir. The challenge can be anything. A duel, particularly violent Scrabble, whatever."

"Otto's challenging your position and if he wins, he becomes your dad's heir and picks up the family business when he kicks."

"Right. Only it's a lot more than business. There's a ridiculous amount of magical power associated with it. It's hard to explain. If he becomes the heir, Dad's going to have to be even more careful because Otto and his allies are going to be gunning for him even harder. As long as I'm the heir, and I know this sounds fucked up, I'm a shield for him. If they kill him—"

"You inherit. But what if they kill you, instead?"

"Even bigger problem. Dad dies without an heir and everything goes to whoever can grab the title and keep it. They'd all kill each other trying to get it, so none of them will make a move on it. He'll end up holding it indefinitely. And if he has more children it starts all over again."

"Okay. I'm still not seeing the big deal. Challenge your cousin to a game of pinochle or hopscotch, then. Hair braiding. I don't know. And is he so powerful you can't take him in a fight?"

"I could wipe the floor with him. He knows it, too." Her face sort of twists up and I can tell she's trying really hard not to start ranting. "The problem is that women aren't allowed to be in this family duel and have to bring on a champion to fight in their stead."

"You're fucking kidding me. This is some Dark Ages bullshit."

"Well, that's when it was written."

It all clicks into place now. "You need someone who would do it and have a decent chance of winning. But why Fireball? Guy's a has-been. Was a has-been. You know what I mean. I can think of ten people who are better fighters than he was in his prime."

"Because no one else will. Money, favors, nothing. Otto's made sure that stories about him in Germany have started circulating here." She stops to hoover up some more fries. Her hands are shaking.

"They're all scared of him," I say.

"And then some. My dad explicitly can't get involved, hell, he can barely even talk to me about it, and most of my frien—people who I thought were my friends are picking sides based on who they think Otto's going to show favor to when he wins."

Fucking politics. "So not only does your fighter have to be strong enough to take him on, they have to be willing to even with all the politics hanging over their heads."

"And be a man," she says.

"Wally Preston," I say. "He's an ass-kicker. And I know he's not affiliated with anybody. Or is there some shit about how it can't be a trans man?" Mages can be as prejudiced as anybody else, and I know for a fact Wally spent way too many years dealing with other people's bigotry.

Most magic gives a fuck one way or the other. It's all intention and declaration. You tell the universe you're a man or a woman, the universe is going to listen and take you seriously even if nobody else does.

"Allowable from everything I can tell," she says. "Except that Wally went to some temple in the Himalayas and nobody's seen him in a couple years."

"Oh. Well, shit."

"I can't find anyone who fits all the rest of the criteria, too. A couple friends, *real* friends, stepped up. But they're not strong enough. And they know it. Volunteered anyway. I said no. I'm not sacrificing my friends to that fucking monster."

"But Freddie was strong enough."

"Yeah. Freddie and I were friends," she says. "I didn't ask him. He heard about it and called me. He was strong enough and I was desperate enough to say yes. When nobody else would be, he was there. And now he's—" She's trying hard to hold back tears. "Now you see the problem. And why I'm asking you to kill Otto for me. You're my only hope, Obi-Wan."

"Otto knew about Freddy," I say. "He killed him to cut off your only real ally. But why make it look like I'd done it? Whether I'd killed Freddy or not, you'd be forced to come to me regardless. If he thinks that's gonna scare me off—Oh. He was trying to scare you off."

"Pretty sure Otto thought that if he could trick me into thinking you'd killed Freddie, I'd figure you'd done it for him."

"Did he eat a lot of lead paint as a child? Because that's stupid."

"I don't think he's actually the one who did it," she says. "If he'd ordered it directly he probably wouldn't be alive. Now that the challenge has been called, if he interferes with it the curse should trigger. I doubt he even knows about it."

"What happens if you don't find someone?"

"I lose by fiat. Otto becomes heir. My dad likely dies not long after that. Otto and the rest of the family move in on the U.S. Makes everybody's lives all the more fucked up. He'll try to eliminate everyone he'll see as a threat."

"Like me?"

"Like you. So really you have a choice."

"Fight him now or fight him later."

"Pretty much."

This is an easy one. "Where is he now? I'll go kill him. Problem solved."

"You think I haven't thought of that? I've got similar restrictions, though not as harsh. Since the challenge has been issued, if he dies before the fight, my head doesn't explode. But he still wins by fiat, and now it's his brother who becomes heir. Believe me, Otto's the safer option."

"Say I fight him," I say. "How does this work? We stand ten paces apart and throw lightning bolts at each other?"

"He called the challenge, so that's all up to the champion. Freddie was planning on meeting him in a boxing gym. Goddammit." She wipes her eyes with the back of her sleeve, takes a deep breath, and the woman made of iron is back.

"If I want to challenge him to pinochle, then that's what we do?"

"If it uses swords, sure. It doesn't have to be to the death, but that's how Otto'll play it. Believe me, there is no way out of this that doesn't end with Otto dead or in charge. I've been going through family history with the lawyers and his claim is rock solid."

"Amanda, I like you," I say.

"Shit. I've heard this speech before. If you're gonna say no, just fucking say no."

"I'm not saying no. I'm saying I have to think about it. When do you need an answer?" I can see a touch of hope brighten in her eyes, but she pushes it down quickly. She knows where that can lead, being hung upside down and gutted in your own apartment.

"Tomorrow morning. I have to meet Otto at noon to either declare a champion or forfeit."

"I'll have you an answer before then." Christ. I honestly don't know what I'm going to do here. I do not want to get involved in family dramas and mage politics. Shit like that, even if I win, I lose.

I do like Amanda. And despite the time he tried to kill me, I like her dad, too. I'm not sure what it says about me that all my best friends have tried to kill me at one time or another.

"Decide tonight, please," she says, bitterness in every word. "I need time to figure out what my surrender speech should be."

"Gimme your number. I'll let you know in a couple hours. Fair?"

"I'll take what I can get." We share our information. I put her in my phone under Peeved Princess. I'm probably something like Dickwad Necromancer in hers.

"You need a ride anywhere?" I ask.

"I have a car," she says. "How about you? I hear you steal all your cars."

"Steal implies that I keep them," I say.

"It really doesn't," she says. "Watch yourself out there. I was serious about people shitting bricks because you and I are having a conversation."

"I'll be fine. I'm more worried about you." She waves it off. "I'll call you in a couple hours." By the time I hit the door she's furiously texting somebody on her phone.

The night's getting cold and the clouds overhead reflect the city's lights back onto itself. Storm coming in. I can smell it. And I'm not just talking about the weather. This whole thing with Amanda screams bad news. I don't see any way it's going to play out well for anybody.

So what do I do? Walking away sounds like the right choice, but I don't know that it is. Running from a problem is something I'm really good at. But maybe it's time to do something different.

One thing's become clear in the last month. Like it or not I'm here for the long haul. I don't get to go back home.

Bizarre—thinking of Mictlan as home. It stings to know I won't see it again.

And now, this crap Amanda's dealing with. I get why she wants me to help. She doesn't have a lot of options. Much as I don't want to get involved, she's right: I'm political by my very existence. Coming back to life can't have helped any.

I'm so absorbed in my thinking that I don't notice the guy coming up behind me from an alley until he's close enough to jam his gun into my back.

"I'm gonna fuck you up," he says, voice full of jitters and speed.

"Funny," I say. "I was just about to say that."

Chapter 4

I don't feel any magic being drawn in or spells being unleashed. Guy's as normal as they come. Doesn't mean a bullet won't fuck up my day.

I drop down, twisting to the left to get away from the barrel and inside his guard. I hook his gun arm in the crook of my left elbow, pull him toward me, and twist the gun out of his hand. I slam my right elbow into his face with a satisfying *crunch*. At this point the fight's already over, but I hate doing things half-assed, so I knee him in the crotch. Then I pistol-whip him.

He drops to the ground screaming that I'm killing him. Now that I get a good look, I can see what's going on. He's filthy. Long, scraggly beard. That stink you get from too much meth and too many weeks on the street. He's wearing three coats and two mismatched shoes, one of them held together with duct tape.

"Jesus, man. I didn't break your arm." I bend down so I'm level with his face. Now I feel like an asshole. "You need money? Place to sleep? Your next fix?"

"Please don't kill me. Please don't kill me. Oh my god. He said it would be fine. Please don't kill me."

"I'm not gonna kill—" Then I notice the gun I'm holding, a shiny new SIG Sauer P228 that looks like it just came out of the box. Where the hell does a meth head get hold of a gun like this? "Who said it would be fine?"

"I did," says a voice behind me. And with it comes a flare of magic that almost catches me before I get a shield spell up behind my back. I turn in time to see arrows made of ice shatter against the barrier, the mage casting them about ten feet away.

Somebody I don't know is trying to kill me. Nice to know that some things never change. He's a tall one. Young, blond, blue-eyed. Well-dressed. Too well-dressed to be chatting up alleyway bums in Downtown.

Might as well put this gun to good use. I pop off a couple of rounds, duck around a dumpster, and cast a push spell that hurls it at him. He pushes the dumpster aside with his own spell, sending it flying behind him to go crashing through a closed storefront window.

While he's blocking that I've already set off another spell, and its results are crawling out of rain gutters, under trash, across the street. Every dead thing in a two-hundred-foot radius pops its head up and makes a beeline for him.

Some of them are too decomposed to move, but there are a lot that aren't. Rats, pigeons, crows, raccoons, a coyote, and—Huh. One guy out from a dumpster. Lawyer type. Looks like he was rolled for his wallet and knifed a couple days ago.

They're empty shells, nobody home. I imbue them with a ridiculous boost of speed and they're on him before he can get another shot at me. Pigeons peck at his face, raccoons and rats claw their way up his legs. I hear muffled screaming as one rat crawls up his pants and bites him somewhere I don't even want to think about.

The thing with the animated dead is that they're not limited by overexertion. As long as I can move their limbs, they can keep going. Like with the lawyer who comes up behind the guy, gets him in a headlock, and squeezes. I don't want to kill him, I just want him unconscious so I can ask him uncomfortable questions later. It's easier when they're alive.

But best laid plans and all that. A burst of force blows all of them off him in an explosion of rotting meat that disintegrates them into flakes of flesh and bone before they hit the street.

But not all of them. I haven't brought my shield down, I've used it so many times I don't even think about it. Rotting viscera splats against it.

On the one hand I'm not covered in week-old dead. On the other, I can't see a goddamn thing.

I do pretty much the same sort of spell he just did to blow the guts off my shield. Fucker's taken advantage of it and closed the distance with clearly magically enhanced speed.

He's so fast and hits so hard that it doesn't matter if my shield holds or not. He plows into it and shoves it, and me, back a good ten feet. I lose my footing, hit the ground, and skid, the breath knocked out of me.

He doesn't press his advantage, which is weird seeing as how I'm not going anywhere for a couple of seconds. Then I see why. He's running up the wall of one of the buildings, a red light growing around him.

He reaches the top of the building and flies straight up off it, then twists in the air and starts to dive back down, fire continuing to grow around him, pointed in the shape of a spear. If he hits me, that's it.

I pull out the blood marble I made in Fireball Freddie's living room and chuck it up at him, then blow it like a frag grenade. Tiny slivers of compressed blood pepper him like shrapnel. Pretty useless if that's all I was shooting for.

But I've got a different plan. I push magic into the blood and every bit of it bursts into thin tendrils strong as steel: a spiderweb made of razorblades. He screams as they slice into him, momentum pushing them deeper into his flesh. I was hoping for a frog-in-a-blender situation, but no such luck. The tendrils have fucked him up, no doubt about that, but the same momentum that pushed him into the web is also tearing it apart.

I manage to roll just in time for him to miss me as he hits the concrete. There's a stomach-churning crunch and he bounces. I come up into a crouch, ready to put two bullets into him if he managed to survive, but by the time I get my head up he's gone.

I find out where he's gone to a second later when he slams into me from behind, knocking me to the ground and getting me in a headlock. At this point it's a contest of strength, my magic against his. He's trying to crush my windpipe like an industrial press and I'm pushing out with as much of my own power as I can to counter it.

He at least matches me in power. We both tap the local pool of magic, each of us trying to draw as much as possible. And it's a lot.

This is the wrong strategy. This is unstoppable force, immovable object shit. This will get me nowhere. I need to shake the game up. But how? For either of us to get anywhere one of us is going to have to change tactics, but if I'm not careful to do it just right, he'll just grab all the power from the pool and pop my head like a zit. It's a magical tug-of-war. I can't let him win.

Come to think of it, maybe that's exactly what I need to do. I keep drawing power, but instead of trying to break his stranglehold I slide over to the dead side of the veil. You want all that power, pal? It's yours.

Jet-engine roar, and my connection to the pool is severed as everything goes black-blue around me.

The dead side is an ugly place. Just being here sucks your life away. I've gotten better at blocking that effect, especially since my stint in Mictlan, but I still need to worry about the ghosts. I don't see any Haunts and only a handful of Echoes, but I can feel Wanderers all over the place.

On this side I can still perceive the living, just like when I'm over there I can see the dead. It's not as distinct. Unless I concentrate, people are just human-shaped blobs of light.

This guy is pretty much what I expect. And then he lights up like an arc welder and just as quickly disappears entirely, which is very much not what I was expecting.

When a mage pulls in more magic than they're capable of channeling safely, it can lead to burn out. We lose our connection to magic, our ability to use it. Very few mages get it back. But if he burned out, he should be unconscious. I should still see him from this side. He shouldn't simply be gone.

Did he teleport somewhere? I fucking hate teleporters. Though it's pretty funny when they get it wrong and wind up half-embedded in a wall.

I slide back to the living side expecting to see a body. I do. All over the place.

The ground and walls of the alley are covered in a thin layer of blood and gore that goes up almost a full story. There are bits of bone and a couple almost-recognizable body parts, but for the most part it looks like somebody exploded a cow full of TNT. There's what looks like a chunk of femur embedded into the brick of one of the buildings like an arrow from an overly enthusiastic archer.

The homeless guy is gone, too. Hopefully he freaked out as soon as we started slinging magic around and bolted. Otherwise he's probably somewhere in this mess too.

There's got to be something here that didn't blow up that might tell me who my mystery attacker was, though I have a feeling I already know. When I find half a hand behind a dumpster, I'm almost certain of it.

I pick it up and the hand falls to pieces. That's fine. I only care about the finger with a ring on it.

My phone rings. Amanda. Before I can say a word, she yells, "What the holy fucking hell did you just do?"

"I didn't do anything."

"Bullshit," she says. "Are you okay?"

"I'm fine," I say. "I take it there was a lot of noise? I was too busy at the time to notice."

"I'm getting texts from people up in fucking Chatsworth and out in San Bernardino who felt it. I'm half a mile away and it almost knocked me out. What did you do?"

"Had a spirited discussion. Hey, you got a family crest?"

The change in subject seems to throw her but she recovers fast. "Yeah. It's—"

"Red and black cut crosswise by a white line and there's some big-ass martini glass on it?"

"It's a chalice," she says. "How do you know this?"

"Pretty sure the spirited discussion was with one of your cousins and he just tried to kill me. Besides Otto, is there anybody else in town?"

"Almost definitely, but I don't know who. What'd he look like?"

"Young, blond, sneers like a Nazi."

"That doesn't narrow it down much," she says. "Maybe Reinhold, Otto's son. Shit. But you're okay?"

"Oh yeah, I'm fine."

"What about Reinhold?"

I look at the smear of viscera sprayed across the alley. "He's around. Can't really get much out of him, though."

She seems distracted. "Okay. Thanks for at least hearing me out at the diner. I'll figure something out."

"I'm in."

"What?"

"You heard me. Guy's kid tried to kill me either to impress daddy or under daddy's orders. Either way he's pissed me off. I'm going to kill the guy anyway. Might as well do it like this."

"Oh god. Thank you. We're meeting at the estate tomorrow at noon. Can you get here a little early? And think about how you want to do this and where."

"I got a few ideas. Need to make some phone calls, run a couple errands. I'll see you there around ten?"

"Perfect. Thank you." The relief in her voice is palpable. It's like a dam of stress has just burst.

And then the dam comes back up. "Only, there's one more thing. And I'm an idiot for not asking sooner. What do you want for it?"

"Sorry?"

"Favors, money. I can—"

"Amanda, you don't have anything I need or want. I'm doing this because your cousin needs killing. Also, I like you, but mostly it's because your cousin needs killing."

"I—Thank you."

"Don't worry about it. I'll see you tomorrow."

I hang up and get ready for a long night of negotiations.

Chapter 5

Powerful mages, like rich normals, like to show off what they've got, and one of the easiest ways to do that is with real estate. And as with rich normals, privacy is a big deal.

Problem for mages is that we can't let it all hang out. Having Willy Wonka land visible from a drive-by of Bel Air Road isn't really an option. So what's an obscenely wealthy, powerful, narcissistic mage to do?

Simple. Get a pocket universe.

They're expensive as fuck and I don't mean in money (mage currency is favors, "gifts" of stupidly powerful magical tchotchkes, and so on). They're a lot of effort and only a handful of mages, or collective mage families, have the ability to make them.

The cheap (hah!) ones aren't completely self-contained. Having to generate your own air supply and sunlight can be a pain in the ass. The more contained your pocket universe is, the more you can impress the mages next door.

But how do you show it off? Just like the rich normals do. You have parties and invite everybody to them. Extravaganzas that would make Jay Gatsby cream his jeans. So many mages in one place that nobody dares try to kill anyone lest everyone else get in on the action. A mage brawl is something to see, but not something you want to be in the middle of.

The mages who hold these parties are, as you've probably figured out, compensating. Lots of flash and glitz to wow the crowds so they'll marvel at your might.

Meanwhile, the mages with *real* power are content in their own fully self-contained realities without having to show them off. They'd be laughing at all the other yahoos out there, if they ever bothered to notice them. And nobody notices their universes, either.

The Werther Estate in the Hollywood Hills is one of those. It sits at the end of a cul-de-sac near Mulholland Drive in the middle of half a dozen multi-million-dollar homes. A wall of ivy and a tall gate behind which is, well, nothing.

Unless you're supposed to be there. If you are, then the gate opens onto a road leading into a completely self-contained, constantly shifting landscape dependent on the will of the owner, Attila Werther.

He controls the land, the water, the light, the weather, the architecture, everything. The world changes at his whim. Nobody has to see the Werther Estate to be impressed. They just have to hear about it.

I head up the driveway to the gate and it opens up for me before I can stop the car. Amanda is standing just inside, looking grim in a black dress and tights with matching flats. She's lost the cornrows, blonde hair falling just past her shoulders; her only adornments are small diamond earrings and a tiny glass bottle wrapped in wire hanging from a thin golden chain around her neck.

Last night she looked almost like a child. Now she looks like a boardroom Xena ready to cut down her enemies without chipping a nail. I'd pay money to see that.

"Thanks for coming," she says. "You doing okay? You look a little rough."

There's no trace of the stress of last night, the desperation. She had a problem and now she has a solution. If she's anything like her old man, she also has one or more contingency plans, which probably have nothing to do with me.

"Late night. Had to get some details ironed out," I say. "Happy to be here."

I am, or at least a close approximation. I feel like I'm re-learning how to operate in society, trying to remember what it was like to be human. I'm not sure I know how to do that shit anymore.

Honestly, I'm not sure if I ever really did.

But killing people? Fuck yeah, I know how to do *that*. Plus it gives me something else to focus on besides contemplating the realities of existence and identity like poking at a rotten tooth.

Last time I was here, this place was pretty much Willy-Wonka-land. Now it looks like a respectable English country estate. I can see the main building ahead surrounded by lush gardens and hedge mazes and can just make out the greenhouse dome of an arboretum and an observatory.

"Very *Downton Abbey*," I say.

"More *Game of Thrones*, really. We're expecting guests over the next couple of days. It's going to be . . ."

"Interesting? Tragic? A nightmare?"

"Yes," she says. "Family reunion. If we're lucky some of us will survive the weekend."

"Sounds to me like a good time to hit the Bahamas."

"If only," she says. "Otto's not here yet. He'll probably have someone with him. A lawyer. Maybe Reinhold, unless you killed him last night."

"I did not kill him," I say truthfully. I didn't. Technically, I wasn't even there at the time. She starts to say something, then stops, probably realizing that you'd better be prepared for the answer if you're about to ask an awkward question.

She leads us to a black Mercedes. We get in the back. The doors close on their own and the car starts to roll. There's a smoked glass partition between the driver's compartment and us, so I can't tell if there's a driver. There probably isn't.

I feel a small flare of magic and recognize the feeling of a privacy spell designed to block scrying or any other method of listening in on us. I'm a little surprised she feels the need to do it since this is her home, but given what she's told me about her family situation, I really shouldn't be.

"What's the plan?" she asks.

"Depends. Is there anything you haven't told me?"

"I don't think so. Otto's made the challenge. You set the conditions of the contest. All of them. Location, time, rules, everything. It doesn't have to be fair, but if it's blatantly not, Otto's lawyer will likely throw a fit. The only actual requirement is that it happen within a week of my, fuck I hate this word, 'champion' declaring the conditions. Sooner would be better."

"Oh, it'll be sooner."

"When?" she says.

"Sooner."

"You're not going to tell me, are you?"

"It's a surprise."

"Which means I won't like it," she says.

"No. It means that I don't know for sure yet. I'm waiting to hear on a couple of things. What's with this family reunion? It can't be a coincidence that Otto threw this at you now."

"It isn't," she says. "It's less a reunion and more of a conclave. Every ten years the heads of the different factions—Dad hates when I call them that, but it fits—get together for a weekend to discuss family business, debates over alliances, and shit like that."

"And kill each other?"

"Yeah. Some of the conditions of the curse shift and a lot of restrictions are lifted. The last one was bad. Really bad. But I've heard of one where literally no one survived the first day. Caused a family war that lasted twenty years."

"When was this?"

"Early eighteenth century," she says. "I'm hoping this year is better."

"You gonna have to kill anybody?" I ask. "It sounds like maybe you should set explosives in all their rooms and just set them off when they get here."

She smiles. It's barely a flicker, but it's there. "You're the second person to tell me that," she says. "I'm seriously considering it." The car glides to a halt. The doors pop open and we step out.

Up close the place is even more impressive. It looks a few hundred years old and should have a name like Rumsbottomsmythe Hall. It's a sprawling Tudor monstrosity of brick and battlements, chimneys and towers. If Werther was going for imposing, he nailed it.

Amanda smooths out her dress and takes a deep breath, and we head toward the house. A tall, immaculately dressed butler opens the door for us.

"Miss Amanda," he says. "And you must be Mister Eric Carter. It is a pleasure to make your acquaintance, sir."

"Uh, likewise?" I say.

"Do you need anything, ma'am? Sir?"

"Not right now, Bigsby," she says. "Thank you."

"Very good, ma'am." He disappears with a pop. One second he's there, the next he's not. Magical butler.

"That's handy," I say. "What is he?"

"Bigsby's part of the estate. No matter what configuration Dad puts it in, he's a constant. If you need him, just ask for him. You won't take him away from anybody else. He can spawn off as many of himself as he needs."

"Like ask him to get me a cup of coffee? Or murder an annoying cousin?"

"Yes to the first, no to the second," she says. "I've tried. He's as much a security system as he is a butler. If we try to kill each other he'll intervene, unless my dad or I tell him not to."

The country manor vibe extends into the house. The foyer is fuck-ing enormous, with a high, arched ceiling and hanging chandeliers. I can't decide whether it has a Bruce Wayne vibe or an Agatha Christie one. Given what Amanda's been saying, maybe more Anne Boleyn.

"This won't work," Amanda says as she leads me into a dining hall with a table that will seat twenty people easy. "Dad! Room's too big."

I hear a distant "Sorry" from somewhere in the house, and the far wall and ceiling rush toward us like colliding freight trains. The windows get shorter and wider and the table shrinks down to seat six.

"Thank you," Amanda calls out. "When he throws these things together, he always has rooms that he doesn't pay much attention to or even know about."

"Like putting something down and forgetting about it?"

"More like leaving a bunch of sawdust on the floor and not looking down. They're leftovers."

"Must make navigation a little difficult."

"For guests, yeah. Bigsby can get someone where they need to be if they get lost, though. I never have a problem."

"When Otto gets here, do I get to slap his face with a glove?"

"If you want," she says. "As long as you don't kill him until the fight you can do whatever you like. My head won't pop."

"Is that literally what happens when the curse triggers?"

"It's not always the same, but head-popping is pretty common."

Bigsby appears next to us. I find it a little jarring, but Amanda doesn't even blink. "Excuse me, miss. Your cousin and his attorney have arrived."

"Thank you, Bigsby. Can you show them to this room, and let my father know?"

"Absolutely, miss. I've already taken the liberty of informing Mister Werther. I'll usher in the guests." Then he's gone.

"You know," I say, "this would be an ideal location for an ambush."

Amanda sits in one of the chairs and I slide into the one next to her. "There will be," she says. "Just not the way you're thinking. Otto's expecting this to be a very different meeting."

A moment later Bigsby leads in two men, one tall and blonde with a familiar chiseled face, the other almost as tall, with a Clark Kent vibe to him. Nondescript suit, nondescript haircut, nondescript glasses. It's like he's beneath my notice. My eyes want to slide off him and when he stops moving it's like he becomes part of the background.

There is absolutely nothing remarkable about him at all, which sets off every goddamn alarm bell I have. I will be making sure I know where this man is at all times during this discussion. Unremarkable people are really good at sliding a knife into your ribs.

"Misters Otto Werther and Jonathan Salvatore, miss. Would anyone like a drink before the proceedings?"

"No," Otto says. His kid looks just like him. Or did, until he was splashed all over the alley. Otto's even got the same sneer. "We won't be here long enough to finish it."

"You can go, Bigsby. Hello, Otto," Amanda says, oozing the sort of politeness that says "fuck you" and means it.

"I am here and I expect your concession," Otto says. "Jonathan here has the necessary paperwork for you to sign. Your attorney can handle the rest of your affairs."

He thinks I'm the lawyer. I know I'm not shabby, but unkempt at the very least. My tie's loose, my tattoos are plainly visible. But then again, mage lawyers are mages first, so maybe it wouldn't be all that surprising.

He hasn't so much as glanced at me and I don't say anything to disabuse him of that notion. I understand now what Amanda meant about an ambush. He doesn't know about me.

"I'm not conceding," she says. "Despite your best efforts, I have a champion." She tilts her head toward me. I give him a little wave, then blow him a kiss.

"This is highly irregular," Jonathan says. "We have it on good authority that your champion was killed last night. You can't do anything but concede."

"I don't know who you're talking about," Amanda says. "A friend of mine was murdered last night, but he had nothing to do with this. When I find out who all were involved in his death, I'm going to end them. How do you know about that, Mister Salvatore?"

Salvatore turns a little green. He's suddenly much easier to track. Interesting. Amanda has her full attention on him, and he doesn't seem to be able to shake it.

"I must be thinking about someone else," he says, lowering his eyes. Being the focus of all of Amanda's attention must be like getting hit with a firehose. There's just so much there.

"Yes, you must be," Amanda says. "I never formally declared a champion. Eric Carter is my champion." Otto still won't look at me.

"I prefer hired ass-kicker, myself," I say, "but y'all have your own fancy way of saying it."

Otto's very white skin begins to turn a lovely shade of pink. Between him and Salvatore it's starting to look downright festive in here. "Jonathan?" he says. The lawyer is going through a briefcase filled with paperwork that I hadn't noticed he brought in.

"Very irregular," he mutters. "Very irr— Oh." Crestfallen, he looks at Otto. "She's right, sir. As she didn't formally declare a champion, she can do so now. The duel continues."

Otto bangs both fists on the table and stands up, ready to loom over everyone. I bet he's a great loomer. He doesn't get very far, though.

"Is there a problem, Otto?" Attila Werther says from the doorway. Otto is physically straining to keep his rage in check.

"No, Uncle. Everything is fine."

"Excellent," Attila says. He looks like he's in his late fifties or early sixties. I'm not sure, but I think he looks younger than he did last time I saw him. But what the fuck do I know? I'm pushing fifty and look like I'm thirty.

"Hello, Eric. It's good to see you."

"Likewise," I say. "Like what you've done with the place."

"Thank you. I just threw it together from odds and ends. Nothing special. Family's coming over, you know. No reason to get fancy." There's no love lost between these two sides of the family. "Now as I understand it, you get to set the terms of the duel. Have you come up with anything?"

"I have a couple of ideas."

"This is the challenge," Otto says. "If the terms are not made then the duel is forfeit."

"Otto," Jonathan says in warning, but Otto's not listening.

"We can finally put to bed this whole ridiculous notion that you could find someone who could best me in a duel. Concede and this man won't have to die."

My phone rings. "Excuse me. It's the caterer," I say. I turn away like that's going to keep anyone from hearing the conversation, but it gives Otto my back. I may not know rich mage etiquette, but I am a master at pissing people off.

"Alice. Good to hear from you. Do we have—Fantastic. I'll talk to you soon." I hang up and slide the phone into my pocket. I turn back to everyone staring at me.

"Last minute details," I say. I let the silence go on too long to see who breaks first. Unsurprisingly, it's Otto.

"What are the terms? Tradition suggests a single attack with a spell from twenty paces. Or a fight with ensorcelled rapiers. Or—"

"Pit fighting," I say.

"What?"

"Pit fighting," Amanda says, not missing a beat, as if she'd been in on the plan the whole time. "You know, Thunderdome, the Octagon?"

"Two men in, one man out," I say. "Goes on until one of us taps out or dies. The rules are pretty straightforward. No holds barred. We go in wearing pants—I'd suggest MMA shorts or gi pants. Nothing else comes in with us. No hidden knives, guns, saps, rhinos, whatever. Not that that matters for mages. I mean, if you don't try the whole sword-of-swirling-energy trick, I'll honestly be disappointed."

"Where will this be?" Jonathan says.

"Quick Change Alice's Bar and Brawl," Amanda says. I'd hoped she'd figure out where I was going with this when I answered the phone. "It's in Long Beach in a space-shifted airplane hangar."

"This is outrageous," Otto says. "I will not—"

"Yes, you will," Attila says, his voice filled with warning. For a second I think Otto's going to challenge Attila, but apparently he's not that stupid.

"Of course, Uncle. I take it this space is adequate and private enough for this"—he makes a face like he's blowing a warthog—"pit fight."

"Adequate? Absolutely," I say. "Private? Oh hell no. This is gonna be the event of the year, my friend. They're already starting to make book on this one and it doesn't start for another twelve hours."

"It's tonight?" Jonathan says. "But he needs time to prepare."

"Well, if he can't meet the terms of the duel—" I say.

"Tonight," Otto says, standing and walking away. "Call Jonathan with the details." All this time and he still hasn't looked at me.

"Oh, hang on," I say. "I know I've got it here somewhere. I think this belongs to you." I toss him a plastic baggie with Reinhold's ring in it. "Sorry. I couldn't get it off the finger."

He picks up the bag and stares at Reinhold's severed finger for a long moment, then finally looks me in the eye. I can see murder in that look. I give him a wink and a smile. He stalks out without saying a word, and if he hadn't already been the angriest he'd been in his entire life, I think that might have pushed him over the edge.

Like I said, I am a master at pissing people off.

Chapter 6

"Pit fighting?" Attila says.

"I was leaning toward lucha libre, but I need to get my mask and cape dry-cleaned."

"Being a smart-ass isn't going to save you, boy," he says.

"No, it won't," I say. "But it will keep him on his toes. I need any edge I can get. If he can't think straight because he's too pissed off at me, I'll take it."

"Understood," Attila says. "One last thing. I take it Alice is expecting my call."

"They're expecting somebody to call to make final arrangements. Seating for the Emperor, shit like that. I was planning on doing it, but you might not like what I come up with."

"Indeed. It's been too long since Alice and I have chatted. I'll give them a call. And here my involvement must end. I can't offer advice or be privy to any discussions on either side. I'm the one who has to judge this debacle. All I can say is what I'm obligated to say to my nephew. Good luck."

"Thanks, Dad," Amanda says. Neither one of them is happy about this situation.

"I'll leave you to it," he says and leaves the room.

"I hope you know what you're doing," Amanda says.

"Me too. Look, when it comes down to it, whether we're flinging fireballs at each other atop a mountain range or trying to stab each other with lawn darts, this is to the death. I don't know that I'll win. I might not walk out of there. But if I don't, I promise you, neither will he."

"Thank you," Amanda says. She looks at me like she's trying to figure out a troublesome piece of machinery and not getting very far with it. "Last night you said you didn't want anything for this."

"I still don't. You're having trouble with this idea. Why?"

"Everything's got a price," she says.

"Maybe some things shouldn't. Why was Freddy going to do it? What did he want?"

"Nothing," she says. "I'd known him since I was a kid. He and Dad knew each other. He came over all the time and taught me how to fight. He was like an uncle. More family than my family ever has been." Amanda's voice cracks but snaps back just as quickly. She'll do her grieving in private.

"And we're not friends is what you're saying."

"No, not like—"

"I get it. We barely know each other. You've known me for a month. Hell, I've only known me for a month. I just came back from the dead, so why am I risking dying all over again to take on some Aryan asshole over wizard politics? You're thinking maybe this is some kind of trap. That I want to have something to hold over you, and by extension, your dad."

"Is that what you want? A favor? More than one? Done. Anything you want."

"No. If I wanted that, I'd have told you. It'd be stupid not to," I say. "Amanda, you don't have anything I want."

"He could kill you."

"And? We all die. Some of us get to do it more than once. Dying is not the worst thing that can happen to me."

This is something I've been thinking about since I was brought back. If I die, my soul isn't going to merge back with Mictlantecuhtli. I don't get to go back to who I was. I know this.

But I also know there's a hell of a lot more than alive or dead. When I die again, I have no idea where my soul will go. I've been told my existence is so jacked that death doesn't know what to do with me. If anything, things are a lot more complicated now, not less.

My soul has to go somewhere, but I'm not sure any afterlife will have me. Fine by me, gods are assholes. Take it from one who knows.

Or it could go the other way. With a case of double deicide on my record, I'm on a whole lotta divine shit lists. They might fight over who gets to eat me.

But do I belong here? Do I belong on Earth with thousands of years of death god memories bouncing around in my skull, half of which are so obscured I can barely see them?

I'm an Eric-Carter-shaped piece of soul that was peeled off of a Mictlantecuhtli stand-in and shoved into my grandfather's dug-up corpse. There is nothing in me that's original. Nothing that's actually mine. I am a man made of bits and pieces and I'm not sure who, hell, *what* I am.

So no, dying is not the worst thing that can happen to me.

"You want to die?" Amanda says.

"Not really," I say. "But if it happens, it happens." It takes her a second to process this.

"Okay. So where do we go from here?"

"Fight's at midnight. Your dad's handling the logistics with Alice. I'll be there around ten. You might want to get some sleep. Bound to be a long night no matter who wins."

———

I'm sorry Freddy's dead, but there's no way he would have survived a fight against Otto. From what I hear, Freddy knew how to fight in a ring, not murder somebody in cold blood. If Otto's half as powerful as his kid was, Freddy would have been dead before he could so much as think about a spell.

He was planning on using a regular old boxing ring, with the standard magic. I'm not. That's going to even things out a little. A wizard fight that uses a boxing ring is a reputable fight. The wards on the ring keep the audience safe from stray magic, but they're designed so that if a mage has to pull in additional power to keep from getting killed, they can. It'll just count against them in points.

At Quick Change Alice's you can't do that. The Pit's an octagon about ten feet in diameter. A chain-link cage is shaped into a sphere, sunk underneath the Pit and ensorcelled to keep everything out, and everything in.

The only power Otto and I are going to have is what we take in with us. There will be a one-minute warning for us to top off before the fight. I can pull in more magic faster than most mages can. But Reinhold and I were pretty evenly matched. No reason Otto won't be just as powerful, if not more so. There's really no concept of cheating in a fight like this. If you can do it, it's legal.

Quick Change Alice's has been a staple on the mage fight scene for almost a hundred years now. Ever since the airport opened. People walk by it all the time and completely miss it. Even the security guards don't know it's there, and they let people into the place. Soon as a car goes in, they forget about it, and security footage shows nothing.

I arrive a couple hours beforehand and it takes me a second to realize something's different. The hangar's there, the parking lot's there. Only they're both much bigger than they should be, but at the same time somehow completely unchanged. Old Man Werther is good with transdimensional spaces, and I can see his handiwork all over. He's taken the spells already in place and beefed them up by a factor of ten.

Good thing, too. Because the lot is full and growing in capacity for more cars. It took me almost half an hour just to get off the freeway. A radio traffic reporter is talking about delays off the 405 and 710 Freeways for construction. There's no construction, it's just Quick Change Alice's customers.

I find a parking spot way in the back. Parking might be a nightmare, but the second I set foot on the pavement, I'm at the hangar entrance.

It occurs to me that if Otto is even close to as powerful as his uncle, I might actually be in trouble.

I pull out a HI, MY NAME IS sticker and write JUST SOME GUY on it with a Sharpie, slap it on my chest, and pump some magic into it. Everybody in this place is a mage, or at least enough of a mage to know how to get here and into the hangar. That probably means a lot more people who know about magic than people who can really do much with it. The sticker should let me get through the crowd easily without most of them getting in my way.

More powerful mages will see right through it, but I'm not worried about them. If Amanda's right about my reputation among the elite out here, it's probably better if they do see me. Goddammit, I hate this shit.

"Sir," one of the bouncers says as I come up to them. They're in uniform and easy to spot. Red polo shirts, white pants, bulging muscles.

They're talents themselves, so they see right through the Sharpie magic. "I'll have to ask you to leave any guns, knives, fetishes, talismans, or artifacts with us. We'll give you a ticket to retrieve them later." Awfully optimistic to think I'll be alive to get them back.

I hand them my Sharpie and the three or four blank stickers I had in my pocket. It's all I have. I don't even have a cell phone or car keys on me. It's not like it was my car I drove here.

Still, they have to check. I get it. Rules are rules. They do a quick pat down and I feel a small flare of magic from one of them as he gives me a once-over for anything I might be hiding. "Thank you, sir. Go right in. Alice has requested to speak with you when you arrive. You can find them in their office."

I pass through the doors of the hangar and Quick Change Alice's turns into something I don't recognize. It's the same layout, only not. Stadium seating that reaches up near the ceiling looking down at the Pit in the middle. Concession stands selling beer and hot dogs and whatever else you're looking for.

Only the place is bigger, a lot bigger, than I remember, and I was here just last night. It's hard to focus on some parts of the bleachers, like they're bending away and twisting at impossible angles. Looking at multi-dimensional architecture can you give you a headache, but this is quality craftsmanship. I doubt most of the people in here even notice it.

I've seen enough at this point that I can tell that it's Werther's work. He's twisted the space inside to accommodate the ever-growing crowd. There is enough space for everyone. There's no over-crowding. And wherever I go I can see the Pit perfectly, with nothing blocking my view. Nice touch.

That said, it's already packed. Christ, how many people are in here? The landscape shifts too much for me to get a good count, but hundreds? Thousands? Fuck. Are they all here to see me get my ass kicked? I never realized I was such a draw.

Making things even more interesting, the crowd is completely sauced. Drunk mages are like football hooligans, but when they throw the seats in protest it's usually with gale-force winds. Here it's kept under more control. The bouncers all carry powerful paralysis talismans. You step out of line, be prepared to spend the next eight hours frozen in a heap in a back room Alice had specially made for it. And then she'll ban you, which is an even bigger threat.

I head down a walkway splitting one level of seating from the other and stop to watch the action below. There's a match already in progress. Two women in sports bras and wrestling tights, one black, one Asian, are trying to kick the shit out of each other. At least I think so. They're a little blurry.

It's a speed match. Same as any other pit fight, only they're both using magic to increase their reflexes to insane levels. Moving so fast they're hard to track. These fights usually end with just one punch. When you're going as fast as they are, one punch is all it takes. Like getting hit with an elephant.

The trick is landing that punch. They're each dodging every swing, kick, jab, knee, or elbow the other throws. Speed matches have no rounds and last three minutes. If somebody isn't unconscious or dead by then, it's a draw. At that point both fighters would be so exhausted they'd have to be taken out on stretchers anyway. I hear it's great for weight loss and cardio, provided your heart doesn't explode.

The black woman finally tags the Asian, slamming a fist into her jaw so hard I can hear it crack over the noise of the crowd. She bounces off the chain-link and hits the mat unconscious or dead. There's something about the winner that looks familiar.

"Quite the match, isn't it?" Gabriela says behind me.

"I know that fighter," I say, hopefully covering up the fact that I just froze for a second. I was wondering if Gabriela was going to show up, not that I had any real reason to. I've been avoiding her, but I'm pretty sure she's been avoiding me, too.

"You should," she says. "You're the one who told her to talk to me."

"That's Indigo? Holy shit." I met Indigo a couple days before I died. She's got a twin sister and a cousin who were all shaping up to be pretty powerful mages. I suggested she connect with Gabriela, see if they could work out some kind of training deal. Her knack was that she could move really fucking fast. She seems to have gotten better.

"My protégé," she says. "She's a lot more versatile these days. So, you're really doing this? Fighting for a young lady's honor?"

"Right, because that sounds so like me," I say.

"It really doesn't," she says. "You doing all right? You look like you could use some sleep."

"I'm fine," I say, a little too quickly. "I have to go see Alice and get ready."

"Talk after," she says.

"Sure." That is so not gonna happen.

"Good luck. And—just don't die, okay?"

"I'll take it under advisement. Say hi to Indigo for me."

Jesus, that felt awkward. I make my way toward the betting booths. I can't tell if it's my imagination, but it feels like Gabriela's burning a hole through my back with her eyes. I haven't talked to her in a couple of weeks and the last conversation we had was kind of strained.

I have mixed feelings about her. She pulled me out of Mictlan. I can't fault her reasons. She needed to take care of Darius, an eight-thousand-year-old djinn who was about to break free of the prison where he'd been locked up by Mictlantecuhtli. The seals were failing and the only one who could do anything about them was Mictlante-cuhtli himself.

She couldn't get all of him, so she settled for me. She ripped me from the only place that ever really felt like home, away from too many things to forgive her for.

But she's my friend. And she risked a lot to bring me back. And she kissed me. That spun me a hell of a lot more than it should have. But now's not the time to think about it.

The seating in front of the betting booths has been rearranged to create a box seat that looks down over the Pit. Werther and Amanda will be sitting there. It looks like there are a few more seats in the box, though. Not sure who else is showing up from the family.

I go to one of the bouncers, some guy I've never seen before. "I'm here to see Alice," I say.

It's clear he recognizes me instantly. "Yes, sir. They're expecting you in their office. Please follow me." He takes me past the betting booths and into a short corridor. Last night there was only one betting booth. Not six, or maybe sixty, I can't tell. Each booth has a line of twenty people, easy. A few take notice of me, mages strong enough to see past my thin disguise.

"You've made some changes," I say.

"Really?" the bouncer says. "I hadn't noticed." We stop at a red door and for a second I flash to a different red door, with the world's worst nightmare behind it. But Darius is dead. Destroyed when I collapsed an entire universe on him. And a few thousand people he thought he could use against me as human shields.

Yeah, I know. Have the butcher add it to my tab.

"Right through there, sir. Have a good fight, and for what it's worth, I hope you win."

"Appreciate it," I say. "But you didn't bet on me, did you?"

"No, sir." He turns and heads back out.

I knock on the door and go in without waiting for a response. Alice is sitting behind their desk, still wearing the Persian woman's skin.

"You wanted to see me?"

They wave at a bar cart in the corner. "Pour me a gin and tonic and have a seat."

"This sounds serious," I say, once I've given them their drink. I considered pouring one for me, but alcohol and fights to the death are not as great a combination as you might think.

"You should know what the betting looks like. Four-to-one on the Kraut," they say.

"And me?"

"Ten-to-one."

"Jesus, seriously? The hell is that based on?"

"You know what they say, 'The race is not always to the swift, nor the battle to the strong—'"

"'But that's the way to bet.' Yeah, I know that one," I say. "But the odds are that stacked?"

"You hear some of the shit that guy's done? He made some big river in Germany flow backward for a week. I saw footage of him taking on three other combat mages and all he left were smeary puddles. He made an entire town disappear and none of the normals have noticed.

Not even the ones with relatives who lived there. It's not even on maps anymore."

"I killed two gods," I say. "That's not nothing, you know."

"Yeah, but I've never seen footage of it," they say. "Ten-to-one. Not a lot of people are betting on you."

"That's not surprising," I say. "What's the audience like tonight? Hard to tell with all the non-Euclidian shit you got going on out there."

"Last I checked, about five thousand out there and another ten thousand on pay-per-view."

"You're streaming this?"

"Hell yeah. I mean, not just anybody can access it. By the time we get going, we'll have another ten thousand watching, easy, probably more. We got people from all over the world out there in the stands or tuning in."

"No idea I was such a draw."

"Nah, it's the story that's the draw. Knight in shining armor comes to rescue a young lady's virtue from her evil whatever-the-fuck-he-is? People eat that shit up."

"For fuck sake. She can handle her own virtue. I'm just helping her get out of a bullshit loophole."

"Uh huh. Sure. Hey, it true you're bangin' her?"

"The fuck? No. I hardly know her."

"Damn. I had twenty bucks riding on that."

Chapter 7

I change into a pair of blue gi pants in the locker room, a barely furnished space made of cheap drywall with a couple of lockers and a shower with disintegrating grout.

I don't like pre-planning fights. It's too easy to second guess yourself trying to prepare for everything. There's only so much you can remember to do when somebody's trying to rip your head off.

According to Amanda, everyone in the family tries to keep their knack quiet. So she doesn't know what he's good with or what he's likely to use. He could channel his power into the physical and move faster, hit harder. He could use it to push or pull, set shit on fire. There's no point in putting too much planning into a strategy for this.

I lie down on the bench and stare at the ceiling. I feel like crap. I need sleep. But if I sleep—well, nothing I can do about that right now. I get up, dig into my messenger bag for a bottle of Adderall. I shake out a couple pills. Fuck it. I shake out another two and dry swallow all four.

A knock on the locker room door. "Come in," I say.

"Hey," Indigo says, peeking her head around the door, like she's afraid I'm going to blow it off, which, let's be honest, I would have had she been someone else. "Got a second?"

Her left eye is swollen half-shut and a nicely stitched slice on the left side of her face goes from her scalp down to the edge of her ear. She's got the kind of proud smile that only someone who's beat the living shit out of their opponent has.

"Yeah, come on in," I say. "Saw your fight out there. Nicely done."

"Thanks. Gabriela's been training me up. I'm better at the physical stuff so she's been having me focus on that."

"Glad it's working out."

"Me too. But that's not what I came here for. I saw your man Otto sparring this afternoon. I don't know if this is going to help, but he really tried to avoid anything physical. Everything he did today was all magic. Big, flashy spells."

"Anything in particular?"

"He did this lightning storm thing like three times. You know, clouds gathering, bolts shooting out of them. I could tell he'd toned it down for the guys he was working with, but it still fucked 'em up pretty bad. But it also took him a while to get it going. A good two seconds easy. They got some licks in before he set it off. Seemed to fuck his concentration a lot."

"Good to know," I say. I have a couple ideas how I might be able to use that information. She's looking me over and I know what she's going to say before she says it.

"Goddamn, you look like a horny peacock. I'd heard about your tats, but goddamn those are bright. Is there any piece of skin you don't have covered in ink?"

When I came back from the dead I still had all my tattoos, which was a little weird considering it wasn't my body. Weirder still was that they had all gone from black or dull green to bright reds and blues, vibrant greens and yellows. I'm not sure if I look more like a Yakuza boss or the scene of a tropical bird massacre.

I wink at her. "Only one way you'll find out."

"Pass," she says. "I'm taken. But seriously, you don't look to me like a guy who goes for jewel tones."

"I'm not," I say. "It's kind of a going-away present from somebody I used to know. It's a long story." An airhorn blows outside. "And that's my cue."

"Good luck. Don't die," she says. "But if you do, make it entertaining. I missed it the last time."

―――――

Noise and light and the stink of sweat and spilled beer. Fifteen thousand people, maybe more, are staring at me as I walk half-naked out of the locker room. There are at least five thousand in the bleachers and another ten to twenty scattered across the world. I make my way up the chain-link covered walk from the lockers to the fighter's entrance. Otto and I each have our own. The crowd's screaming but I can't tell if they're cheering or cursing. Nobody's throwing beer bottles at me, so that's a good sign.

Why do I even care? I'm here to do one thing, and whether people are watching hoping I get murdered or not is irrelevant. And if they are, that's certainly not new. Even before the fires I had mages gunning for me, when they thought I was some kind of serial killer murdering other mages. Even Werther got in on that action.

The walkway opens up into a larger chain-link-covered space with a stool, a bucket of ice water, and a first aid kit. Like I'm going to get a chance to use it.

An airhorn blows and a scoreboard above the Pit starts to count-down from sixty seconds. I reach out and seize the magic from the local pool, drawing in as much as I can as fast as I can. Though I can't see him, I can feel Otto doing the same. We're like two kids shoving each other out of the way to get to the drinking fountain.

How much a mage pulls isn't actually a good indication of how much they *can* pull. You don't know how much they started with. Maybe they've got more capacity. Maybe less. And just because you can fill up the gas tank doesn't mean you can use it all. But people will bet on anything.

The timer ends and the airhorn blows again. The gate to the Pit slides open and I step inside. It's showtime.

Stepping into the Pit is a little like walking into one of those sound-proofed rooms covered in baffles where all you can hear is your own heartbeat—only for magic. It disappears around you and the only power you can feel is your own and your opponent's.

I scan the audience and find the box that Werther is in, grim-faced, looking like he's about to officiate at a funeral. Jonathan, Otto's law-yer, sits to his left, looking jittery and nervous. Next to him are two men who are almost the spitting image of Otto. One's clearly older than the other, looking more like Attila. I'm betting that's Amanda's uncle Liam and Otto's brother Hans.

Amanda sits to her father's right in a black dress. Her face is blank, and I can't even imagine what she's thinking.

It takes me a second to realize who the woman sitting to her right is. Gabriela's changed out of her punk princess attire and exchanged it for a simple black dress similar to Amanda's. They're holding hands. Huh.

Otto steps into the Pit wearing wrestling tights. The guy's ripped, I'll give him that. But from the way some of his muscles bulge in weird spots I'd say they've been enhanced a bit for tonight's performance. He's got his way of getting an edge, I have mine.

He pauses for a second, surprise flashing across his face. I'm bet-ting he's never been in a shielded space, though maybe he just doesn't like it. Most mages don't. It's unnerving if you're not used to it. He recovers quickly and gives me that now-familiar sneer of superiority.

"We can end this without you having to die. All you have to do is concede." He has to yell above the crowd to be heard. The wards keep out magic, but do fuck-all for sound.

"You seriously think I'm going to believe that after I tossed your dead kid's finger at you this afternoon?"

"Reinhold went against my wishes. He knew not to meddle. A son who disobeys his father is less than useless. You did me a favor."

"You people are really fucked up. Let's get this started. The sooner I kill you, the sooner I don't have to see your ugly face."

Otto throws his hands into the air theatrically and I feel a flash of magic. The air above him starts to shimmer and fill with gray clouds, lightning sparking through them. Confronted with the majesty of his control of the weather, I do the only thing I can think of.

I tackle him. He hits the mat hard and I hammer at his face a good five or six times before he gets his shit together and throws me off with a push spell that sends me crashing into the chain-link on the other side of the Pit. I hit the mat, roll back to standing. He's still trying to catch his breath and get to his feet.

His face is a mess. Busted nose, already-swelling left eye. Blood pouring from a gash in his cheek where a tooth has punched through. His eyes are so full of hate it's almost comical.

I'm back on him before he can get all the way up. I don't think it's going to work, Otto's too powerful to let something like this through, but I slap the flat of my hand against his cheek and look for a hook into his soul. Either he doesn't have one or he's got a good lock on it, because I can't even find it.

So instead I catch him with a punch followed by an elbow strike. Not enough to knock him out by a long shot. Neither one of us is going down that easy, but I've definitely thrown him for a loop.

I block a half-hearted jab and follow it up with my own, realizing too late that it's a trap. His left hand and forearm have morphed into a wide, flat blade with a hooked barb like a fat harpoon.

I spin out of the way, but he scores a long slice along my ribcage. My tattoos help with the pain and in minimizing the damage, but I can still see bright red meat and bone through the wound. Blood splashes onto the mat.

My balance is already fucked. He hits me with a quick jab. I trip over my own feet, land hard on my back. He moves in like lightning and leaps at me, his full weight on his left arm. I manage to roll out of the way just in time. The Pit shakes with the impact.

Miraculously, he doesn't follow up, and when I get to my feet I can see why. He's punched into the mat so hard that half his forearm is sunk into it and the barb is sticking. He can't pull it out.

Far be it for me to see a prize-winning opportunity and not take it.

I aim a kick at his elbow, snapping it sideways with a satisfying crack. His weight takes care of the rest as he falls the wrong way over his forearm, ripping bone, meat, and sinew out through a tear just below the bicep.

Otto screams, clutching at what's left of the ruin of his arm. That has got to be agonizing. I wouldn't blame him for calling the fight, but I really don't think he will. Still, I give him the chance.

"We can end this without you having to die," I say. "All you have to do is concede."

In answer his right arm morphs into a sword blade, and with one quick slash he severs his shattered arm just above the break. Blood sprays across the floor as he raises the stump of his left arm and calls fire to dance across it, cauterizing it.

"That's a no?"

Otto screams and runs for me, slashing with the blade. He tags my left forearm as I twist away from him, but I get my fist up into his right armpit and, with some extra power from a push spell, slam it into his brachial plexus.

His right arm goes dead and he howls. I cut that off with a follow-up elbow strike to his throat. He staggers back, gagging.

It's not going to keep him out of the fight for long, but I need the break. I pull back, breath coming in rapid gasps. Even if he doesn't kick my ass, this fight sure as hell will.

"You think," he says, coughing between words, "that you're hurting me? You think you can win?"

"To be honest, yeah, I kinda do."

"No, I don't think so." He disappears.

Fuck. Invisibility. I hate invisibility. I can't hear anything over the crowd. I try to track him from the indentations his feet leave in the mat, but I lose him fast. I push myself into one of the corners of the octagon and go low. There's no way he's going to come after me head-on and this at least covers my back.

I feel something move to my left, so I roll to my right. There's a momentary shimmer where I see him as the blade slams into the chain link, and then he's gone again. I have to do something about this fast.

Then it hits me. There's an awful lot of blood all over the floor. I reach out with my magic and pull it all into a wet ball floating in front of me. Then I throw it up into the air.

The ball of blood explodes, filling the space with red rain. It coats everything. Me, the mat, the chain-link, and most importantly, Otto.

He doesn't seem to realize that I can see him perfectly fine now, so when he comes at me with his sword-hand I'm ready for it. At least I think I am. He slashes. I sidestep. He recovers and twists around to stab me in the side, missing by a hair's width. He sweeps his leg, taking my feet out from under me, and I hit the ground.

He slashes and punches at me with lightning speed. I raise a shield to ward off his attacks, but he's pushing a lot of power into his strikes. I'm not going to be able to keep this up much longer.

Time for Plan B. My shield finally breaks. He pulls back and stabs, but I'm not there anymore.

Though Quick Change Alice has been around for a long time, the Pit's relatively new. She had it built in the nineties and hired people from all over to ward the fuck out of it against every type of magic she could think of. Fire, lightning, scrying, curses, hexes, whatever it was, she thought of it.

Except for one. See, necromancers are rare. In the last hundred years there have been five of us at most in Southern California. And so it never occurred to her to ward it against ghosts. More importantly, she didn't ward it against anything crossing the veil.

There's a rush of noise and everything turns to shades of grey and blue as I shift to the other side. I get to my feet, dizzy, bruised, and bleeding. Which means I've already gotten the attention of all the Wanderers in a ten-mile radius. I don't have a lot of time.

I can't see the cage around me. It hasn't been in place long enough for its psychic footprint to solidify over here. Which is one of the reasons I picked this place for the fight.

I can see everyone in the seats, though, and Otto is right where I left him, glowing like a bonfire. I was here last night, dropping off a package in the middle of the Pit in case I needed some backup.

The straight razor is one I've never used before. Honestly, I've been afraid to touch the damn thing since I found it in a storage building with a bunch of other magical tchotchkes that ranged from the dangerous to the stupid, heavy on the stupid. I inherited the building and its contents from my parents but didn't know about it for decades. Not until I came back to Los Angeles. There's a ledger for all the crap in there with an entry for every item. And for all that, I still can't figure out what half the shit does. Most of the entries are along the lines of, "Winter Coat—Do not wear for more than two hours at a time," or "Hat—Randomly changes overnight between fedora, trilby, derby, boater, and tricorn."

When I'm summoning and talking with ghosts it helps to offer a little something to entice them. A few drops of blood are perfect. So

I carry around a straight razor and cut a little into a bare patch on my left forearm without any tattoos. I had years of scarring, but this body hasn't been cut up enough yet.

Since I almost always have a straight razor on me, I've learned how to fight with one. I don't recommend it if you don't like cutting the shit out of yourself while you learn.

So I'd been really interested in an item entered in the ledger as "Straight Razor," then crossed out with the words "Vorpal Razor" handwritten above it. There wasn't much detail in the entry itself, but plenty of notes in the margins to suggest that's as good a name as any for it. Most of the notes were variations of "Don't fucking touch this thing," or "Frank took his hand clean off yesterday when he wasn't paying attention." At least three mentioned decapitation.

I'm a little nervous, but nobody ever said I was smart. I've got one chance at this, and if I fuck it up, Otto's gonna be pissing inside my ribcage.

He's moving around the Pit looking for me, swinging wildly from side to side. I open the razor, stay behind him, wait until he stops moving, then slide back across the veil.

I grab his hair and yank to the side to hold his head in place, then slash across the back of his neck. If this thing works nearly as well as I'm expecting I should be able to sever his spine without a problem.

The blade bites through his skin, goes through tendon and muscle and bone like tissue paper. And before I realize what's happened, I'm standing there with Otto's severed head in my hand.

Blood fountains out of the stump of his neck as his body sways, falling to its knees and then the rest of the way, landing with a wet plop in a growing puddle of gore. My little blood shower was nothing compared to this. I swear he must have had high blood pressure, because this shit is coming out like a firehose.

The audience is dead silent. I cast around until I see Werther sitting stoic in his box, Otto's lawyer next to him looking like he's about to throw up. Liam is, like his brother, unreadable, but Hans's face is pure rage.

Amanda looks stunned and Gabriela—well, Gabriela looks like she's trying really hard not to laugh. I raise the head, its eyes still blinking, toward them.

"Does this mean I win?"

Chapter 8

I rinse out the cuts with a bottle of Jack Daniels I found in the locker room. I just want it clean enough to see what I'm doing when I start sewing.

With all this blood on me, I'd probably have to stand in the middle of a car wash to get it all off. You think sand is bad? Blood gets into places you didn't even know you had. And once it dries it might as well be paint. You can feel it pinching your skin every time you move.

Nobody tells you these things. You pretty much have to figure them out on your own. You'd think by now some enterprising mage would have written a basic manual on shit like this. "Chapter 7: Clean-up Tips After Sacrificing a Black Ram at Midnight to Dark Entities Unknown."

I pull out a suture kit from a first aid kit on the wall. Last time I stitched myself up I had a sewing needle, dental floss, and a gash in my cheek where some asshole decided to go to town with a dental pick, so this is quite an upgrade. My life is a glamorous one.

I have more cuts than I realized. Three on my chest, one of which looks pretty significant. My left leg has a slash in it. Two slices on my ribs haven't completely stopped bleeding, but I slapped on some gauze from the first aid kit in my corner of the Pit when I walked out, and they've slowed enough that I can work on them.

Between the blood and my tattoos it's hard to see where exactly I'm bruised. I assume "everywhere" and decide to worry about that later.

I'm about to start stitching, the needle just over the skin, when the door bursts open. Without thinking I put my hand out, and the straight razor, which I thought I'd stuck in my bag, flies across the room to slap into my hand.

I go low into a crouch, ready to fire off a spell, jump, or cut the guy who just walked in. He's young-ish. Late twenties, maybe. Brown hair, green eyes, glasses. Wearing a doctor's lab coat and carrying a black bag—like I'm gonna fall for that.

"Oh, for god's sake put that thing down before you hurt yourself," he says. "What the hell kind of hack job are you trying to do?"

"I don't know who the fuck you are, but you got five seconds before I start cutting off limbs."

"It's all right, Eric. Doctor Hilliard is with me." Attila Werther steps into the room behind him. "Thought you might want to have a professional look you over."

"Last one did that told me I had brain damage."

"They were clearly right," Hilliard says. "You're seriously trying to sew yourself up? Do you even have any anesthetic?"

"Your bedside manner sucks."

"Good thing you're not in bed, then. Now put that goddamn thing down so I can take a look." I do what he says, fold the razor and put it down.

Hilliard looks me over, asking me to move for a better view at a couple cuts I missed. "Okay. These are easy," he says. "If you really want to sew yourself up, knock yourself out."

"I'll leave it to the professional."

"Oh, I'm a professional? Thanks for noticing. Close your eyes, take a deep breath, and shut up." I can feel the flare of magic as he performs a spell.

"Am I gonna live, doc?"

"Only if you fucking shut up like I told you. All right, open your eyes."

He's typing notes into a cell phone. Or hell, maybe he's texting somebody and sending dick pics, I dunno.

"Yes, you'll live," he says. "You've been knocked around some, but you don't have a concussion. You're bruised all to shit inside and out, though. One of your kidneys took a beating. Probably be pissing blood for a few days. Don't worry about it. Your left vertebrochondral ribs are bruised, so try not to get hit on that side for a couple days or one of them's going to crack. Take some ibuprofen and ice whatever hurts. Other than that, you're alarmingly healthy."

"Alarmingly?"

"How old are you?"

"Depends on how you look at it. Couple thousand years, pushing fifty, or just over a month."

"Are all your people this much a pain in the ass?" he asks Werther. "I'm gonna go with a month. Your mental capacity certainly fits. You don't have any of the damage I would expect to see in anyone who looks like you. No arterial plaque, no scarring, no sun damage." He turns to Werther. "You sure he's human?"

"More or less," he says.

"All right. Instead of ripping through your skin with a needle and thread we're gonna do it the right way." He places one hand about an inch over each of the rib slices, casts a spell, and I feel a weird sensation, like a jacket being zipped up.

The slices have been replaced with new, pink skin. He tapes Steri-Strips over everything and transparent Tegaderm patches over those.

"This shit's still gotta heal," he says. "It'll be fast, maybe four or five days, but only if you don't fuck with it. You go getting yourself into more fights, there's no guarantees."

"Thanks," I say.

"Yeah, whatever. Attila, anything else?"

"No, thank you, Walter. I appreciate you coming in on such short notice."

"Sure thing. And you"—he looks me up and down—"I don't know what the fuck you are, but you creep me out." He grabs his bag and pushes his way past Werther.

"The fuck was that all about?"

"Walter is a physician I have on retainer," he says. "He can be brusque, but he does good work."

"If that's brusque, I don't want to know what qualifies as an asshole."

"There's an adage about pots and kettles," Werther says, "but I don't recall what it is just now."

"Fine. Yes, I get your point. And thank you." Not having to sew myself up feels a little alien, but I'll take it.

Werther comes over to the bench to look at the razor. "May I?" he says.

"Knock yourself out." He picks it up, unfolds it. For the most part it looks ordinary. It's straight-razor-shaped, at least. The handle is mother of pearl with brass fittings, the blade has whorl patterns in it like Damascus steel. A line of runes is carved into the blade, a language I don't recognize.

"I haven't seen this thing in ages," Werther says. "You know we locked it up for a reason."

"I been meaning to ask you about that. You and my grandfather built the storage unit, right?"

"Oh, a whole cadre of people," he says. "Sadly, most of them died in the war." He folds the blade and places it back onto the bench. "Most of the items in there were shipped over from England after the war. Some of the more dangerous pieces we moved after Dunkirk. Like that razor."

"Don't worry, it's going right back in the box I pulled it out of," I say.

"No, I don't think that's going to happen," Werther says.

"That sounds ominous."

I grab a thin towel from a stack, step into the shower, and close the curtain. The water pressure sucks, but much as I adore walking around covered in blood, it's starting to lose its charm. I let the water soak into the pants for a bit before I try to peel them off.

"You're the first person to use that blade in over a hundred years," Werther says. "You've spilt blood with it. You've murdered with it. It's consecrated and bound. It's yours whether you want it or not. It's never going to be far, no matter where you are."

"What, like a puppy?"

"I've heard it described that way, yes. Or a very annoying cat. Be careful about who you let handle it. One wrong move and they might kill themselves just opening it up."

"What about me? Am I gonna lop off a hand if I nick my thumb?"

"You'll be fine. You can even shave with it if you want. If you don't want it to kill, it won't."

"Well, that's handy."

Beats a Nazi murder gun that wants to kill everything. Had a Browning Hi-Power from the war, before the Belgians started sabotaging their own factories. It hadn't started talking to me yet, but it was damn near. I could feel its emotional states and they were never good. It was destroyed when I killed Darius. Good riddance.

"I'm not here to talk to you about dead people and angry razorblades," Werther says. "I wanted to ask, 'Now what?'"

"Well, I'm gonna finish getting cleaned up, put some pants on. Probably go get a burger or something." I know what he's talking about, I just don't want to think about it.

"You just murdered one of the most powerful mages in all of Western Europe as the proxy of the daughter of one of the most powerful mages in the Americas, in full view of at least twenty thousand people and easily two or three million more streaming the fight on hidden YouTube channels."

"Fuck." I knew it was going to be bad. I didn't know it was going to be this bad.

"Indeed. I don't think you can claim to be apolitical anymore," he says. "So, now what?"

That's a good question. My life has been upside down since I came back. Now it's taken a sudden left turn into territory I have only the barest understanding of.

No matter how many times I run water through my hair, it keeps streaming to the shower floor tinted a dull rust. Did Elizabeth Bathory have this problem? Screw it. I finish and start toweling off.

"You tell me," I say. "I don't know what any of this really means. I know I already had a reputation."

"In Los Angeles, absolutely. Now it'll be the world. Right now, people are trying to figure out who you are, where you came from, whether any of the rumors about you are true, and just how terrified of you they should be."

"As long as one of those rumors is 'he's hung like a bear,' I'm okay with it."

"A lot of people respect you now, whether they like you or not. A lot more are simply frightened. And some are going to come at you to make a name for themselves. I'd hate to see you die like some Old West gunfighter."

"What, ambushed in a saloon and shot in the back of the head during a card game or penniless with tuberculosis? I don't play poker and I take my vitamins."

"Joke all you like—"

"I will," I say. "I have to or I'll start screaming. There are whole states I can't set foot in without risking my hide. I have pissed off one or more very powerful people in every major city east of the Rockies and more than a few minor ones. Other countries, too. Mages in Port Au Prince would love to see me fed to sharks, but they'll have to get in line behind the Cubans who want to do the same thing. This really isn't any different than what I deal with now."

I learned that paranoia pays years ago. Getting out of Los Angeles after I'd killed Jean Boudreau was a crash course in how not to get murdered. Word had been spreading that I'd taken him down and some of his people thought if they could bring my head to the new boss they'd get a seat at the table. Trouble was, the new boss was the one who told me to get out of the city. Not that he was any help, of course. If they'd brought him my body filled with holes, I don't think he'd have minded. I survived through luck, desperation, and paranoia. And I see no reason to change things now.

"You might see a higher class of killer than you're used to," he says. "But younger and brasher is my guess. At a certain level of notoriety, we all run into them eventually. In this case, though, a lot of people are going to think you're allied with my family."

I get out of the shower with the towel around my waist, pull a change of clothes out of the locker, and start to get dressed. For once they're not completely covered in blood.

"Yeah, I figured that part out on my own, thanks." I realized that would happen the moment I decided to take on Otto. I don't like it, but as mages go, Attila's not that bad, and there's actually a chance Amanda won't grow up to be a raging asshole.

"I can help with some of that," Werther says. "By way of saying thank you, I've set up an account for you offshore with two million dollars in it and signed over the deed to a property in Big Sur."

"I don't need the money," I say. "Or a place in Big Sur. I didn't do this for anything like that." And then it clicks. "You've leaked this information already, haven't you. You're making me look like a mercenary for hire instead of your bitch."

"Colorfully phrased, but yes," he says. "This should throw a bit of a wrench in how people see you. Some will still believe we're allied, but word should get around that you're an independent contractor, not under the Werthers' thumb. I'd suggest moving some money back and forth through that account. Maybe sell the property. No doubt someone has already hacked into the account and is watching to see what you do with it."

"Appreciate it." I sit down to tie my shoes.

"Not to undo what I've just done, but I have a proposition for you."

"Will it make things worse?"

"Undoubtedly. My family is in town for a conclave. One of them is going to try to kill Amanda. I'd rather that not happen." I don't ask him how he knows. He's probably just playing the odds.

"I thought you couldn't kill each other."

"During the conclave most of the restrictions are eased."

"What keeps you all from murdering each other during a conclave?"

"There's still a restriction against directly murdering each other. But if we can get someone to pull the trigger for us, we can target whoever we want. That said, it's mostly me. As the head of the family and the controller of the property where the conclave is being held, I have a certain amount of control. But constant infighting between alliances and factions inside the family helps. There's no real unification. Any killing will be, if not discreet, at least not in public view."

"You want a bodyguard for her," I say.

"Yes."

"No."

"Can you take some time to consider it?"

"Nope. Not my pig, not my farm. I helped Amanda because this whole thing was stupid and she was getting the shaft. She's still young enough that maybe she won't turn out to be a total prick like the rest of us. I'm sure she can do just fine on her own."

"Think about it," he says.

"Already have," I say. I put my jacket on and head to the door, then stop. Something's not adding up. Then it clicks.

"You don't think Amanda's in danger," I say, "at least not any more than she usually is. You think somebody's gonna kill you. If that happens, sure, she inherits, but then she's stuck with your family. They won't kill her, but they might try to manipulate her."

"My daughter is far more formidable than they realize. But if something were to happen to me, I would like to see her surrounded by allies."

"Jesus. You just paid me two million and a house to make it look like I was some gun-for-hire rather than a Werther ally, and now you want to invite me to the family reunion?"

"As security. Exactly the sort of thing a gun-for-hire would be hired for."

"I can't," I say. "I'm sorry. I really am. But I'm not the guy you think I am and I'm sure as hell not the guy you need. Good luck this weekend. And keep your head down."

"Aren't you forgetting your puppy?" Werther says as I open the door. He's holding the straight razor out to me.

"If it really wants to, it can catch up."

Everything hurts down into my bones. I knew this was going to be an ugly fight, but I don't think I was prepared for just how ugly it got.

I don't have a problem with having killed Otto, but I shouldn't have underestimated him. Just because somebody's a pompous fucknugget doesn't mean they can't kick your ass.

A fight like that, I usually don't plan. Sure as hell don't have an audience. Like in the alley with Reinhold last night. He tried to kill me, so I went and tried to kill him right back. It was honest. This felt a little . . . dishonorable? That's not the word. Dammit, what is it? Cheap. It felt cheap.

Don't get me wrong, I'd totally kill him again if I had to.

Walking from the locker room toward the exit I can definitely feel every one of the bruises I got in that fight. Bruises are part of the cost of doing business, but damn, these are pretty fucking epic.

As I get closer to the exit I can hear that the crowd hasn't really thinned out much. I'll have to pass by the betting booths. Christ, Alice, this whole layout is a fucking nightmare.

To be fair, usually there's only maybe fifty people in here, drinking shitty beer and watching a couple of mages whale on each other. Weekends can top a couple hundred or so, but that's nothing compared to this. I don't know how they even staff for this.

I'm not in the mood to deal with a bunch of pissed-off mages who lost a lot of money because of me. I go to pull a HI, MY NAME IS sticker and a Sharpie out of my pocket and remember that I gave them to the bouncers. There's got to be another exit.

Or I could just make my own. There aren't any Haunts here and I only see a few Wanderers nearby. A couple Echoes of people who died in plane crashes, which are always weird. I can see the person, but not the plane. It's like watching Superman do a nosedive into the tarmac.

I'm about to slide over when I hear someone say my name. I'm tired. It's making me slow. As I turn to see who it is, I get a face full of fist.

It's a solid right hook that connects on the side of my head, snapping it to the side and taking the rest of me with it. I stagger, get my footing, and catch the next punch in my hand, which I pump up with a strength spell. I hear bones pop.

Usually when that happens people make some noise, a scream, a grunt, something. But not this guy. At first I think I made a huge mistake and it wasn't Otto whose head I cut off. This guy's got all the same Aryan Nation features. Then I remember Hans was in the audience. Standing behind and a little further back is another man. The family resemblance is unmistakable, but he looks a lot more like Attila.

The guy I assume is Hans pulls his hand back for another shot and I let him have it. But not before hexing his fingers to burst into flame. Now he makes noise. His flaming hand has all his attention. He's not prepared for my jab to his face or my foot in his nads.

Now he's on the floor, on fire, with a busted nose and ruptured testicles. He doesn't look like he knows which problem to deal with first.

"Nicely done," the older man, who I'm assuming is Liam, says.

"Thanks."

"No, thank you. This one's even more of a shit than his brother. Liam Werther. I'd offer to shake hands, but I prefer mine to stay flame free."

"Liam," I say. "And that's Hans?" The flame is spreading, though slowly. It's easy to put out and it's not going to do much more than hurt. He should be more worried about his nuts.

"Unfortunately, yes," Liam says. "Oh, Hans, my boy, if you ever wondered if you were set on fire, would anyone so much as piss on you to put you out, I would say the answer is an emphatic no."

Hans gets to his feet, glares at me, then runs back the way he came. Hobbles, really. Yeah, he needs to get his nuts looked at.

"He seems nice," I say.

"He is a perfect example of the worst my family has to offer."

"And you're not so bad?"

"Oh, my boy, I'm ten times worse. We both know I'm not to be trusted and I won't insult you by saying otherwise. But it doesn't mean I can't be civil about it."

"I appreciate the honesty," I say. "And in the spirit of transparency, I'm more than happy to murder you."

"I, too, appreciate the honesty. I enjoyed the fight. Clever. I see your reputation is not unearned."

"Which reputation is that?"

"Oh, I hear things now and then. I was in Vegas several years ago for a short bit. Your name came up quite a lot."

I tense and force myself to relax, certain I didn't manage it before he noticed. Vegas is one of those times in my life I prefer not to think about. I learned a lot in Vegas. Mostly that I shouldn't be in Vegas.

Not a fan of the place. And that was before I lived there. It stinks of desperation, of people right on the brink of everything falling apart. It's a good place for luck magic and spells that are stupidly ambitious, provided you're okay when they fail spectacularly. I did a ritual like that once. It seemed to work fine, but I didn't stick around to see how it all turned out.

"Haven't been there in about thirty years," I say. "Can't imagine who would drop my name."

"Oh, people," he says, dismissing it with a wave of his hand. "You made quite the impression on a few."

"Must be thinking of somebody else," I say. Alarm bells are going off in my head because there's only one thing I ever did of note in Las Vegas.

Vegas is where I washed up when I bolted from L.A. after killing Jean Boudreau, the guy who murdered my parents. I laid low, assuming—rightly, as I would be reminded from time to time—that some of his old organization would come after me.

I was twenty years old and hadn't gotten a lot of training from other necromancers, on account of having only met necromancers who either wouldn't talk to me or who were actively trying to murder me. Everything I knew about my knack I'd learned on my own.

As luck would have it, the ghost of a necromancer was haunting a jail cell in a North Las Vegas police department. Guy got drunk, passed out, tossed in a cell and had a heart attack. Pretty embarrassing. I hung out a couple years until he'd pretty much said everything he was going to say and moved on. I just didn't move on far enough fast enough.

I got in with a couple of psychopathic mages—redundant, I know—who needed a necromancer for a ritual. It was . . . unusual. And that's saying something, for necromancy.

Only those two other people were there when I did the spell. Three if you count the guy whose head I had to cut off as part of it. Four if you count the demon I stuck in the head to keep his soul company.

Far as I know at least one of them is dead. And it's not the guy missing his head. He was fine when I left him. Sort of.

"I was misinformed," Liam says. He looks behind him and sighs. "I should go see if my idiot nephew has managed to burn himself to a crisp. It was very nice meeting you."

Liam turns and heads down the hall after Hans as Attila is coming out. They really look a lot alike. Attila says something I can't hear. Liam answers, looks back at me, and gives me a broad smile before walking away.

Okay, what the fuck? I haven't heard shit about Vegas in thirty years. So why am I hearing about it now from him?

My thoughts are interrupted by the sound of running footsteps. Great, now who wants to take a shot at me? I turn in time to see Amanda coming at me, Gabriela in tow. She throws herself at me with an enthusiastic hug and it takes everything I have not to scream.

"Oh god, you're a hugger," I say through clenched teeth.

"What? Oh, shit. I'm sorry. Are you all right? Of course, you're not all right. Thank you. You have no idea how relieved I am that that's over. Thank you. Especially for not dying."

"Told you if I kicked, I'd make sure Otto went first," I say. "And you can stop hugging me now, please."

"Shit. Are you all right? I asked that already."

"For him," Gabriela says, "this is all right."

"Pie," Amanda says.

"I beg your pardon?"

"We need to go get pie. I know a place that's open twenty-four hours and they have amazing pie. All three of us. We're gonna get pie to celebrate. We'll take my car." Amanda hurries down the hall, looking over her shoulder. "Come on. Pie waits for no one."

"Pie?" I say.

"She likes pie," Gabriela says.

"Well, how could I refuse such enthusiasm?"

Gabriela laughs. "She can be a bit much sometimes." In all the time I've known her, I've hardly ever heard Gabriela laugh. Like genuinely laugh, relaxed. The kind of laughter that lets you forget the bullshit of the world for a few minutes. People like us, we don't really get the opportunity.

"Two of you are looking like BFFs," I say. "Didn't you only meet her last month?"

"Yeah," Gabriela says. "Kinda took me by surprise, actually. She grows on you fast. If the world doesn't shit too much on her she might actually turn out to be a decent human being." One can hope.

"What was the deal with you being up in the box seat with her?" I say.

"Oh, we're getting married." I stop mid-stride and Gabriela laughs again.

"The look on your face. We're not, we're just telling her family we are."

"Attila's not gonna try to marry her off, is he?"

"No, it's all for show. He's in on this. But there are at least five different situations where she might be forced to marry."

"The fuck is wrong with this family?"

"Right?" she says. "Anyway, she wants to nip that shit in the bud."

"And scandalize the family?"

"And scandalize the family. They're very old-school. You know. Homophobic. Racist. Shitbags. The usual."

Up ahead Amanda takes a left at the wall and disappears. Gabriela heads toward the same spot and pauses when I don't follow.

"Attila put in a door especially for us," she says. "Now you won't have to walk past your throng of screaming fans."

"I have fans?"

"I don't know what else to call a gaggle of terrified mages who want you to officiate at their goth weddings. They're calling you the Black-Eyed Devil."

"My eyes went dark?"

"As the void. Soon as you started the fight your eyeballs went all Nietzsche. Come on." She steps through the wall and disappears. I follow and come out onto a still full parking lot.

When I first married Santa Muerte, my eyes went pitch black and stayed that way. As time went on, I eventually was able to turn them back, but ever since, whenever I channel Mictlantecuhtli's power it happens again. Sometimes I can feel when it happens and will them back to normal. But I had other things on my mind this time.

Amanda's a few car lengths ahead of us heading toward a silver Aston Martin with no other cars around it. The benefits of being the star of the night, I suppose.

"Great. The Black-Eyed Devil. I'm the monster under the bed, the Big Bad Wolf, and Baba Yaga all rolled up into one." In Mexico some years back the Cartel heavies started calling me The Gringo With No Eyes.

"Anybody who saw you covered in blood, standing over Otto's corpse with his head in one hand and that straight razor in the other, is going to think twice about fucking with you."

"You would know." Gabriela knows how to make appearances stick. That's totally the sort of thing I can see her doing. She has cut off people's heads and skinned them alive: sometimes to send a message, and sometimes just because they annoyed her.

"Honestly," she says, "it was kinda hot. Speaking of which—"

"Did you feel that?" A sudden flare of magic, so slight it's almost unnoticeable.

"No, I—Shit."

I operate without thinking, maybe she does, too. Years of paranoia have honed our instincts to the point where we'll do something and not know why until it's done.

Amanda's approaching her car when Gabriela reaches out with a spell and yanks her back over the top of the intervening cars to slam into her arms. Gabriela ducks and turns to shield her.

At the same instant I shove her car across the veil. It disappears, but I can just make it out over on the other side. I've sent over bigger things, like a speeding SUV. But I've never done it at a distance. I'm a little surprised that it worked.

Nothing happens. "What the hell?" Amanda says, pulling away from Gabriela.

"Give it a second," I say. I see the car shimmer, go bright, darken. I pull it back. It's barely recognizable as a car, just a twisted mass of still-melting steel and bubbling plastic. Thick, black smoke billows up from the wreckage. If it had gone off on this side it would have taken out a few rows of cars, and we sure as hell wouldn't be standing here.

Amanda looks at the hulk that used to be a very nice Aston Martin. Any trace of the girl who ran up and nearly tackled me with a hug is gone. The Iron-Willed Princess is up to bat.

"Well, shit," she says. "So much for pie."

———

Werther brought a limousine to the event, because of course he did. Not that I'm complaining. The four of us are in the back, we have a driver, and most importantly, the car is not on fire.

"Is anyone else from your family in town?" I ask.

"By now? Certainly. The conclave begins the day after tomorrow."

"Do you know who all's going to be there?" Gabriela says.

"There aren't that many left," Attila says. "The last ten years have not been kind to my siblings. My sister Helga and her son Hans, who you've met."

"You ran into Hans?" Amanda says.

"Yeah, he punched me, so I kicked him in the nuts and set him on fire. I'm not good at de-escalation."

"There's Liam, who you also met."

"He needs killing," I say. He's the most dangerous thing I've met tonight. I know Attila's strong, but I get the feeling Liam's nasty.

"Yes," Amanda says, her voice surprisingly subdued.

"Then, of course, there's Otto."

"Wait," I say. "Otto? Otto whose head I'm pretty sure I chopped off? That Otto?"

"You did," he says. "And yes."

"And it was awesome," Amanda says.

"He was dead for about a minute and a half before a stasis spell kicked in," Werther says. "His medical staff have him. I hear he's alive now, but I don't know what state he's in."

"Do all your irritating family members have Get Out Of Dying Free cards, or is he special?"

"Special? No. Just lucky. We all have something, but there's a limit on what they can do. Now if you'd pulped his brains . . ."

"I'll keep that in mind for next time."

Fantastic. Maybe I should track him down before he gets back on his feet and take his head off again. Speaking of which, there's an unusual weight in my jacket pocket that I'm certain is the razor even though I left it in the locker room. It feels oddly comforting.

"Hans's son Tobias will be there," Amanda says. "He's nineteen. I've met him before. Nice enough kid, I suppose. Hans and Otto treat him like shit, and Helga barely acknowledges his existence."

"Just because they're assholes?"

"Because Tobias has no power," Attila says. "I think they like to let him run around in the hope someone will kill him for them."

Jesus. My sister had no magic. But we didn't hate her, and we certainly didn't want to kill her. We didn't lock her in the attic, though for a while we might as well have. We changed her name, never went out in public together. For the most part she stayed with another family, went to a regular high school. It was hard, but if we hadn't, she never would have made it to her tenth birthday.

I left L.A. because of her. After I killed Boudreau I knew she was going to be a target. She was the most vulnerable. Eventually somebody would link the two of us and that would be that. She knew about magic, and how it worked, and theory, and all that. She just couldn't do it. The safest thing for her was for me to not be there. So I left L.A. I came back to L.A. because of her, too.

"Tobias is the one they're going to try to marry you off to?"

Amanda starts to say something, but Attila talks over her. "Likely," he says. "But with Miz Cortez's help that's not something we should have to worry about."

"Then there's Siobhan," Amanda says, jumping in before her father can cut her off again. "She's a wild card. Not a lot of the family like her, so she tends to keep to herself."

"She has a different mother than my other siblings," Attila says. "Because of that and a few other things she has no claim to the inheritance, and she's never shown any interest in pursuing it. As Amanda says, not many in the family care for her."

"She handles businesses in Ireland and Wales," Amanda says. "But beyond that she doesn't have much involvement in the family. She's a powerful mage but prefers to keep to herself. No partner, no children so far as I've heard. I think she has a half-brother, but I'm not sure."

"She hasn't been to a conclave in almost a hundred years," Attila says. "I don't expect to see her."

"She comes to visit on her own every once in a while, though," Amanda says. "She's the only one I get along with. She's a painter. She's very good. I have some of her pieces."

"Anyone else?" I ask.

"They can bring whoever they want to the conclave," Amanda says. "Family and guests. I'm bringing Gabriela, Hans is probably bringing his lawyer."

"Is that the sleazy one who was working for Otto?"

"Yes," Attila says. "Watch out for him."

"Good phrasing," I say. "My eyes keep sliding off him. That a voluntary thing, or is it just something about him?" I prefer to keep track of the people I'm in a room with, and he raises all sorts of alarms.

"Like your seeing the dead, you mean? I don't know. I have some people looking into him. He appears to be fairly incompetent at everything besides law, but I can't afford to underestimate anyone coming to the conclave."

"I wouldn't be me if I didn't suggest this, but why can't you put bombs in all their rooms, or something? You know they all want you dead. Maybe take care of the problem before it becomes a problem?"

"I told Amanda the same thing," Gabriela says. Of course she did.

"A few reasons," Attila says. "At the moment we have a stability of sorts. The family is split, but we've had several losses over the last few years so no one has the numbers to turn things into an all-out civil war. The conclave helps ensure this."

"I don't see how," I say. "You're coming together to kill each other, not circle up and sing Kumbaya."

"Limits the casualties," Amanda says. She turns to look out the window. "Or so I've been told."

Werther spares a glance for her before continuing. "We aren't coming together to murder each other, much as it might seem that way. We have traditions to uphold, vows to renew. Large-scale business ventures that the family has to vote on, and so on."

"Crimes to be judged," Amanda says. "Or not."

"The point is that it's a framework that keeps the peace," Attila says. "It has rules that need to be respected. And if they're not—"

"Nothing happens," Amanda says.

"Amanda."

"No, Dad. This is bullshit. It was bullshit ten years ago and ten years before that and ten years before that. No one 'respects the rules.' They twist them so they can get away with whatever fucked-up depravity they come up with.

"If it were up to me, I'd murder every single one of them. Blow them up, slit their throats, poison, I don't fucking care. Not a goddamn one of them is worth two shits. You know it. And worse, you let them get away with it."

"What she said," I say. "Just the little bit I've learned about you and your family, she's got the right idea. You people are worse than the fucking Borgias. They're all going to be in one place. Gas them. Drop a bomb on them. Shrink all their rooms until there's nothing left but smears."

"I believe we're at your stop," Werther says as the car pulls over. His voice is icy rage. But I don't think he's upset at me or even Amanda. I think he's pointing that directly at himself.

The limo's door pops open. I can take a hint. "Think about it is all I'm saying."

"Which I believe were my words to you earlier this evening," he says. "Good evening, Mister Carter."

"Eric," Gabriela says. "Call me."

"Sure," I lie. "Amanda, don't get yourself killed over this archaic bullshit. Night, all. I've had a lovely time. Let's never do this again."

Chapter 10

Attila kicked me out of the limo on Washington Boulevard half a mile from my stop in Venice Beach, which is fine by me. I need some cold air to clear my head.

I've been staying at my sister's house along the Venice Canals. It's weird thinking of it that way, in the present tense, like she still owns it. But it feels accurate. Dead isn't always dead. She's somewhere, even if her meat suit's in an urn.

This house is where she was brutally murdered, god, ten years ago? More? I can't keep track of time anymore. She left a ghost, an Echo of her death repeating over and over again. It was cruel, and agonizing, and was done entirely to leave me a message. To push me over the edge. It worked.

The place has been fixed up, new furniture, paint, the works. But in the middle of the living room, Lucy kept dying. So I never stayed here.

A few years later, after I went up against Mictlantecuhtli and Santa Muerte, killing one and changing the other into something completely different, I came back to this house and I exorcised her ghost.

It was hard. This was the last thing, the only thing, to show me the woman she had grown up to be. I cherished the first minute of the Echo before everything went to shit and then agonized over the next half hour as it was all taken away.

And now I'm staying in her house. Even without her Echo, her presence is embedded in the place. She designed it, had it built, decorated, everything. Dead or alive, it's always going to be her house. At the moment I just happen to be sleeping in it.

I head down Ocean and cut across to the Howland canal. It's four a.m. The only noise is the lapping of the water in the canals and the bumping of rowboats against their tiny docks.

The house is warded, of course, and it looks like nobody's messed with it. I bring enough of the wards down to enter the property and unlock the door.

Which is when the assassin makes his move. He's good. I didn't feel any magic. He was hiding somewhere nearby and I totally missed him. I usually get a feeling when someone's watching me, and I'd like to think my situational awareness is fairly good, sucker punch from Hans notwithstanding, but it appears his is better.

The knife skims along my left arm, the tattoos I depend on for defense doing their job. More or less. They're not perfect, but without them that knife would be in the back of my skull.

I spin around, the straight razor, which I don't recall grabbing, open in my hand. But gift horses and all that.

The assassin is white, older, not too tall. Has a well-trimmed mustache and beard. He's wearing, of all things, tweed. And a bow-tie. It gives him an academic air. Like he teaches at some posh Ivy League school but does wet work on the side.

"Can we reschedule this for tomorrow? I've had a really long day. I'm sure you can understand. I'm really not in the mood. Whattaya say? Rain check?"

He answers by flicking his fingers at me, three blades flying from his hand. They're easy to avoid, and I know they're not his main attack. He wants me to focus on them so he can come in with something bigger.

I step to the side and as he comes into where I'm going to be with a wicked-looking Bowie knife, I use a little magic to slide back where I started and take advantage of a clear shot at his neck.

I step in and slash with the razor, but he's too fast. He'd be too fast even if I wasn't exhausted. He ducks below the slash, brings his arm up over mine, trapping it, and yanks. Pain explodes inside my arm as he dislocates my shoulder.

The razor falls from my fingers. He kicks it behind him into the canal where it hits the water with a plop. I try for a knee to his crotch but he blocks it with his leg.

I hit his arm with a push spell that I've narrowed into a small enough area with enough force that he loses his grip on me and falls back. Instead of taking a bath in the canal he rolls and does some acrobatic shit I can barely follow.

And we're back where we started, several feet apart, my back to the door, his to the canal. Only now I have a dislocated right shoulder, a slice in my left arm from his first attack, and no weapon. I don't know what magic I have that might counteract what he can do. He'll find some way around a shield, he can probably dodge anything I throw his way. If I slip to the other side that just delays things. He likely caught that move earlier in the fight, so he's going to watch out for that kind of thing.

But then I have an idea. I put out my left hand. Let's see how loyal the puppy is.

In a ridiculously posh accent he starts to say, "Hans Werther sends his re—"

But there's a splash and a whipping sound followed by a meaty snap, and he never gets to finish his sentence.

His eyes go wide, body limp. He falls forward onto his face, the straight razor sunk halfway into his spinal cord somewhere around C6. He's not dead, but he's not going anywhere.

He might still be able to talk. But I'm not sure I have anything to ask him. Hans sent him to kill me. That's really all I need to know. After this one there will be others. That's how it always works until there's some sort of détente or one of us is dead. I don't get the feeling détente is on the table.

I walk over to the door, take a deep breath and careful aim, and slam my shoulder into the frame as hard as I can. There's a loud pop that echoes in my head, and the pain subsides as the shoulder snaps back into place.

I search my would-be murderer and find a wallet with ID, credit cards, some cash. Cell phone, five knives, a derringer . . . Seriously? A derringer? They still make these things? And a hold-out .38 in an ankle holster. I pocket all of it.

The ID's clearly fake. Archibald Leach. A Cary Grant fan. Same for the credit cards. The derringer's a neat little two-shot number chambered for .44. Good lord. Firing that thing could break your hand. I roll him over so I can look him in the eyes.

"Okay, Archie. I know you can hear me. But just in case, blink if you can." He does. "Awesome. Here's how it's gonna go. You're already dead, so we're gonna make it official. Don't worry, it'll only take a couple minutes or so. Granted, a really shitty couple minutes, but you pissed me off."

Nobody seems to have heard the fight, or if they have, they're playing it smart and staying away. Half the neighboring plots are nothing but vacant weed-choked patches of dirt and rubble left behind by the L.A. firestorm, their owners dead or simply gone. Hardly anyone lives in the remaining houses, and those who do are probably squatters. I might as well be alone. Still, it always helps if nobody sees a corpse as a corpse.

I don't have any HI, MY NAME IS stickers or even a Sharpie, so I dip a finger in the blood seeping out of my arm, and use it to write I'M JUST A LOG on his forehead. I pull the razor out of his back. There's some blood and spinal fluid, but it's pretty clean overall.

I wipe the blade on his tweed coat, fold it, and put it in my pocket with a "good dog." I wonder what sort of treats magical murder razors like.

I drag Archie over to the canal and slide him into the water. I wait a couple minutes until the bubbles stop breaking the surface, then cast a couple spells that will keep the body fresh for a day or so and push it drifting down the canal toward Ballona Lagoon.

Tomorrow, the day after, somebody will figure out he's not a log. If Archie's a real professional, they won't be able to identify the body. I wonder if his credit cards work.

I have to open the door with my left hand. I can move my right arm, but it is fucking agonizing. I've got some salve inside that should dull the pain enough to allow me to move it and cut the healing time from a few months to a few days. It's mostly herbs, with ensorcelled goat's blood in the mix, plus the blended-up tongue of an innocent man imprisoned, which is surprisingly easy to come by. Or maybe not so surprising. This is the U.S., after all. There's a lot of menthol in there too, of course.

Exhaustion is pulling at me like an undertow. I stumble up the stairs into the bedroom, sit on the bed, grab a bottle of Adderall from the bedside table. A couple should keep me going a few more hours. I know I can't keep this up, but I was hoping I'd have figured out a different solution by now. I start to shake a couple tablets into my hand—only the bottle's gone, the pills are gone, the room is gone.

I fucking hate dreams.

They started about three weeks ago. No vision, no sound, just a vague sense of unease. As days passed unease turned to terror, silence turned to a tremendous tearing and crashing like the mother of all woodchippers. I'd wake up soaked in sweat, my heart hammering.

Then about three, four nights ago I saw it. A landscape where the ground is made of shattered bone, broken femurs, cracked skulls. Three rivers of blood flowing thick through paths carved out of the skeletal remains.

And in the middle of it all a massive sinkhole. It grows, sucking the bones down into its hungry maw. The rivers become falls, blood pouring thousands of gallons a second into the darkness. Freud would probably say it's about buttholes and try to find something he could identify as a penis and call it a day.

Except I know this place. It's Mictlan, only not the one I left. As

Mictlantecuhtli I traded bone for green forests, blood for cool, flowing water. Something is happening in Mictlan, but I don't know why I'm seeing it. Is this a leftover from Mictlantecuhtli? Is it his terror and not mine that wakes me up screaming in the middle of the night?

That's when I stopped sleeping. I've been running on magic, meth, coke, and caffeine since. I knew I couldn't keep it up forever.

This time it's not just the sinkhole. There's Mictlantecuhtli, me, standing at the edge watching bits of bone shake into the void. We still look kind of alike if you look closely, basic features and such. He's changed so much that someone might peg us as second cousins, but probably not.

He's gaunt and gray, wearing a loincloth and a necklace of eyeballs strung on a cord. Skin so taut I can see each rib. His organs push against his flesh as if threatening to burst out and escape.

"You need to choose," he says. I can barely hear him over the grinding of acres of bone. I'm tempted to kick him into the hole.

"Choose what?" I yell.

He says something but I can't hear it. He says it again, his face contorting in anger, but whatever he's trying to get across is lost in the noise. Furious, his hand snaps out like a snake, grabs me by the throat, and as if I'm a stray piece of trash he casually tosses me into the hole.

Choose.

I snap awake at the sound of a ringing phone. Heart hammering, adrenaline spiking through my veins. Gabriela. I hope Alexander Graham Bell is roasting in some nightmare hell of constantly ringing telephones and Alvin and the Chipmunks ringtones.

It takes some fumbling, but eventually I manage to answer. "Yeah, I'm here. What's happened?" Because of course something's happened. Nobody calls at four in the morning to tell you you've won the lottery.

"It's Attila," Gabriela says.

"Shit. Hang on." I put the phone on speaker and roll off the bed. With apparently more grunting than I realized.

"What the hell is that noise?"

"Me," I say. "I'm old."

"Your body's, like, twenty-five, thirty tops."

"I've had a long night in case you've forgotten. Just tell me what happened." I'm still dressed, thank fuck. Buttoning your shirt with one hand is not easy, and don't get me started on shoelaces. If I can keep from fucking up my shoulder any more, it might actually heal right, but I doubt things are going to work out that way.

"We're not sure. Amanda bursts into my room screaming that he's dead and we go to his study and his corpse is sitting in an easy chair."

The open bottle of Adderall is lying on the floor, pills scattered like discarded peanut shells at a baseball game. I scoop as many as I can back in the bottle, but I get too woozy and have to stand back up. I toss back the ones in my hand and choke them down.

"How did she know he was dead?" I ask.

"The inheritance. It's not just money and status, it's power. I don't know what all it does, and I'm not asking right now. It woke her up when it hit."

I really do look like hell. There's blood on the shirt, I assume from the assassin. I don't remember him bleeding on me. Oh, right. It's mine. Whatever. I'll just say it's my brand. It's pretty much true at this point.

"Any wounds on the body?"

"Not that I could find. Tried to resuscitate him. Nothing."

"Okay. I'll get going in a couple minutes. I have to find my shoe. Should be there in—"

Thunder rips through the room, a tear in the space in front of me, and on the other side is Amanda in a parlor, arms wide, blue energy coursing from her fingers to the edges of the tear. Gabriela, behind her, phone in hand, stares at me in shock.

"Uh. Appreciate the ride, but I need a couple minutes if that's okay?"

"Oh. Yeah. Yeah, just let me know." She nods and the tear closes. I need to get stronger wards on this place.

"Did you know she could do that?"

"I did not," Gabriela says. "I'm not sure she knew she could do it either. Teleportation isn't her knack." I'll have to find out what it actually is. The only magic I've seen Amanda do was make Vicodin appear in her hand. I don't know if she summoned the pills, created them, or what. But I don't know anything else about her abilities.

At some point since I got inside one of my shoes came off. I have no idea how.

"What the hell is this about your shoe?" Gabriela says. I must be thinking out loud. Great. An unreliable inner monologue always makes things easier.

I give her a summary of what happened with Hans's assassin. I find the shoe, still tied, just outside the bedroom door. I get halfway through untying it when I finally say fuck it and just use both hands. My shoulder screams at me, but the salve has kicked in enough to make it barely tolerable.

I check the wards on the house. They're all intact. They should keep out pretty much everything. It's like Amanda's spell slipped right past them. Concerning, but I can't think of anything to strengthen them.

I toss the Adderall and some Oxycontin into my messenger bag. Reinhold's P228 is in there along with a couple loaded magazines and ammunition. The .38 and the derringer follow it, both already loaded.

"How's Amanda taking this?"

"How do you think?"

One thing I've taken to not packing when I leave the house is a pocket watch, a 1919 Illinois Sangamo Special. Keeps perfect time, and lets you twist it around, too.

It's not as useful as you'd think. It makes things you point the face at age very quickly. A hundred years or more in under a minute. It's gotten me out of a few scrapes, but it has all the accuracy of a grenade.

"Like a seething volcano that wants to bury an entire island village in her white-hot rage but doesn't know which village to hit so she's thinking about doing it to all of them."

"Add in the occasional fugue-like state where she just stops for a minute and then jerks back to consciousness and doesn't remember what she was doing and you're close."

I must be getting old, because I look at the watch and think it's too dangerous to use. I really need to get it into the storage unit with all the other weird crap.

"All right," I say, "I'm about as drugged up and prepped as I'm gonna be. I'm good to go."

A boom of thunder that shakes the house, a hole in midair with Amanda on the other side. I actually have a ring—it was two rings, but I gave one to Gabriela—that does something similar, but nowhere near as powerfully.

Amanda's opened a passage between the Hollywood Hills and Venice Beach from a self-contained constructed universe into a specific bedroom of a warded house she's never been in. I can't even imagine how much power and skill it would take to pull that off.

I step through the hole into the parlor. Amanda closes the hole. Stone-faced, she says, "He's this way," and turns like an automaton to walk down the hall.

"I'm here," I say into the phone.

"I'm in the medical suite," Gabriela says. "See you in a minute." She clicks off.

Who the hell could have even gotten to Attila? And how? It'd have to be an ambush. I can't imagine anyone sneaking up on him in his own house. Or getting into his house in the first place.

Whoever it was would have to be so well hidden that he'd never see them coming. Or they'd have to be so well trusted that he'd never see them coming.

I'm gonna set that aside for right now. That's not a question I want to ask either Amanda or Gabriela. My gut tells me they're thinking the same thing.

Amanda leads me through a hallway to a simple wooden door with a red cross painted on it. I'm thinking some kind of first-aid closet where, I dunno, they keep the Band-Aids or something.

It's a fully equipped medical suite with Attila laid out on one of the half dozen beds wearing the suit I saw him in earlier. His shirt's been pulled open. A defibrillator lies discarded on the floor. Gabriela sits in a chair across from the bed. She looks exhausted.

"How long's it been?"

"Couple hours," Gabriela says.

"I was getting ready for bed," Amanda says. "And then . . . I don't know how to describe it. Like I was on fire and freezing at the same time and suddenly I . . . I knew stuff. Like about this house, and the family, and magic that I'd . . . it all came pouring into me. And there was only one reason that would happen."

"We ran to his study. Well, more she brought his study to us."

"I rearranged the house. I'm still getting used to it. I think I accidentally got rid of the kitchen."

If Attila left a ghost, I can't see it anywhere, or feel it. That's a better sign than you might think. Ghosts are born out of trauma. If it was quick and quiet, at least he didn't suffer.

But it also means I can't just ask him what happened. Dead people can be a real pain in the ass sometimes. I could make him talk, or make the body talk, at least, but I don't want to do anything to it if I don't have to. It'd be more invasive than an autopsy.

I have a spell that slows down decomposition, but it also damages the body like freezer burn if I'm not really careful. I need the brain as intact as possible if I end up having to make him talk.

There's something wrong with this whole scene, though. Something wrong with Attila and the house, but I can't figure out what. I walk around the body, lean in close to take in every detail. That's when I spot it. A glimmer, something on the edge of my vision.

"I'll be right back," I say, and slide over to the other side. I'm a little surprised to find the same exact architecture over here as on the living side. This house is constantly changing, and things that aren't fixed in place for a long time tend to not exist on this side. But then, this is a universe in its own right, so I don't know if physics even works the same here.

I can make out the outline of the body, which I shouldn't be able to see at all. It shimmers, a barely visible glow that coalesces to a single point and shoots a thread out through the wall.

Manipulating objects over here can be tricky, but I've had enough practice that I might be able to push my way through the wall and follow it. The wall's just as solid here as it is over there. Then it occurs to me if the architecture here is the same as over there, maybe there's an easier way.

I open the door just as if it were on the living side, which isn't something I've ever been able to reliably do, and follow the thread through the house, wandering through rooms, tracing it all the way outside, where it shoots into a glass-paneled arboretum and out the other side, fading into the distance.

I reach out and touch the thread and the effect is immediate. It's like pissing on an electric fence. My body locks up, energy courses through me, and the sheer power of it throws me a good twenty feet across the lawn.

Okay. Don't touch the glowing thread. Message received. But I have a feeling I'm going to have to do it again at some point. Along with the rhino charge of power that slammed into me, I got glimpses, words, emotions. A lot of anger. And also recognition.

I pick myself up off the lawn. That didn't do my shoulder any favors. The salve and the Oxy are good, but they're not that good. I don't know how big this place is and there's no point running into the dark until I have some more information. I slide back over.

I limp back inside the house through a pair of French doors that I also went out through on the dead side. They're wide open over here. They shouldn't be. Things don't always translate from one side to the other. If I move something on one side, it doesn't necessarily mean it moves on the other.

The doors open onto a parlor and I find Gabriela holding a sobbing Amanda on a couch. With everything that's gone on in the last 24 hours, she's got to be a wreck. It says a lot about her that she's kept herself together so well until now.

"What are you doing here?" I ask.

"The infirmary door opened on its own," Gabriela says. "Then we heard another door. We figured it was you, so we followed the opening doors. What'd you find?"

"I'm not sure what it is exactly. I've seen things like it, but this is different. I am sure of one thing, though."

"What?" Amanda says.

"Your dad's not dead."

Chapter 11

"**If you are yanking my chain,** so help me I will fucking destroy you," Amanda says, pulling away from Gabriela. Gabriela puts her hand lightly on her shoulder and Amanda's energy goes way down.

"What did you see?" Gabriela says.

"There's something—and I'll admit I could be wrong here, but I don't think I am—tethered to the body that I'm pretty sure is his soul."

I describe the thread and the shimmer around the body. How the architecture of the house exists both here and on the other side. "It just keeps going. I assume all the way to the edge of this world. I don't know how far that is, so I didn't want to do anything else until I talked to you."

"Why do you think he's alive?" Amanda says.

"He's not," I say. "He's just not dead. His soul is still anchored here. I touched the thread—"

"That was stupid," Gabriela says.

"The hell else am I supposed to do with it? Anyway, when I did, I connected with him. He recognized me. Didn't talk, but I got a lot of images, emotions. He is pissed. Not at me, but at whoever pulled this shit. I wouldn't call it communication as such. Point is, he's aware of what's happened and he hasn't moved on. Something's got him stuck."

I sit down in one of the chairs. Slowly. Everything hurts, my shoulder, all the bruises and cuts I got from the fight with Otto, my back after that blast blew me across the lawn. I keep this shit up, I'll die sooner than I did the last time.

"So we can bring him back," Amanda says.

"I don't know," I say. "I think so. I doubt it'll be easy. Mostly because of how long he's been dead."

I don't tell Amanda that he's terrified for her. A raw blast of fear that swept through me. Flashes of what his family's done before, all that he's lost over the years. After seeing that, I'm terrified for her, too.

"Is he in pain?" Amanda says.

"I didn't get any sense of that. Trapped, though he doesn't know exactly where or how. But—and this is why I think we have a chance of bringing him back—it's somewhere physical. I got a sense of a place. Where, I don't know. Could be next door, could be the other side of the moon. But if it's a place, we can find it."

"How stable do you think the connection is?" Gabriela says.

"I've got no way to tell. But if what hit me when I touched the thread is an indication of its power, I don't think it's going anywhere any time soon."

Amanda stands up. "Okay. Let's go see where this thing goes."

"Unh uh," Gabriela says. "You can barely stand. You need sleep. We all need sleep. And he needs more bandaging up."

"But—"

"You can't do anything if you can't think straight," Gabriela says.

"First, though, we need to get the body into a freezer," I say.

"I took care of it," Amanda says. "I stopped time in the room. I didn't know I could do it until I wanted to do it."

"You what?"

"Yeah, turns out I can stop time," she says. Nervous laugh, bordering on hysterical. "Maybe only on the estate. I don't really know. But I can't seem to wind it backward."

"Did this kind of thing happen to you when you became Mictlantecuhtli?" Gabriela says.

"Finding out I could do something only when I needed to do it? Yeah. Gets old after a while."

"That's what this feels like," Amanda says. "I don't know what to do with it."

"Nothing for right now," Gabriela says. "Go to bed. The shit's not really hitting the fan for another day at least. We all get sleep, figure out a game plan, go from there. And the two of you can compare notes."

"Yeah, you're right. I need sleep," Amanda says. "I can't. I can't think."

"Before you pass out, you mind opening a hole back into my bedroom so I can do the same?" I say. "The two of you have a lot of work to do. No point in me getting in your way."

Both of them stare at me like I've just started talking in ancient Nahuatl, which actually happens from time to time.

"I'll talk to him," Gabriela says to Amanda. "We'll see you in the morning." Amanda nods and leaves the two of us alone.

"I'd really rather not have to drive all the way to Venice," I say.

"The hell is your problem?"

"My problem? My problem is that I'm doing what I said I was doing. Not getting involved."

"She needs help."

"And I've helped out plenty already," I say.

"So you're just gonna walk away from this? Right now, we're the only two people on the fucking planet in a position to help her, and you just want to hang her out to dry?"

"No," I say. "I'm doing exactly the opposite. In case you haven't been paying attention over the last several years, whenever I get involved in something, the Shit Fairy comes for a prolonged visit. I like Amanda. I want to help Amanda. The best thing I can do to help Amanda is not be here."

"How fucking arrogant can you be?"

"Excuse me?"

"None of this is about you," Gabriela says.

"You think I'm arrogant because I'm aware of how toxic I am for her to be around?"

"Yes," she says. "I do. Being a god's rubbed off on you. You think you're the most important person in the room. All fucking high and mighty. Hell, you won't even answer my calls."

"Is that what this is about?"

"It was an example," she says, but she looks away when she says it. "What makes you think you being here is worse than leaving?"

"I don't even know who the fuck I am," I say. "I'm not sure I can trust myself, what makes you think you can?" Confusion crawls onto Gabriela's face and camps out there.

"What?" she says.

"You haven't figured this out, yet? Why I haven't been talking to you? You're the one got me in this mess and it never occurred to you. Here's a hint. What am I? Huh? Tell me."

"I—"

"You don't know, either. I'm a slice of soul carved off a god who used to be a man and dumped into a secondhand body, all to take out an asshole djinn. That's it. That's the only reason I exist."

"That's not true," she says.

"Horseshit. If I wasn't the only one who could put him down, you wouldn't have fucking kidnapped me, taken me away from everything I was meant to be, meant to do, the souls that are mine to care for, and leave me stranded here in this chunk of walking meat. Do you even understand what you've done to me? Do you?"

"Okay," she says, with an eerie sort of calm like she's talking down a psycho off a ledge. Her hands are up, palms out. "Okay."

That's when I realize that I'm looming over her, that I've been screaming at her. That my voice changed as I screamed. I know my eyes have gone black. I see a crack in the floor where I'm standing.

She looks a little nervous. I don't think I've ever seen her look that way. She's probably right to be. I sit back down, breathing so fast I'm almost hyperventilating.

"Hey, you're all right," she says. "Take a deep breath. In, hold it, then out. Good. Are you feeling okay?"

"Just tired," I say. "It's been a long day." I try to will my eyes back to normal, but it's not working.

"You're my friend," she says.

"What?"

"You asked me what you are," Gabriela says. "You're my friend."

"You sure about that?"

———

I take a bedroom between Gabriela's and Amanda's. It's very posh. Four-poster bed, its own bathroom, walk-in closet, the works. I doubt I'll be awake long enough to appreciate it.

My shoulder is throbbing. I find more cuts. Gabriela offers to help me, but doesn't push when I tell her I don't want to be around her right now.

My right arm is in no shape to handle anything delicate, like stitches. Huh. I wonder. I use the blood spell to clot the cuts and it works. That's handy. I'm still probably going to have to get them looked at, but for now not bleeding is good enough.

I debate taking more Adderall. I'm probably still out there waiting to ambush me in my dreams. Ultimately, I don't bother. I'm not sure it would keep me awake at this point.

I wanted to hurt Gabriela. Something I haven't wanted to do since we first met, and even that was reluctantly; she thought I was somebody else and tried to kill me, so, of course, I reciprocated. We ended up calling it a draw and celebrated our newfound camaraderie and bruises with shots of tequila until a bunch of Russians showed up and things really went to shit.

But tonight, I wanted to *kill* her. Didn't I? It feels vague. Like the anger is a distant thing. Any other time I can't imagine wanting to hurt her. But I'm not entirely me, am I?

She's sort of right about Mictlantecuhtli rubbing off on me. Only it feels like it's the other way around, like I'm a rock scratching against a boulder. I don't have his power, or I do, just a tiny piece of it.

The problem is the memories. Thousands of years of memories washing in like a storm surge. How many years of Eric Carter's memories are there? How much of Eric Carter is really in here? Is it enough to say that's who I am and leave it at that? Is it that easy?

I'm too tired to answer existential questions. If I dream and I throw myself down a hole again, I don't remember it.

I wake feeling just as raw as I did earlier, but at least I got some sleep. My arm's feeling better, relatively speaking, so that's a plus. Or at least it's more mobile than it was last night. When I go to get dressed I find my clothes are washed, ironed, and pressed, and I wonder if this is something the house did on its own or something Amanda had the house do.

I had a room much like this pocket universe at the ghost version of the torn-down Ambassador Hotel. Every time I'd leave and come back there'd be clean laundry hung up in the closets. Man, I miss that place.

I get dressed and stand at the threshold. I need to decide what I'm going to do before I walk through that door. I know that this isn't the choice my dreams are demanding, but it feels almost as important.

Amanda needs help. Attila made a good point when he asked me to attend the conclave. She needs allies. Gabriela's a good one to have.

I'm not convinced that I am.

Fuck it. Let's do this. Worst case, I kill all her family and go home.

I step out of my room and the house has shifted again. I'm still between Amanda's and Gabriela's rooms, but now there's a small kitchen with a dinette set at the end of the hall. Both of them are eating. Neither of them looks particularly happy.

"Not sure if it was you or the house that did it, but thanks for the dry cleaning." I grab a mug off the counter and pour a cup of coffee.

"Yeah, no problem," Amanda says. "Um. About last night. Thanks for taking on Otto. I really appreciate it. It was a lot, I know. If you want to leave, it's okay. I understand."

"I'm not going anywhere," I say. "Except to get some other clothes to wear, run a couple errands. The conclave starts tonight? Or tomorrow night? It lasts until Sunday, right?" Gabriela's looking at me like I'm a bug under a microscope. Probably wondering when I'm going to snap and go all death god on her again.

"Uh, tomorrow," Amanda says, surprised. "Yeah, it ends Sunday. Most business happens on Saturday, but with Dad . . . how he is, I don't know how it will go. They'll start to show up tomorrow afternoon. We have cocktails and pretend to catch up with each other like we care, followed by an informal dinner outside. There's a formal dinner Saturday night. Do you have a tuxedo?"

Jesus, a tuxedo? What is wrong with these people? "I can get one," I say.

"Don't worry about that. I'll have Bigsby get you new clothes. Just let him know what you need."

"Handy. So what's our play here?"

"Hang on," Gabriela says. "What happened?" The confusion on Amanda's face tells me Gabriela didn't mention any of last night to her.

"Gabriela and I had a heated discussion last night," I say to Amanda. "On what my plans were. I wasn't expecting to stick around. Now I am."

"Thank you," she says.

"You're welcome," I say. To Gabriela, "Don't ask." I'm not sure I could give her an honest answer.

"I won't."

"What are we tackling first?"

"My dad," Amanda says.

"The family," says Gabriela at the same time.

"How about I deal with your dad," I say. "So far I'm the only one who can see what's happened and I don't know what either of you could do to help me just yet."

"The family then," Gabriela says. "Christ. Where do we start?"

"Who gains the most from Attila dying?" I say.

"Me," Amanda says. "I'm the head of the family now. I can't believe that. And there's so much . . . new in my head. I don't know what to look at first. You said this happened to you when you went to Mictlan. How do I deal with this?"

"Something like it, yeah," I say. "Still happens. Not as much anymore. Something that helped was to ignore as much as I could. If I needed to know something, I just knew it. Like it's all off-stage waiting to jump in when I need it."

"But it's so loud," she says. She digs the heels of her hands into her eyes. "I just want to scream."

"I'd recommend not doing that while there's anything breakable nearby for a little while. I did that the first day. Turned half of Chicunamictlan into a crater."

"I—Oh, god. That might actually happen. I stopped time. How did I even do that? What else can I do? It's, ugh. I need it to stop."

I kneel in front of her, take her hands in mine. "Breathe," I say. "Slowly. Big inhale, count to four, exhale. Good. Does anything physically hurt?"

"No. Sort of. I have a headache."

"Bad?"

"Just noticeable."

"Okay, good. It means you're probably not going to explode. Think back to when your magic first manifested. Everyone's a little overwhelmed when that happens. This is the same thing, only bigger. You have the power. The power does not have you. Say it."

"I have the power," she says. "The power doesn't have me."

"Good. Say it again." We do a couple rounds of this and her breathing eases.

"How do you feel?"

"Clearer."

"Whenever this happens, remember you control it. Not the other way around."

"Thank you."

"No problem," I say. "Been there. What do we know about who's coming?"

"I think we can put everyone into two broad categories," Gabriela says. "Those who will try to kill Amanda and those who will try to manipulate her."

"That Venn Diagram's a circle," I say.

"Yeah, but which one each of them tries first is going to tell us a lot. It might help us narrow down who did this to Attila."

"Otto and Hans will try to kill me," Amanda says. "They're blunt instruments. They won't care what it would do to the family or anyone else. I don't think they have anything to do with what happened to my dad. They're not smart enough. And Helga and my dad were close. Close enough that I think she wouldn't try to do something like this. She could pull it off, but it's not her style. She's a manipulator."

"I don't think we should discount her just yet," I say. "Hans's no talent kid is coming, too, right? The one they were hoping to make you marry."

"Tobias, yeah."

"Attila dies," I say, "and Amanda gets the inheritance. So whoever did it either wasn't part of the family, which I seriously doubt, or they're dead now, because the curse would have killed them. And I seriously doubt that too. Something's not adding up here."

"Jonathan?" Gabriela says.

"The lawyer? Enh. Attila told me something about him not being competent at anything other than law. It's possible, but it doesn't feel like it's him."

I'm missing something about what happened to Attila and how Amanda got the inheritance. It comes together like solving a Rubik's Cube and I think I understand at least some of how this happened.

"How does this sound?" I say. "Attila's soul gets pulled out of his body. His body dies, the inheritance triggers. But since his soul is still tethered here, the curse doesn't register it as death, and doesn't kill whoever did it."

"It sounds terrifying," Amanda says. "The fact that direct murder isn't an option is the only thing that's kept this family alive. If that's possible—"

"Then Otto and Hans definitely didn't do it," Gabriela says, steering Amanda away from thinking too hard about the ramifications.

"But it makes Helga a lot more likely," I say.

"How?" Amanda says. "If I die, the inheritance goes to Liam as next in line. How does that benefit her?" Then it hits her. "Then she tries to manipulate me into marrying Tobias. He's my first cousin. I hate this family so much."

"If she manages it, she gets a direct line to you," Gabriela says. "Okay, yeah. Let's keep her on the list for now."

I sit down at the table. Give me something to beat up, kill, banish, call bad names. But this shit? Not my forte.

"You all right?" Gabriela says. "Are you wincing at the coffee or the fucked-up shoulder?"

"Coffee's fine. I'm a mess. But that's nothing new. What about the kid himself? Does he have much control over his situation?"

"I don't know all the details," Amanda says, "but no, I don't think so. He's got no magic. What can he do?" A lot, but I get her point.

"And Liam, right?" Gabriela says.

"Liam. He could do it," Amanda says. "But I think he would try something more direct and final. Even if he's trying to avoid triggering the curse, I doubt he would have left that connection to the body."

"Kind of a prick?"

"He murdered my mom at the last conclave," Amanda says. "So yeah, I'd call him kind of a prick."

"That's a wrinkle we should explore," I say. "Are we killing him?"

"I . . . No," she says. "The restrictions on the curse are eased, but not as much for me as head of the family. None of us can kill each other directly, but we can be more directly involved. If one of them asked you to kill another outside the conclave and you did it, they'd get hit with the curse. During the conclave that won't happen."

"They can aim the gun but they can't pull the trigger," I say. "But it's different for you?"

"I have to be at least one step removed. I could ask you to ask Gabriela to kill one of them."

"What sort of restrictions do we have?" Gabriela says.

"You can do whatever you want as long as I don't ask you to do it, and I'm not going to. I hate these people, god how I hate these people, but killing them all would cause more problems than it solves."

"With more of them in the picture, the infighting keeps them occupied," I say.

"Something like that. If they all banded together and went up against me—I don't think I could stop them."

"Okay," I say. "I will try not to kill any of them. Unless they piss me off."

"Same," Gabriela says. "Just know that it's pretty much guaranteed they're going to piss me off."

"Back to Liam. You don't know if he's bringing anyone with him."

"No clue. He could bring a whole entourage, they all can if they want."

There's a pop over by the door and my first instinct is to grab Amanda and run for cover, but it's just the house butler, Bigsby.

"Sorry to trouble you, ma'am," Bigsby says. "But your guests have begun to arrive."

"Oh no," Amanda says. "They're not supposed to be here until tomorrow. Fuck. Fuck fuck fuck. Which one is it? Liam? Otto? They're already in town. Goddammit."

"Deep breath," Gabriela says.

"It is Miz Siobhan Werther," he says. "Shall I let her in?"

"What? No. I mean, yes. Let her in. I'll—I'll be there in a few minutes. One second." She blinks. "There's a new reception room just off the foyer now. Have her wait there."

"Very good, ma'am." Bigsby disappears with a pop.

"Isn't she the one no one's seen in years?" I say.

"Yes," Amanda says. "Only one I get along with, but I don't know if I can trust her. Not with this."

"Wild card's in play," Gabriela says. "Game just got more interesting."

Chapter 12

We agree that it would be best if no one knows I'm here until the conclave officially starts. Everyone's been told about Gabriela, but no one is expecting me. There's already a sizable surprise with Siobhan showing up. I'll stay out of sight until the festivities start tomorrow. It'll give me a chance to run some errands and spend more time investigating that thread to Attila's soul. I slide to the dead side outside the house and see it heading off into the distance.

The layout here is still exactly the same as the other side, which creeps me out a little. There are no ghosts, of course. There's no way Amanda or Attila would allow that. That does give me an idea, though.

"Bigsby?"

He appears in front of me looking as professional and proper as always. It's a little startling. The only people-shaped things I ever see on this side try to eat me.

"How can I be of assistance, sir?"

"Had a couple questions," I say. "Can you see this thread?"

"I can indeed, sir. It extends through the arboretum, out past the woods to the border of the estate. Presumably, it is attached to Mister Werther's body, but since Miss Amanda has frozen the room containing said body, I cannot be certain." Interesting. Whatever Bigsby is, it's not omniscient.

"Are there places you can't go?"

"Private rooms unless specifically requested by the rightful occupant, restrooms, and the like, as well as areas that have been locked through magic, such as the medical suite holding Mister Werther's body."

So he's got eyes and ears almost everywhere on the estate. I assume Amanda knows that, but I'll want to check.

"Was Werther's study one of those areas?"

"I don't believe so, no."

"You don't know?"

"During the transfer of ownership certain of my abilities were temporarily curtailed. I have been given to believe it is much like the process of rebooting a computer. Unfortunately, my most recent memories are unavailable until the process completes."

"And that takes how long?"

"Unknown, sir. This is the first time in my existence that this has happened."

This can't be a coincidence. Whoever took Werther's soul had to know that the estate wouldn't remember who or even if someone was in Werther's study. Triggering the inheritance to move to Amanda might be part of a larger plan, or just a side-effect of Werther's—I have a hard time calling it murder, but I suppose that's technically true. Kidnapping? I'll go with kidnapping.

"Do you know what this thread is?"

"I do not, sir. However, I-I-I—" Bigsby stutters. First his voice and then his entire body flickers. Before I can blink, he is nothing but a man-shaped mass of jagged lines and smears of color.

I have no idea what's happening or what to do about it, which usually means I should get the hell out of there before whatever it is gets worse.

It gets worse. Bigsby moves like lightning, grabbing me by the throat and lifting me off the ground. I try to slide back to the other side, but whatever Bigsby is now isn't letting me go.

I crank up a push spell and try to force the things that used to be Bigsby's fingers off my throat. Nothing. My vision is starting to go dark around the edges.

A sudden weight in my hand, and without looking I know what it is. I swing the straight razor at the thing's wrist, but it passes right through. At first I think it's done nothing. Then I fall to the ground with the severed hand going slack around my throat.

I go after the legs next. There's no resistance, like I'm slashing at smoke, but the legs sever at the knees and the thing falls to the ground. It's still going, its remaining hand reaching out and the body writhing toward me like a fat, staticky snake.

I cut off the arms, the rest of the legs, the head. Not only is the torso still moving, the rest of the pieces are getting in on the action.

I could just slide back to the other side and let it do whatever it's going to do, but I know I'm going to have to come back here and I don't want to get ambushed by a pissed-off hand.

On this side, if I really need to get rid of a ghost, I'll pull it in and devour it. Not as bad as an actual soul, but never fun. There is no way I'm going to try that with this thing.

The other option would be to trap it. Ghost traps are relatively easy.

You can use anything from a bottle to a piece of cloth. I trapped a few thousand ghosts in a pallet of paper in Hong Kong years back.

I don't know if a trap would work here, but I'm willing to give it a try. Trapping a ghost in an actual container, like a bottle or a box, works better than trying to place it within a solid object, like embedding it into a piece of paper. I rifle through my messenger bag and the only thing I come up with are the bottles of Vicodin and Adderall I tossed in earlier. I really need to start carrying stoppered vials again.

The pieces of ex-Bigsby are still moving toward me, but slowly. Hard to go very fast when you have to wiggle your way around like a maggot. I empty one bottle of pills into the other, then take the empty and place it on the ground, open end toward the oncoming body parts. I kick a couple of them closer to the torso; a hand grabs onto my pant-leg and I have to pry it off and toss it back near the others.

I don't know if this thing can re-form, so I don't want to waste time, but I take a moment to look around to make sure I'm not missing any parts. With a ghost I'd spill some blood to help the magic along, and also as bait. Might as well do the same here.

"You lop my hand off and you're going back in the box," I say to the razor. "You know that, right?" If it's sentient enough to understand, it doesn't give me any indication. Here's hoping Werther was right that it won't slice off *my* hand.

A quick slash on a patch of my inner left forearm devoid of tattoos. On my old body it was a mass of keloid scars from decades of cuts. But there are only a few barely visible scars from the few times I've done this on the new one.

I let a few drops fall onto the bottle and cast a binding spell. I don't know what to expect, but it seems to work just as well as it would with a ghost. The spell draws all the pieces toward the bottle, where they turn to smoke before being sucked in. When the last one goes, I stick the cap back on. Using the child safety cap side, of course.

I don't know why that worked. Not saying I'm not glad it did, I just don't understand it. Ex-Bigsby wasn't a ghost, but apparently it was similar enough that I could trap it the same way. I just hope it won't figure out how to escape.

Now that that's handled, I finally notice how much my throat hurts. If the razor had waited a moment longer, Bigsby probably would have crushed my trachea. But that'll have to wait. If Bigsby changed on this side, what the hell happened on the other? I flip back to the living side—though I'm starting to wonder if the idea of sides even applies here—razor in hand.

"Bigsby?"

"Yes, sir?"

It appears behind me and I spin, ducking low and cutting it off at the knees. Instead of falling to pieces, it turns to smoke.

Another one forms behind me. "I take it something's wrong, sir," it says. It doesn't seem any more murdery than before it changed on the other side.

"You don't know?" I say. "Turning into some technicolor static thing and coming at me?"

"No, sir. I don't recall that happening." It pauses. "However, I have just noted a gap in my memory. It's less than a second, but it appears some part has been erased and stitched back together. I fear I may be compromised."

"Yeah, I'll say. Where are Amanda and Gabriela?"

"Speaking with Siobhan, sir. I'm informing Miss Amanda of my state now."

"Can you do it discreetly?" Bigsby changed after Siobhan showed up. Could be coincidence. I don't like coincidences. Either way, I don't want to tip her off to anything that might be wrong.

"Yes, sir. Only Miss Amanda will get the message. She's told me to go to sleep until she can get things sorted out. Do you need anything before I go, sir?"

"Yeah. Let Amanda know I have to leave for a while. I'll be back later tonight. She can call me if she wants."

"Very good, sir. She's received the message. Goodbye."

And like that, Bigsby's gone. I need to talk to Amanda about what happened, get a better understanding of what Bigsby is, maybe figure out how someone fucked with it.

Speaking of, what the hell even happened? It was about to tell me something about the thread when it went all murder-butler on me. Either I triggered a trap that was already in place, or somebody's paying attention. Whether to Bigsby, me, or just what's happening around Werther's soul, I don't know.

Where does it go? The edge of the estate? When I touched the thread, I got the feeling that Werther's soul wasn't here. Could take me hours to find it. What's outside the estate? I don't know how pocket universes are built. My only experience with them is the room in the ghost of the Ambassador Hotel. That one was a trap, designed to collapse in on itself. It was built using the forces of other worlds pressing on it in equal measure, so that if one part was breached the whole thing imploded like a black hole.

Werther built it. I can't imagine he didn't build this one, too. If he used the same technique, then there's something on the other side of the boundary. I wonder if the thread is weakening the structure. This one is a thousand times larger than the hotel room. Werther wouldn't live here, or especially let Amanda live here, if he didn't think it was a fortress.

What sort of magic could drill a hole through a universe? It had to come from someone who knew how the universe was built, understood what it could and couldn't withstand. My money's on one of his siblings, but I don't know enough about any of them to make a guess as to which.

The thread is really more like a cable, thin strands all woven together. I walk back to make sure I'm seeing it correctly. It's noticeable, but only because I'm looking for it. Why? How far does it go? Where does it lead? More questions than answers. Anything I come up with is sheer guesswork and I've no way to know what's true.

I need to talk to Amanda about it, but I can't right now. Not while she and Gabriela are with Siobhan. I text Gabriela, telling her to call me when she has some time. Less suspicious if she gets a text than if Amanda does. I get a text back with a thumbs-up emoji.

Great. Now if the rest of the day can be less mysterious and murdery I'll count it a success.

———

My first night back from the dead I wound up at a church. There are so many levels of irony there I don't know how to even start unpacking it.

A small community of refugees from the fires had set up in the parking lot of a half-burned church. The pastor was apparently Unitarian, which I never really believed existed except to give out online minister certificates so people could officiate weddings. Shows what I know.

The next morning I met one of the people there, Lani, still don't know her last name, and her ten-year-old son, Matthew. They're close to the South L.A. Toxic Zone, where all the chemicals that got thrown into the air when the city of Vernon exploded hang like some magical, horror-story mist.

Which it is. A group of mages contained it and have been trying to figure out how to safely get rid of it without killing everyone else in the county. Tall order. Disaster like that, coupled with the fires and enough magic being thrown around the city to crack a planet, it's turned into way worse than just a toxic cloud.

For starters nobody can go in. Literally. Twenty feet in and they keel over. Doesn't matter what kind of protective gear they're wearing. Gas masks, NBC suits, airtight APCs. I saw a downed helicopter in there one time. Somebody flew too close and came tumbling down like Icarus.

The only gear that keeps people alive is magical. I've got a set of talismans Gabriela gave me that lets me survive the place. With those, the air, if you can call it that, is breathable, the killing magic doesn't touch me.

Without those I'd just be another not-rotting corpse lying in the street. That's one of the weirder things about it. Bodies don't decay. I've been tempted to try animating one to see what would happen, but a place like that make the chance it could go horribly wrong more than I'm comfortable with.

There are a bunch of egghead mages living inside a protective bubble at the emptied-out USC campus trying to figure it out, but they need to get their asses in gear. It's been hovering over that section of the city like an immobile stormfront for the last five years.

Of course, people have noticed. All sorts of conspiracy theories about it. Every news story is just one more theory, the weirder the better.

That's because of us mages. Compared to the rest of the population we're not that many, but more than enough to infiltrate high positions all over the world and control at least some of the messaging and media. They've been pushing every theory imaginable online except the one we don't want to get out there: magic. Honestly, I'm a little surprised that they've even contained the cloud itself. Not that they were able, but that they cared enough to do it.

Hiding magic on that big a scale is like our number one priority. Not that I necessarily care one way or the other, but letting the normals know we exist isn't really a good strategy for keeping us all from being rounded up to be burned at the stake. That would not go well for anyone, particularly the normals.

Which is why we tend to stay away from them. Lots of them know we exist and what we can do, or they've got just enough magic to call themselves a talent, if not a full-on mage. Wizard. Witch. We don't really have a good naming convention on that front.

So it's a little weird that I've been coming back to this camp every few days and bringing food, water, fuel for the generators. City services aren't online everywhere, and this close to the Toxic Zone isn't a priority. I show up, I drop stuff off, and I linger just enough to acknowledge the overenthusiastic thank-yous.

I brought this calamity down upon them, least I can do is make sure they can eat. There are a couple other reasons; one of them is Lani. She's nice. I like her. She's normal. Almost too normal. But it feels comfortable to be around her. I'm not getting close and I'm not interested in any sexual way. Being around her just feels a little grounding.

That's started to spread to the entire camp. I'm a regular. I get offers of food, drink, dates. I politely turn them all down.

The other reason I show up is Rosalie.

"Hey, Rose," I say, tapping on the rainfly covering her tent. It's been sprinkling, which of course for Angelenos means Noah's flood is upon us, but it hasn't gotten too heavy, yet. "It's Eric."

"Come on in," she says. Voice a little cracked, a little weary. I hear her shift over to the far side of the tent before I unzip the entrance, step inside, and zip it back up.

It's a roomy tent. Three compartments that act as semi-private bedrooms. She's done her best to make this place a home, her sparse belongings that have spent years in a shopping cart finally laid out for all to see. I wish she wouldn't. She can't stay here.

She looks the way she always looks when I come by. Jaundiced skin, sunken cheeks, hair a dishwater gray with clumps falling out. She doesn't leave her tent most of the time, and never during the day if she can help it.

"Wish you'd let me take you to the shelter," I say. "Gabriela's got a standing offer for you."

She looks at her feet like a guilty five year old. "I know. I just . . . I just can't, okay?"

"Okay." I don't push. Some days Rosalie inches my way on the topic and other days it's like moving a boulder. Not my job to change her mind.

"Got your stuff." I hold up a little Coleman cooler with dry ice and a supply of bagged blood inside. "Clean needles, too. Not even out of the package."

Rosalie is, if you haven't guessed, a vampire. Vampires live on blood, sure, but they're not like you see in the movies. Most drink their blood, but a portion of the Los Angeles vampires can't, and I've never been able to get one of them to tell me why. I don't know vampire politics, but I can tell when people are getting screwed by the system.

These vampires can only feed by getting it directly into a vein. To call them junkies isn't an exaggeration. And that's how they live, in places usually worse than this, the only places that will take them in.

"I got my works," she says. "But yeah, I'll take the needles. Thanks." I pass the cooler and bag with the syringes to her. The needles don't matter to her. She takes them as a gesture. She can't get any diseases, but she can pass them along. And if she feeds on somebody, she's going to stab a syringe into their neck, almost guaranteeing they get Hep C or HIV unless she's careful.

"You mind?" she says. "I think better when I've had a hit."

"Go right ahead." She pulls a bag of blood and draws a little from her syringe, finds a vein and pumps in that sweet shot of life.

The effect's immediate. Her hair regains color, features fill out, eyes brighten. She sheds thirty years in thirty seconds and goes from withered crone to stunning 1920s flapper with a bob haircut and a predatory gleam in her eye. Her eyes roll up and she takes a deep breath.

"God, that's good. You have no idea." The vamps claim it's better than sex, though most of them will agree that sex is pretty great, too. "Thank you."

"Happy to help," I say. More like, "Happy to keep the vampire from going hungry and starting to stab people in the camp trying to get her fix."

She looks into the cooler with eyes that can see straight and a brain that works. "This is like a month's worth," she says. "You going somewhere?"

"Just got a feeling things are going to get a little weirder than usual. Might not be able to get out here as often."

"What? Not even to see your sexy lady friend?" She laughs and it's light and breezy and I can see how she could have made many a man or woman follow wherever she wanted.

"I get accused of bangin' a twenty-year-old mage yesterday, and now you think I'm goin' for a single mom in a squatter's camp. The hell is with everybody?"

She laughs again. "I know it's not her. Or me. But if bringing me blood and staring at that ass in those tight jeans of hers helps you feel less guilty, who am I to judge?"

"You good to talk?" I say, changing the subject. Much as I want Rose to not be here, as long as she is, I'm going to use her.

"Yeah. No more of that weird green blob coming out of the fog. You either took it out or scared it off good. Haven't seen it all week."

"That's a bright spot of news."

The night I stayed here Lani told me about a glowing green blob that came out of the Toxic Zone and would roll down the street, split off pieces of itself, reform, and eventually go back in. Hadn't hurt anybody but it was only a matter of time. The only things that go into that fog are stupid, and the only things that come out are dangerous.

"But—" she says, and there's a long pause. "It doesn't really matter to me one way or another." The hesitation in her voice tells me that's bullshit. She won't admit it, but she likes these people. As much as someone who sees humans as lunch can, at least. "But I've been hearing some stories."

"Yeah, what kind of stories?"

"El Cucuy," she says.

For most people, El Cucuy's another name for the boogeyman. The thing under your bed, comes for you in the night. For mages they're bad news.

El Cucuy, or a dozen other names they go by, are magic eaters. In their normal form they're tall monstrosities with heads like horse skulls and arms like tree trunks tipped with foot-long razor blades. But they can squeeze themselves into a hollowed-out corpse. They don't look all that human up close, but if they're up close you're already fucked.

I fought one back east—they call them Jersey Devils out there—and I know Gabriela has fought at least one in Mexico. Neither one of us thought we'd make it out of those scrapes alive. They're tough fuckers and you have to be careful about the magic you use, because a lot of it they'll just eat like you're tossing them treats.

"I don't like hearing that," I say.

"Nobody does. Right now just stories, but they fit. Heard from a guy in another camp, kids are going missing all over. Never the same place twice. Other night, something stole some woman's baby."

"Mage?"

"No. But the guy said it looked like some old woman and then it turned into a monster. Coulda been high, though."

Could be about a dozen different things I can think of just off the top of my head. I don't like the old woman angle, though.

El Cucuy love to eat baby mages. They don't put up a fight, but they'll pretty much leave anybody else alone unless they catch a scent and can't narrow it down. You get a mage baby in a maternity ward or an orphanage, anywhere with normal children, and they'll keep showing up in the night and stealing kids until they get the right one. But it could be something worse.

"Also sounds like a Baba Yaga."

"Okay, now I don't like hearing *that*." Rosalie shivers. "I'll keep an eye out, and with this"—she gestures at the cooler—"I can hang around the camp more often at night. Maybe scare whatever it is away. Somebody needs to take it down."

"I'll talk to Gabriela. The people here need to know about it, too." But how? They know there's something off with me, but they really think there's something off about Rosalie. She only comes out of the tent at night when no one can see her or after she's had a hit and looks human. Nobody here has seen her as a withered old crone as far as I know, but vampires just give off a predator vibe.

"No," she says, panic in her voice. "I got a good thing here. Don't fuck it up for me."

"Rose, it'll be fine. I won't tell them about you. Just to keep an eye out and run if more weird shit happens. They've already seen weird shit."

"Fine," she says. "You'll do whatever you do, let everybody else get fucked. You're harshing my high. Get out of here. Go see your MILF in the tight jeans. And zip the door up on your way out."

The hell of it is, she's right. She's found good people and as long as she keeps to herself she'll be fine. Vampires are adaptable if nothing else. Also really hard to kill, so she's got that going for her.

I leave her tent, carefully zipping the tent closed so it doesn't snag. Sunlight wouldn't kill her, but it'd definitely be uncomfortable as her skin flakes off, and I don't want to mess up her living room.

The people here need to know. Vague warnings should be enough. Most of them saw the green blob thing, a nature spirit, if you can call it natural. I've seen similar. With trees you get forest spirits, cities get city spirits, toxic waste sites, you get the idea.

I head over to Lani's RV, where she's sitting under an awning enjoying the cool, misty air and a beer. Lani's an Asian woman with a ten-year-old who's afraid of me. Kid's got good instincts. I ignore Lani's tight jeans.

"Hey," she says, pushing a lawn chair toward me with her foot. "You've been away too long. Was starting to get worried." She smiles. It's a nice smile.

"I was here like three days ago," I say. The smile's infectious. I don't have anything to smile about, but I do it anyway and it feels good. I lower myself into the chair and all my bruised and tightened muscles scream at me.

"Are you okay?" she says. Concern. She starts to get up and I wave her back.

"Rough couple days," I say. "How are things here?"

"Good," she says. "Little exciting. Matthew and I might be leaving." I'm surprised. Not that she's leaving, but that I'll miss her.

"That's fantastic," I say. "Where you thinking?" A look of disappointment flickers across her face and then it's gone.

"I've got a cousin in Denver. Her husband's looking for a job for me where he works. They've got a couple kids and she's a stay-at-home mom. We can stay there for a while. Get on our feet."

"Do it," I say. The words come out a little too quick. A little too urgent. She needs to leave. I need her to leave. But there's a pinprick in my gut when I say it. "Now. I'll give you money for a flight, a bus, whatever. What do you need to make that happen?"

"Whoa. Eric, you're scaring me a little. What's going on?"

That was probably a little too insistent. How to say this? "Sorry. You know that green glob that was coming out of the Zone? There's worse out there. A lot worse."

"Oh," she says. "That's why you've been coming around?"

"Not the only reason," I say.

She's thinking. I have a feeling that what she's about to say next is something we're both going to regret.

"Come with us. We'll make it a roadtrip. I know you think Matthew doesn't like you, but he does. He's a little shy is all. Think of it as a vacation. You don't have to stay."

"Lani—"

"We'll be stopping in Vegas for a bit on the way to see some friends and you and I can hang out. Maybe."

"Lani. Stop. I can't. You don't know me. I like you . . ."

"But not enough?"

"That's not it," I say. And realize it's true. It sounds like a great plan. Get out of here. Get away from the politics and the bullshit. I know Denver. Nice town. Good people.

But Vegas? That brings it all to a screeching halt. Vegas, Denver, Los Angeles, doesn't really matter. She's normal. I'm so far from normal I can't see it from here. Me and her? She and Matthew would be dead in a week.

"Vegas and I don't get along. It's complicated." Which is easier than saying, "Last time I was there I almost didn't make it out and going back to deal with the shit I did would be bad for everybody."

"Always is," she says. "Sorry. I didn't mean to throw that at you. I just . . . I've been thinking about the fires, how lucky we are to be alive. How easy it is to say, 'Oh, I'll do that tomorrow,' until there's no tomorrow. I don't want to keep doing that."

"Believe me, I get it. And I'm not saying I don't like the idea. I do. A lot." Stupid though it might be. I've spent all of maybe a week total in Lani's presence. Even less in her son's. But there's an allure to it. Life isn't calm or easy for anybody, but normal people don't have to worry about being assassinated for lopping some magic asshole's head off.

I think I understand where Letitia's coming from a little better now. I still think her keeping everything secret from her wife for so long was a dumb move, but what if she hadn't? Would she even still be with her?

Normals believe in magic. We could all come out of the closet tomorrow and most of them would just nod their heads and go, "Yeah, and?" Magic they wouldn't have a problem with.

Mages, on the other hand? The first time an overly zealous mob with pitchforks comes after the wrong hedge witch and ends up a bubbling smear on the pavement, folks are gonna get a better idea of just what they're dealing with.

And that's before they find out how sociopathic so many of us are. How many murderers there are among us. It's not that we're necessarily more bloodthirsty than anyone else—except for the ones who drink blood, of course—it's that for the most part we simply don't care. Mages see normals pretty much the way most vampires see humans. A necessary evil. An annoyance. Peasants.

"I know I don't understand your life," she says. "And I get that it can be dangerous. But everyone is in danger. All the time. Maybe think about it?" she says.

I plaster a smile on my face and lie like I've never lied before. "I'll think about it." Neither of us says anything for a little while and it's a comfortable silence.

"You want to come by tonight?" she says. "I was thinking we can hang out, just you and me. One of the other parents can watch Matthew." I'm saved from having to answer when the pastor comes over to us.

Pastor Nancy Grimm runs the church here. Nice black lady, sixty years old, maybe? Grandma vibe. Built like a fucking oak tree. Probably arm wrestles Marines for fun. She's a no-bullshit sort of woman. I avoid her as much as I can.

"Mister Carter," she says. "I was wondering when you'd show up. It's very nice to see you again." She gestures toward a third lawn chair. "May I?" she says to Lani.

"Of course. Uh—"

"I was just leaving," I say. "I just came to drop off some more stuff."

"Where do you get all that food and whatnot, I've been wondering," the pastor says.

"Where else? I steal grocery trucks." She laughs like a seal barking.

"Lani, could I trouble you for a cup of tea?" the pastor says. "Don't worry, Mister Carter won't leave until he can say goodbye."

"Oh. Of course. I'll be right back." She gives me that smile but now it feels like a twist in my guts.

"She's sweet on you," the pastor says once she's out of earshot.

"I know," I say. "I'd appreciate it if you'd steer her away from that particular line of thinking."

"I will. She's not for the likes of you. But I do hope you'd keep coming by. You're a good man, Eric Carter, even if you don't believe it. You solve problems that need to be solved and I appreciate that. Even if I question the methods."

"Might be gone a little longer than expected," I say, wondering what that last bit meant. I don't know why, yet, but that gnawing in my gut tells me I won't like it when I find out.

"I've gotten the word out about the El Cucuy, already," she says. "Some of the folks out at USC are friends of mine. They're looking into it." I'm so shocked I don't know what to say. She laughs again.

"You're a mage."

"Of course I am," she says, like it's the most obvious thing in the world. "And I know who you are. And I know what you've done."

"You don't know the half of it."

"The half that matters," she says, sweeping her hand to take in the entire camp. "This half. The one that's taking care of people."

"You knew this was happening," I say, suddenly angry. "And you're doing fuck all about it? I don't want to get into a pissing match with you, especially here. But I'm leaving. Now. Deal with your own problems. You won't see me again."

Lani steps out the door with a steaming mug in her hand, not sure what's going on. The pastor mimes putting glasses on her face and I hurriedly get my sunglasses on before Lani can see that my eyes have gone black.

"Everything okay?"

"We're good," I say. "Thanks for the chat, Pastor. It was illuminating. And watch yourself. It might be a Baba Yaga." The pastor's hand stops centimeters from the cup Lani's handing her and her eyes go wide.

"You sure?"

"No," I say. "But ask around. And ask yourself, if it were an El Cucuy, why you of all people haven't seen it on your doorstep." I turn on my heel and leave, Lani looking back and forth between us. She calls my name, but I ignore her. Being here, being involved in any way with these people, I was afraid I was endangering them, endangering Lani and her son. Poisoning the well.

Turns out somebody beat me to it.

Chapter 13

Mages and normals don't mix. It never goes well.

Everything I said about understanding Letitia marrying one? Yeah, forget that. She's an idiot. I don't even understand how she managed to keep her wife from knowing magic existed for their entire relationship. I let the cat out of the bag when she asked who I was, and being a smartass, I told her.

She didn't believe me, but she believed Letitia, who finally realized that all the years of lying to her wife was going to get her killed. And almost did. As relationships go, I'd call theirs "rocky."

A lot of normals know about us. Some more than others. The best interactions are strictly business. Sometimes they become friends. But like everyone else, friends die, and normals are more fragile.

Even the word we use looks down on them. We're a bunch of bigoted assholes who should be looking up at them as the paradigm of humanity, not the other way around. It's not that they're normal, it's that we're monsters.

I don't even understand why I care so much. So what? The pastor's a mage. We don't go advertising what we are even to each other most times. And she's actually doing some good, right?

Or is she? Why did I have to be the one to deal with that toxin spirit? Why didn't she have someone she knew deal with it? If she knew who the fuck I was, why not tell me and save me a ton of trouble going in and out of the fucking Zone?

I suppose none of that matters. She didn't cause my predicament, I did. I started to care about these people. I thought I could help, after the shit I brought down on them when Quetzalcoatl burned the city.

They're as tight a community as any I've seen. They share childcare, take turns cooking, getting groceries, pooling resources. Quite a little sixties hippie commune they got going there. I just wanted to help.

Or maybe I just want what they have. Mage communities are a fucking joke. We're a bunch of backstabbing narcissists who measure everything by how much magic we can use. That's like measuring self-worth based on who can piss the farthest. Amanda's family might sound like an extreme case, but they're not. They've just got some added wrinkles.

The pastor's making her community work. She's part of it. She's not creating a cult of personality, which automatically makes me not trust her. There's something pretty fucked up when you don't trust some-body because they might be trustworthy.

I head into Inglewood not far from the church or the Toxic Zone. Peeling billboards that haven't been replaced in years tell me about the magic of Disneyland, warn me about the dangers of syphilis, beckon me to gamble in Las Vegas.

I stole a beater car decades ago, ugly as fuck. An old Honda with a weird aqua-puke blueish-green paintjob. Couldn't recall ever seeing one like it. Didn't really think about until I got on the road. All of a sudden they're everywhere. Same car, all over the place. I didn't notice them before, but once my attention was drawn to it, I couldn't stop seeing the damn things.

The Vegas sign makes me think of that. So do the other signs I go by, an ad for the Bellagio on the side of a bus, the Venetian on a public bike rack, and two benches for some washed-out entertainer showing at the Venetian. I haven't thought about Vegas in a long time, but now that it has my attention, I can't stop seeing it.

Maybe. One of the problems with being a mage is we attract magi-cal shit. It sort of seeks us out. I knew one girl whose knack was con-trolling insects, butterflies mostly. They loved her. She fucking hated them. Couldn't get rid of the damn things. Butterflies, moths, June bugs. Buzzed around her head like it was a hundred-fifty-watt bulb. She spent more time zapping the fuckers than she did anything else.

That's what omens are like. They buzz around us whether we see them or not. Or maybe they don't. That's the problem. Humans are pattern-matching monkeys. We'll see dragons in clouds, rabbits in a popcorn ceiling. Am I just noticing it more, or is something trying to draw my attention to it? By the time we're sure that something's an omen, it's usually too late to do anything about it.

I pull into the old Forum parking lot off Manchester. It's an indoor sports arena and concert venue. Or it used to be. It's seen better days. It took a hit in the fires, though not as bad as a lot of places. Now it's more of a backdrop for a huge open-air market that sells everything from brand new washers and dryers to black market weapons.

Was a man, Jack MacFee, I called him a friend a time or two, who used to run a booth at a drive-in-theater-turned-swap-meet before the whole place burned down. He sold New Age tchotchkes to the normals and more useful items to the magic set. He died a month ago. I killed him. It was a mercy, but it's still a gut punch. He was looking at a few more weeks of life in agonizing pain from the cancer that had spread through his entire body. My way, he went quiet, peaceful, and with family who loved him.

His granddaughter Cassie runs his shop now, relocated to the Forum parking lot. I've only seen her once for a few minutes since that day when she asked if I could ease his pain and I said yes.

She made it plain that though it was the best thing to do, she didn't want to see me after that. Don't blame her. Well, business is business, and I need something only her grandfather, and now hopefully she, can provide. Finding Cassie's booth takes a while. She's moved, and the place has become more of a maze since I saw it a month ago.

The Forum Lot, as it's known now, isn't too far from the edge of the Toxic Zone. Close enough to remember it's there, far enough to not have to think about it too hard. With that hard edge blocking the east, and nowhere else big enough or open enough that wasn't razed in the fires, it's become the main place to hawk your wares. One part carnival, one part Bartertown, it's a lifeline for a lot of people. Things previously taken for granted have become essential survival tools.

It isn't that L.A. hasn't recovered from the fires, it's that it hasn't recovered equally, which nobody with half a brain expected it to. The same people getting screwed before are still getting screwed, only worse.

I haven't seen how the last five years have played out, but from what I've heard it's been a nightmare. Violence, food and water shortages, vigilantism, rampant crime. Not enough manpower to police the city so people started doing it themselves. You can imagine how well that's worked out. Though let's be honest, the police would have done a hell of a lot worse.

L.A. used to be a bunch of towns that got swallowed up and turned into neighborhoods. Now a lot of them have reverted. Some have put up their own walls and have their own security. The city's broken along the lines you would expect. Rich white neighborhoods on one side of a wall, poor Black and brown neighborhoods on the other.

The Toxic Zone makes it all worse. It's stuck over where the majority of Blacks and Latinos lived before the fires. The racial implications haven't been lost on anyone, not even the mages. I've heard of fights breaking out between mages who say they're doing everything they can to fix it and those who think they're stalling because that way they

can kill more black and brown people. It's not that simple, and at the
same time, it is.

But for all that, the Forum Lot holds together. Only place I know
with more than a few thousand people that doesn't have a weekly
double-digit body count. People don't just work here, they live here
too, and any racial strife seems swallowed up in a sea of every ethnic-
ity in L.A.

I'm sure it'll go to shit soon, these things always do. But for now I
can't go ten feet without seeing every shade of skin color there is. I
pass food stalls with smells of every cuisine in the world, though some
of their ingredients might be a little suspect. People sell electronics,
clothes, medication, appliances, scrap. Only things not blatantly out
in the open are guns, but if you want a grenade launcher, I can point
you to three different dealers within fifty feet of each other.

Cassie's booth is near the Forum building itself. It's partitioned off
from everyone else by big, blue tarp walls. She has a couple long tables
out front as counter space and a big tent in the back. If she's kept up
the store philosophy, she sells anything and everything, with a specialty in hard-to-find magic reagents, knickknacks, and the occasional
"How The Fuck Did You Get Your Hands On That?"

Parked to the right is a bright green 1963 Buick Invicta. Thing
shines in the sun with a mirror polish. She loves that car. Almost as
much as she loved her grandfather.

She's got help now. I go up to a woman at the table who's reorganizing a large jewelry display. There's a family resemblance and the age
is about right that she's probably Cassie's mom.

"Hi," I say. "Looking for Cassie. Need a specialty item that Jack
had at one time. Was wondering if she still had it."

"Specialty item?" she says, confused. Ah. Might not be in on the
real family business.

"Cassie would know."

"Sure. She's in the tent. I'll just go back and—" Her face goes a
little blank and then brightens up. "I'm sorry, can I help you?"

"It's okay, Mom," Cassie says, coming up behind her. "I got this."

MacFee's granddaughter has his eyes, but that's about it. MacFee
was a bear of a man. Big bones wrapped in big meat, a massive red
beard that spilled down his chest. Cassie's slender, lean-muscled. Her
mohawk is swept down one side of her otherwise shaved skull.

"Okay, honey," the woman says. She looks a little confused and
then smiles, goes to the other end of the table, and starts reorganizing,
Cassie's eyes on her filled with concern.

"I take it she's not up to speed on the family business?" The tent is also a portal to a warehouse up in Lancaster where MacFee kept all his special merchandise. I can see where she wouldn't want anyone to wander in there.

"Most of them don't know. This is just to get her out of the house. With Granddad gone . . ." She seems to remember who she's talking to and her eyes go hard, voice curt. "What do you want?" She doesn't want me here. I don't want to be here. We're both equally unhappy with the situation.

"I'm looking for an item Jack had for tracking ghosts." One eyebrow ticks up a notch.

"Isn't that the sort of thing you already do? What do you need that for?"

"For something it's not meant for," I say. If it were Jack, I might feel comfortable telling him. He was someone who took confidentiality seriously. That's why people did business with him. I've met Cassie once.

"Brass disk about the width of one of those mini-CDs. Splits in half on a hinge," I say. "One side has a compass, the other side has a gauge for distance. Should be a button on one side."

"Huh. Gimme a minute." She heads into the tent. I people-watch as I wait. Haggling, bartering, paying through the nose and thinking they got a great deal. People adjust to a new normal by throwing the skin of the old on top of it.

"Got it," Cassie says, stepping out of the tent with a hinged brass disk in her hand. She comes to the table and cracks it open.

The compass is spinning like mad and the gauge is springing back and forth across the chart. Time to see if this thing actually works. Like Cassie said, tracking ghosts is the sort of thing I can already do on my own.

The Forum Lot has some Wanderers in it, but the Forum building itself is packed with Haunts. The building didn't take a lot of fire damage, but there was a church service meeting inside at the time. Some three thousand or so people went to meet their maker from smoke inhalation.

I pick up the device and point it at the building. The compass goes a little more steady, sweeping in a narrower range, but there's still too much background noise. Or it just doesn't work.

I focus my attention on a nearby Haunt in the parking lot not far from the booth. The compass needle snaps to a stop and the gauge shows me that it's about twenty feet away. I press the button on the side, triggering some mechanism inside. I hope this isn't really a grenade.

I move a few feet to the right and left, a few steps closer to the Haunt, a few steps further away. The needle and distance gauge stay locked on the ghost.

"Mind if I check this out for a few minutes?"

"Knock yourself out," she says, and heads back into the tent. I walk through the crowd focusing on Haunts, Wanderers, the occasional Echo. It seems to track whatever I've got my attention on. I press the button and it stays locked on until I press it again.

Neat trick, and might be what I need, but maybe not as useful as it sounds. I don't see how anyone but a necromancer could use it easily, and we can pretty much track a ghost like a bloodhound. Another mage could cast a spell to see ghosts and track them from there, I suppose, but it'd be kind of a pain in the ass.

Still, might come in handy. I'm hoping I can repurpose it to track Werther's soul outside the estate. No idea if I can, but it's the only thing I can think of right now. If I can lock in on him from inside the estate pocket-universe and then come back out again, theoretically it could stay targeted on him and lead me to the location, if there is one, of his soul. Maybe.

Cassie's behind the counter when I get back, talking to another customer. I see her slip a Hand of Glory into a bag under the table and hand it to the man who looks furtively back and forth before taking it and scurrying back into the crowd. I step into his place and set the brass disk on the counter.

"What do you want for it?" I say.

"Nothing," she says. "Take it."

"That's not how this works," I say, surprised she's offering it to me for free. "I know you don't want to see me. I don't want you to have to see me. If you never want me here again, you want me to just walk away, no problem. But if this is a transaction, then it's a transaction. Money, goods, favors, whatever. But I can't just take it."

"You've already paid," she says, not looking at me. "For life."

"I—"

"No," she says, pitching her voice lower. "You're paid up. My dad died of the same cancer. I know what the end was going to look like. Granddad had friends and people who helped him live through it, sure, but you saved him from . . . You just saved him, all right? You need anything I can get, just tell me. I'll get it."

Now she looks at me. There are tears in those eyes, but there's fire, too. I can argue with her, walk away, or take the deal, but I know she won't change her mind.

"Two conditions," I say. "Sometimes, third parties have to be involved. Specialty items you just can't pick up. I pay those expenses."

"Fair enough," she says. "The other?"

"It goes both ways. You need a hand with something I can help with, you call me. I owed Jack. And now I owe you."

"No, you—"

"Yes, I do. Deal?" I put out my hand to shake, she takes it.

"Deal," she says. "You want a bag for that?"

"I'm good," I say, picking up the disk and sliding it into my messenger bag. "Thank you."

"Now go before I have to make my mom forget shit again," she says.

"Gone." I turn around and walk away like I'm just another customer.

———

I spend the next two hours driving around the area alternately checking the compass on different ghosts and looking for signs of an El Cucuy or a Baba Yaga.

I try the compass on the Haunts, Wanderers, and Echoes scattered around. Five years after the fires and there are still so many it's sometimes hard for me to differentiate all of them. Two or three years on most of them would have deteriorated. But then thousands of them weren't created in one night, either.

The compass seems to work best on Haunts, possibly because they're stationary, and Echoes it doesn't pick up at all. It locks onto Wanderers immediately, though it can't keep track of them unless they stay in close range, and if they move into a cluster of other ghosts then both needles go batshit and start spinning wildly. Sometimes the disk can find them again and lock back on, but there's still the problem of distance.

Triggering it is easy enough. I see a ghost and think about tracking it, and it homes in on them. But I've been in this area enough times that I've gotten the names of some of the Haunts and Wanderers, and when I try to focus on one of them by name, the compass does nothing.

If I have to see a ghost in order to track it, I don't know how it's going to do my any good. I can't see Attila's soul. Unless the tether is part of it?

I don't get why anyone would make this. If a ghost has to be seen to be tracked, then the only people who could use the device easily would be necromancers. But like Cassie pointed out, tracking ghosts is the sort of thing we already do.

So if this is going to be at all useful, then it needs to be able to lock onto a ghost I can't see. But then, how do I know which one it's targeting and whether it's the one I was thinking of?

I need a ghost I know, or at least know about. There's the White Lady in Griffith Park. She shows up whenever there's a brush fire out there. She's been getting a workout lately. There's the Knickerbocker Hotel just north of Hollywood Boulevard. Place is brimming over with ghosts like turds in a backed-up toilet bowl. I know a few of them.

I need something closer. Not as far as Long Beach. Somewhere in the South Bay. Then it comes to me.

In April of 1992, four LAPD officers on trial for the beating of Rodney King were acquitted despite video showing them beating the shit out of the guy in a clear case of police brutality. The response was the '92 L.A. riots. More than sixty people died, over a thousand buildings burned. Smoke got so thick LAX had to shut down because they couldn't guide planes in for a landing. More than twenty years later Quetzalcoatl would swing by, say "Hold my beer," and show everybody how it's really done, but at the time it was huge.

One of the people who died, Omar Saleh, was a Jordanian immigrant whose charred body was found two days later in a burnt-out house in West Adams. Smoke inhalation killed him and then the fire cooked him.

At least that's what it was supposed to look like. Hear Omar tell it, he was drugged, tossed into a corner, and set on fire to make it look like he was a victim of the riots, instead of the asshole cousin who was banging his wife and wanted the corner liquor store Omar'd started about twenty years before.

He left a Haunt, a surprisingly cogent one. Most ghosts can barely remember one moment to the next, but Omar's sharp. And pissed. His cousin got everything. The store, the house, his wife, his three kids. If he could have somehow gotten out of that house and over to our side he'd have chewed through his cousin like a starving shark on a diver with a papercut.

But fate beat him to it. I checked on the cousin and found out he'd pissed off the wrong people and pretty much shared the same fate Omar did. Only with several hours on the receiving end of a baseball bat first. I've never seen a ghost so happy as when I told him that.

Omar's ghost isn't far from the Forum. A mile maybe, a little ways out of the Toxic Zone. I concentrate on him and click the button. The needles point in the direction I remember and about the right distance.

I know where I'm going, but I want to find out how well this thing works. I drive around a bit watching the needle move and the distance change. If it's not locked on him then it's locked on something near him. After half an hour I decide to find out if I'm right.

He's still there when I pull up. He's got a lot of leeway for a Haunt. A lot of them are stuck in a room, or a house. Omar can go as far out as the street.

Recognition when he sees me get out of the car, and he's in front of me in a flash. The distance needle drops to zero. I'm gonna call this one a win.

Omar's starting to deteriorate. All Haunts will over time. Some take longer than others and I've never really understood why. He's going fuzzy around the edges, awareness drifting. Most of the time you don't notice it. Ghosts aren't really all there to begin with.

"Eric," he says. I haven't seen him in a few years, so maybe my memory's off, but I don't remember Omar sounding quite so hollow.

"Omar," I say. I pull out the razor and cut my arm, let a couple drops of blood fall to the cement. His attention immediately snaps to the blood and I let him have it. He's a blur as he kneels to get it and less than a second later he's back, looking a little sharper, a little more there.

"Thank you," he says. Then his awareness drifts again. "Eric. When did you get here?"

"Just now," I say. "Wanted to check on you."

"Thank you," he says. Then, "Eric. When did you get here?"

Ghosts aren't people. They're leftovers, snakeskins shed by a soul as it moves on. But some of them are hard not to see as people. Omar's one of them. And seeing him go like this is like watching a friend with dementia slowly fade away.

"It was good talking to you," I say. I close the tracker and slide it into my pocket. "I'll see you around, Omar."

"Goodbye," he says. Then, as I'm opening the door and sliding into the car, "Eric. When did you get here?"

I'd like to say it doesn't get to me. It's bad enough when someone slides into oblivion, but watching it happen after they're already dead feels just as cruel somehow. Like, didn't they go through enough? But they're not people.

No matter how many times I tell myself that, I can't quite make myself believe it.

———

I get a lock on what I hope is Werther's soul once I get on the road. If this tracks souls the same way as it does ghosts then he's somewhere to the northeast. It might be pointing at the estate, but I think it's a little too far to the east for that. I'm going to have to go there to know for sure.

I have less luck tracking down a possible mage/child eating monster near the Toxic Zone. I find a couple out of the way places that either might use as a lair. By the stink and spatter of dark, dried blood on the ground something was, but they're long gone.

Gabriela calls me after I've done a third sweep of the area. Whatever the thing is that's grabbing kids in the camps, I'm not going to find it out in the open.

"How go the intrigues at court?" I say.

"Jesus, these people," she says.

"More showed up?"

"Yeah. Siobhan was the first. I like her. Don't necessarily trust her, but I like her. Amanda says she has no claim on the inheritance. Different mother than the rest of them. Even if everyone else dies she gets nothing."

"That's fucked up. So, what, she lives off their table scraps and magnanimity?" I ask.

"She's still a mage, and from what I hear from Amanda, a pretty powerful one. She's carving her own way through life, and the rest of the family seems content to let her."

"Does she know about Attila?"

"No. Amanda's keeping that until tomorrow night. She's telling everyone he's unavailable, and playing the gracious host while avoiding answering questions. Right now, we've got Helga, Hans, and his son Tobias. No sign of Otto yet. Liam is supposed to be here later with his wife and his mistress, or something like that. Then there's the lawyer." Her voice turns to venom at that last one.

"You gonna kill him?" I say.

"Probably. Fucker's poking around all over. Doesn't seem to realize Amanda knows every move he's making and deliberately rearranging the house so he gets lost. It's actually kind of funny."

"Sorry I'm missing all the fun."

"Don't be. These people are insufferable. When Helga showed up, she assumed I was a servant and tried to get me to take her luggage."

"And she's still alive?"

"Yeah, but I had Bigsby toss her shit into a lake."

That's a surprise. "Bigsby's back?"

"Amanda looked him over inside and out. He's fine. Whatever that thing that attacked you was, it doesn't seem to be inside him."

"Which means either there was a trap set for him if he talked about the thread," I say, "or somebody was watching me on the other side and hit him with a spell."

"I don't like either of those options," Gabriela says. "I hope it wasn't a trap. There's never just one trap. I'll talk to Amanda about it. How's your day going?"

"Well, I bought a magic tchotchke I'm hoping will help me locate Attila's soul. So far, signs point to guardedly hopeful. I'll know more by the time we all meet tomorrow night."

"About that," she says. "Call me and let me know you're coming. When you get here Bigsby will get you into your room without anyone seeing you. Can you be here by three?"

"That depends," I say.

I'm on the fence about which is the bigger priority, the Werther Murder Party or the kid snatcher. Somebody else should be able to deal with the latter. The pastor says she knows some of the mages at USC. They should be powerful enough to track that thing down and take care of it. No need for me. Still.

"What happened?"

"Been hanging around a homeless camp of normals out near the Toxic Zone last few weeks. You know a vampire named Rosalie?" She pauses a second before answering.

"Rosalinda de la Guerra y Noriega," she says. "Yeah. Been around a long time. Rancho days. She stayed at the hotel for a while. She there? She becoming a problem?"

"Nothing like that. If anything, she's probably the least dangerous thing out here. I've been bringing supplies to the camp, and blood to Rosalie to help her keep a lower profile. The camp's on a church parking lot."

"I know the one you're talking about. Mage runs it. Nancy . . . Grimm? A pastor, right?"

"Yeah. Just found out about the mage part today. Anyway, Rosalie tipped me off to a possible El Cucuy in the area. Kids are going missing. Some of them are being snatched openly. Talked to the pastor and she already knew about it. Little annoyed about that."

"You don't sound convinced," she says.

"I think it might be a Baba Yaga."

"Shit." If this thing stalking kids is an El Cucuy, it's bad. But if it's a Baba Yaga, yeah, "Shit" is the right sentiment.

"I don't know if the pastor's the only mage in the area," I say, "but if there's an El Cucuy around I would have expected it to have made a play on her by now. I don't know if any of the missing kids are mages, but it's hitting a camp and moving on. Not over and over until it gets what it's looking for."

Russian folklore, right? Baba Yaga's this old witch who flies around in a cauldron, lives in a hut that hops around on a giant chicken leg, eats children. The eating children bit is true, the rest not so much.

They're rare, thank fuck. Really hard to get rid of. See, they soul hop. Shit gets too heavy, they leave one body they've chewed the soul out of and jump into another one. As escape hatches go, it's pretty convenient. Some mage goes to take your head off and you just hop into somebody else.

It's not all bad news. They die easy. Knife, bullet, drop a piano on them. They're easy to spot, too. They'll twist the host into the bent-over, gnarled form of an old woman. The longer it sticks around, the more it looks the part.

Back in the days when they got their name, seeing a hunched-over old babushka walking down a midnight road to the next village over might not raise suspicion. You might even get close enough to have a chat, or let your kid go over and take the sweet it holds out as an offering, and then you'd be fucked.

These days the lures have to match the times. They still do the old lady schtick. I've never heard of one changing its routine and I'm not sure it could. Ingrained hunting habits can be a bitch to turn around.

But "Don't take candy from strangers" is so ingrained into our culture now, they need something with a little more pep. You know, fun, in a razor-toothed psycho clown sort of way. They might go around like street vendors selling bright-colored balloons, cotton candy, blinking LED bracelets. You can tell if one's been in a body a long time by all the crap they've festooned themselves with. And—if you get too close—by all the children's bones they have sewn subtly into their clothes.

Mages are naturally resistant to that soul-hopping thing. It just sort of slides off of us. Weaker mages can get hit, but they'll fight back. They'll still die, but they'll make the Baba Yaga pay for it. A normal will pop like a water balloon.

There are a couple silver linings. Baba Yagas don't eat children raw, and they won't kill them until they can get them to their lair to cook them. Once they've got hold of a meal, they're not likely to let go, taking the soul-hopping trick off the table. In theory, at least.

It all boils down to the best way to take one out is hit it after it's grabbed a kid but before it's killed them. That's not a big window.

"You ever take one on?" I say.

"No."

"I ran into one in El Paso. It was acting as a homeless woman selling knockoff Mexican toys on the street. Fake balloons on plastic straws sticking out like porcupine quills, a garland of blinking, multi-colored LEDs wrapped around its body, bags of rancid cotton candy hanging from a belt."

"That worked?"

"Weirdly, yeah. Every couple of years a town would get hit and a few kids would go missing. Then it'd move on. Chased that fucker across half the state and once it was onto me the body-hopping started. I think it jumped to ten, twelve people inside of an hour."

"Did you get it?"

"Honestly, I don't know," I say. "I killed something. Whether it was in the body at the time or not? Couldn't say. Anyway, the pastor knows. Says she has friends who can help."

"Yeah, but I wouldn't be surprised if you're the only one around who's actually run into one before. If there's ever been one in L.A. I haven't heard about it. Do you think they can handle it?"

She's thinking what I'm thinking. Priorities. Amanda's nice and all, but the problems of one-percenter mage elites kind of take a back seat to having something like a Baba Yaga on the loose.

"I'm hoping I don't have to," I say. "I'm staying down here tonight."

"At the camp?"

"No. I won't be going back there." That comes out harsher than I intended. "I'll be in the area, though."

"Call me if you think you need backup," she says. "If they're as bad as I've heard—" There's a sound of genuine worry in her voice.

"I'll be fine. Go give Amanda some tongue and scandalize her relatives."

She laughs. "Not as fun as putting a hatchet in all their heads, but it'll do," she says. "Be careful."

"This is me we're talking about."

"That's why I'm saying it."

"Fair point."

"Hey, real quick," she says. "I'm sorry about last night. I'm sorry about—Look, can we just fucking talk? Not now, obviously, but soon?"

"Yeah," I say. "Soon. I mean it. It'll happen."

"Thank—"

I end the call before she can finish. I know I should talk to her about—well, shit, everything. Maybe I'll get lucky and die again before I have to.

Chapter 14

The rain clouds growing over the city fat and dark have finally decided L.A. needs some flooded sewers and open up like a busted dam. The kind of rainfall that hits once every ten years or so. Within an hour the L.A. River's going to be worthy of the name and the accident rate will triple.

Just as well I'm not planning on going back to the estate tonight. It'd be a good three hours easy. This Toyota I snagged hasn't been washed in weeks. Dirty water cascades down the windshield barely touched by the wipers. Visibility has gone to almost nothing and late afternoon might as well be midnight.

Dammit. Now it's even more pointless trying to track down a monster. It could run in front of the car with sirens and flashing lights and I probably wouldn't even see it. I pull over and check where I am on my phone. Not far from the church. This is as good a place to hole up for a bit as any and wait this out.

My phone rings. Lani. I stab the answer button hard enough to jam my finger. Lani isn't going to call unless there's something really, really wrong.

"I'm about five minutes away," I say before she can get a word out. I'm already on the road swerving past the other idiots driving tonight. "What's happening?"

"The pastor," she says. "There's something wrong with her. She's shaking and feverish and we don't know what happened. She went for a walk a couple hours ago and came back like this."

"Not a seizure?"

"Bob says it might be, but it's the weirdest one he's ever seen." Bob. Who the fuck is Bob? I know this. EMT. He's an EMT. Okay, that's good.

"Is anything changing?" I miss another car by inches. Their blaring horn is barely audible over the hammering of the rain on the roof. "Like her hands, arms. Her face?"

"I—I don't think so. Hang on." She calls out to Bob and gets a muffled answer in return. "Bob says yes. Her arms are longer. She's shaking really badly."

Fuck. It's a Baba Yaga. Pastor probably tried to find it and instead it found her. She must have hurt it badly enough that it needed to jump into another body, and hers was the only one available.

"I'm almost there," I say. "Is she inside? In the church? One of the trailers?"

"We have her in the church. Bob's trying to strap her into a chair—"

"No. Don't restrain her," I say. "In fact, get everybody the fuck away from her and out of the building, and don't let her out. I don't care if you have to park a truck in front of the doors. And for fuck sake, don't let it see anyone through the windows."

If it feels trapped, it'll do the same thing to someone else that it did to the pastor, only it'll be worse. A normal will die immediately and change. Then it'll kill anyone it sees.

But the pastor's putting up a fight. She's ultimately going to lose, but if she can buy me a little time, I might be able to take the thing down.

Lani yells away from the phone what I just told her and Bob is having none of it. An argument is about to erupt and I need them out of there now.

I hear a yell in the background, a scream from Lani, then running footsteps and slamming doors. "What's happening?"

"She bit Bob," she says.

"Bitch chewed through half my finger!" Bob yells in the background. Maybe the pastor heard Lani and she's giving me a hand. Or Bob's just got really tasty-looking fingers.

I turn hard around a corner and see the church just ahead. I fishtail into the driveway, sending a wave of water across the lot.

Everyone's standing outside the church, terrified. The doors are closed and someone's driven their camper up the steps to block the doors. They open to the inside, but nobody's getting through the camper. As long as the Baba Yaga can't see anyone, it can't hop into them.

"Everybody, get to cover and out of sight," I yell. It's hard to hear through the downpour, but I put some magic into my voice and it cuts through the noise. Everyone but Lani and Bob starts to scatter. The inhuman shrieks inside tell me the pastor's almost out of the fight.

"Are there any other doors?" I ask.

"A couple," Bob says. He's holding his left hand to his chest, but looks ready to jump back in there if he has to. I like your moxie, Bob, but not your brains. "Couple of the RVs backed up against them."

"All right, both of you get the hell out—" The screaming suddenly goes from angry-punk-band loud to skull-shattering loud, blowing out all the windows. Silence.

Shit. There are still some people out in the open, hiding behind a dumpster, behind a lamppost. Jesus. "Everyone, get into your trailers. Lock the doors. Close the windows. Don't—"

The church doors burst out, the blast flipping the camper end over end to land on its roof in the middle of the yard. The Baba Yaga launches itself over the crowd. It hits the pavement and tries to run, but it's struggling. Not enough that I can catch up to it, though. Before I can get near, it leaps through one of the RVs. Punches a hole like it's a Bugs Bunny cartoon. There's a crash, then another, and another, the RVs swaying with each impact.

It hits one and stops. There's a high-pitched scream and I can't tell if it's coming from the RV or from Lani, who's running like she's on fire.

Matthew. Fuck.

"You," I point at Bob. "Get everyone into the church. If you have guns grab them and cover the door." I point at another guy, Ted? Todd? I don't remember, but he's built like a block of cement and that's what I need.

"You go stand in front of the altar and get ready to catch."

"Catch what?" he says.

"I don't know yet, but if something comes at you, you fucking catch it." He nods like it's the most reasonable thing anybody's asked him to do all night and runs for the church.

I catch Lani inside her RV, screaming for Matthew. The Baba Yaga's already got him, and it's already gone. The windshield has been blown out.

"What happened?" She doesn't know whether to cry, scream, or punch something, so goes for broke and does all three at me. "Where's Matthew? Why did she take him? Why?!"

"I will get him back," I say. I'm not going to tell her any more than that. It would waste time I don't have and it wouldn't do any good anyway. "Get to the church. I will get him back."

"Please—" Crying, lost. Just the threat of that sort of loss is too much for anyone to bear.

"Church. Go. Now."

I race through the spaces between the RVs and into the street where I see the Baba Yaga loping away with Matthew clutched in its arm like a teddy bear. The body doesn't look anything like the pastor anymore. It's a caricature of a human being, shreds of clothing hanging off its body where the changes burst through seams.

The skin has gone a pale, ghostly gray. Its back is hunched over with a pronounced hump, and its arms are long, hands tipped in knife-blade claws. It's the face that's most changed, though. The head is a misshapen lump, large and ill-formed. Long nose with warty growths and a wildly protruding chin. The corners of its mouth go all the way back to its ears and sharp teeth poke out at wild angles.

Matthew is screaming and kicking. Good. Screaming is good. Screaming is alive. Screaming I can work with.

Every few steps the Baba Yaga halts, its feet trying to go in different directions, the arm holding Matthew trying to unfold. It stumbles in the rain.

The pastor is not out for the count. That gives me an idea. Her body is alive, but her soul is being shredded apart. If she were a normal, it would have been instantaneous. But with the pastor it's taking time. When she goes, there's a chance that the Baba Yaga's spirit won't be fully established, won't be dug in like a tick. Just a split second. If I'm right, that should be all I need.

But I have to work fast. First thing is to keep it from getting away. I crouch and slam my palm to the ground. Blue fire erupts in a ring around us, blocking its path.

Physically, it's just fire. If it wants to barbeque itself, sure, it can walk through it. Hell, the flames are low enough it can probably hop over. But its spirit won't go through with the body.

It turns to me, rage and a faint recognition. It opens its mouth impossibly wide, the chin brushing the ground, and lets out an inhuman shriek.

Baba Yagas depend on stealth. Situation like this, it would normally hop into whoever is confronting it, like it did with the pastor. But I'm the only one it can go after. I feel a brush of magic that quickly pulls back, like a finger from a fire.

"Try it," I say, wiping rain out of my eyes with the back of my hand. "I dare ya." It answers with another scream. "Yeah, fuck you, too. You don't have a lot of options right now. We both know you won't kill the kid until you're ready to stick him in a pot, and you know you're not getting across that line in anybody's body. How about you let the kid go and we call it even?"

This time the shriek is even louder. Guess it doesn't like that idea. The arm holding Matthew begins to stretch out while the other arm tries to pull the traitorous limb back.

I'm going to have to do three things at the same time and if I fuck up any one of them Matthew's dead. I've already got the spells in my head, and the portal ring is firmly on my finger.

"Pastor, I know you're still in there, if only a little bit, and you're still fighting. You're going to lose. That doesn't mean this thing has to win. I have to ask you to trust me. And I know how big an ask this is. I need you to let go."

At first I think maybe I'm wrong. She's not in there. Or she can't hear me. Then I feel it. A death, so small it barely registers. She's lost so much in her fight that there's hardly anything left.

There's a blank space where her soul used to be, a tiny gap, insignificant really. A little niche that the Baba Yaga hasn't been able to invade yet, but large enough that for a split second the body is a corpse, nothing but meat.

And in that moment, it's mine.

I release its grip on Matthew, rocketing him toward and then past me with a pull spell, while triggering the portal ring to open a hole to the church where Ted or Todd or whoever waits to catch him. I see a glimpse of everyone staring back at me, terrified. As soon as Matthew is through, I snap the hole shut.

I can feel the Baba Yaga's soul filling the last empty spaces of the pastor's body, but before it can finish I make the body throw all its limbs wide, its head back, its chest out. I bend every joint, strain every tendon, stretch every muscle—far, far past their breaking points.

The Baba Yaga dies as its body shreds itself at my command, an unlucky toy in an angry child's hands. Nothing left but scraps of meat and split bone.

My knees buckle, injury, pain, and not enough sleep finally catching up to me. I don't know how long I stay down. Time gets a little blurry. Someone helps me to my feet, walks me back to the parking lot. Big guy. Can't remember his name.

"Matthew—"

"Is fine," he says. "I caught him just like you asked. He's with his mom back at the church."

"Anyone else hurt?"

"Just Bob," he says. "But mostly that's whining. Going on about how he'll have to get his fingers amputated. He just needs some stitches. The pastor . . . That wasn't the pastor, was it?"

"No, but she was in there. Fighting the whole time. I wouldn't have gotten Matthew back without her."

"Do I even want to know what any of that actually was?"

"No," I say. "Not if you want to sleep at night, at least."

"Thought as much." He helps me up the steps of the church. By the time I get to the top step I'm walking on my own, my energy returning.

Most of the people in the camp are there. I hear a few engines revving up, cars peeling out of the parking lot, as others have decided that this isn't the place to be.

No one says anything. They don't know whether I'm a demon they need to fear or a messiah they should follow. I sit on one of the pews near the door. Keep enough distance and maybe one of us won't feel so awkward.

"I just need to catch my breath," I say. "And I'll be going."

"Is it safe?" someone asks. "Is the pastor—?"

"Pastor's gone. She fought. Hard. Even when she knew she'd lost. She did more out there than I did."

"She almost killed my boy," Lani says, pushing her way through everyone to stand in front of me. She and Matthew clutch each other tight enough to cut off circulation. She has a blanket over her shoulders, sopping wet and shivering.

"No," I say. "That wasn't her. It was something else that took her." Really doesn't matter what I say. Lani's face tells me everything they're hearing.

"What are you?" she says. Fear and betrayal on her face. I tried to warn her.

"It's—"

"Complicated?" she says, her voice hot. "No. It's not complicated. Were you like the pastor? Just waiting for the right moment to take my son? Take any of us?"

"Jesus, Lani. I told you there are worse things out there. Don't say you didn't understand me. Maybe you didn't want to, but we both know you did."

"Things like you, you mean." So quiet only I can hear her.

"Are you human?" someone yells from the back of the church.

"As human as the rest of you," I say.

"Only demons have eyes like that," yells someone else.

Crap.

"Did you turn the pastor into that?" yells a third. Given how he's holding his hand, it's probably Bob.

I can feel the heat rising. Fear turns to rage awful quick in a traumatized crowd. Their pastor, someone they trusted, turned into a monster who tried to take a little boy. They don't want to believe anything bad about her. I don't blame them.

They think they want answers, want to understand and process what happened, but what they really want is for everything to be normal again. For everything to make sense. All we're missing now are the torches and pitchforks.

"No. The thing out there wasn't the pastor," I say. "It was a thing that took over her body and she fought it to the end. She tried to save Matthew, Lani. She tried to save you all." I wonder if maybe she put herself in the path of the Baba Yaga. Maybe she thought she could take it. Maybe she just wanted to make sure it didn't take any of them.

"We're still in danger, aren't we?" Lani says.

"You said it yourself," I say. "Everyone's in danger. All the time." I pull myself up from the pew. Lani is staring at me with burning eyes, shivering, whether with cold or anger I can't tell.

"Go away," she says, her voice cracking. "Don't come back. Don't ever come back."

"I won't," I say. I head out into the rain, leaving them huddled together inside the church, afraid of the dark.

"Eric?" Gabriela says, voice tinny through this crappy phone. "What time is it?"

"About three. How are things going at Casa De Borgia?" I hear mumbling in the background.

"It's—Hang on. I'm putting you on speaker. I've got Amanda here."

"Tell me you've had a better time than we have," Amanda says.

"How about we talk about my night later," I say. "I'm a few blocks from the estate. Can I get in without tipping off the crazy family?"

"Yeah," Amanda says. "I'll have Bigsby meet you at the gate and bring you straight to the room."

"No, I just need to get in," I say. "I'll be back out in about five minutes. I have a thing that might help track down your dad. But I—"

"You can help him?" Amanda's energy cranks up to eleven.

"He said, 'might,'" Gabriela says, her voice pitched down a notch, quieter.

"Right," Amanda says. "Sorry."

"No, it's all good," I say. I don't think I've ever heard Gabriela talk to anybody like that. I didn't even know she could talk to anybody like that. But to be fair, most of the time I've been around her there's been a lot of gunfire and stabbing.

"What do you need from us?" Gabriela says.

"Just make sure nobody's wandering around I might bump into. I think I just need to get inside the gates. Actually, a towel would be nice."

"A towel?"

"It's been raining out here. I'm a little soggy."

"I'll get you a towel," Gabriela says.

"You're clear to come in," Amanda says. "I've shifted the grounds so even if anyone's nearby they won't see you."

"They might notice the magic," I say.

"Don't even worry about that," Gabriela says. "These people are slinging spells around like it's some kind of shit festival at the monkey house."

"All right." I drive up the short road to the estate and the gate at the end opens up for me. "I'm here. I'll call you when I have more information."

"You sure you don't want to come up to the house?" Gabriela says.

"Yeah. Like I said, in and out. I'll call you when I have more information." I park right outside the actual entrance to the estate. No need to drive in for this.

Of course, it's still pissing down rain, so this was probably a stupid idea, but I don't want to make more noise than I have to. I trust Amanda's control of the place, but I don't trust any of her relatives.

On my way here I followed the disk's directions and drove around three times to make sure I had it right. If it's got hold of Werther his soul's somewhere in Union Station. Before I go on a wild goose chase through the station I want to make sure I actually have him.

I pull out the brass disk from my messenger bag and do a quick check. It looks like it's still pointed at Union Station. I step over the threshold and the pissing rain turns into a clear, moonless night on a forest road, stars bright overhead. I wonder what it would take to get a place like this. I'd probably have to kill somebody. Maybe a lot of somebodys.

"Jesus, you are soggy," Gabriela says, standing just a few feet from the entrance. She tosses me a large, fluffy towel.

"Thanks," I say. I wipe my face and hands with it and run it over my hair. I take off my coat and try to shake some of the water off it, but it's useless. It's completely soaked through.

"You look like you've had a fun night," she says. She's wearing sweats, her hair pulled back, sleep still in her eyes. "Go for a dip in the river?"

"Ran into the Baba Yaga," I say.

That wakes her up. "Shit, are you all right?"

I start to say, "Sure, I'm fine," but my brain seizes up. "No," I finally say. "Not by a long shot. But it's dead. And a kid isn't. That's what matters." I don't want to think about it right now. I want to focus what little energy I have left on the task at hand and pop some more Adderall. Starting to think maybe I should just move straight to meth.

I steel myself for Gabriela to push me on it, but she says, "Okay. We can talk about it later. What's the gizmo do?"

"Ghost tracker. Seems to find wayward souls, too. Wanted to see if I could tag Werther's soul out there. Wanted to confirm it's actually him by checking over here."

"Did it work?" she says. I move it around. The needle's spun and locked in the direction where Werther's thread hits the estate wall.

"Looks like," I say. "Want to check something." I slide over to the other side to get a better view of the thread. Sure enough, the needle's locked in the same direction.

"Is it working?" Gabriela says, appearing next to me. She looks a little nauseous.

"The hell are you doing over here?"

"Just because I don't like slipping over to this side," she says, "doesn't mean I can't. But I can't stay long. Jesus, I hate this place. I don't know how you stand it."

"You get used to it," I say. "I think we got him. Come on, let's get out of here."

We slide back and Gabriela immediately leans on a tree, taking deep breaths. I run over to her, grabbing a vial from my messenger bag.

"Breathe this in," I say, pulling the stopper. "It'll help." After she does, the color returns to her face and she stops dry-heaving.

"Thank you. What is that?"

"No idea," I say. "I got it in Louisiana from . . . ya know, the less said of that the better."

"Well, it works. I feel a little fuzzy around the edges, though," she says.

"That'll pass." I hand her the stoppered vial. "Hang onto it. I don't need it anymore. It's supposed to never go bad."

"Is it any good with hangovers?"

"Only if you go drinking with the dead."

"On my bucket list," she says.

"Enh, it's overrated."

"Where is he?" Gabriela says. "Out there."

"Near as I can tell, Union Station," I say. "Now that I'm pretty sure I have him, I'm going back out to see if I can narrow it down." She grabs my arm as I turn back to the estate entrance, not hard, but I can tell that if I want to pull it back neither one of us is gonna be happy.

"No, you're not," she says. "You're coming to the house and you're getting some sleep. Real sleep. Not one of those twenty-minute naps you take when somebody hits you in the head too hard."

"I'm fine," I say. "Besides, you know how it goes: 'Can't sleep. Clowns will eat me.'" She doesn't move. Doesn't say anything for a couple of beats longer than I'm comfortable with.

"This is about Mictlan," she says. "Or someone in Mictlan."

"That's a bit of a leap," I say, hoping she'll buy it and let me go so we don't have to start beating the crap out of each other.

"I've seen you run. You're either running toward a disaster or away from something you just don't want to deal with."

"Seriously? You want to psychoanalyze me now?"

"Something's happening when you sleep. Something so bad you're trying to avoid it altogether. I can only think of one thing that might be, something about Mictlan."

"This isn't your problem to deal with," I say.

"Yeah, it is. Amanda's trusting you to have her back. And I know that no matter what state you're in, you will. But the next couple of days are going to be a shitshow and you need to be on top of your game. Amanda needs you."

"Amanda's—"

"I need you." She lets go of my arm, but she holds me with her eyes.

"You're right," I say, trying to ignore those last three words. "Amanda needs as much help as she can get. And to help her I need to have my shit together."

"Yeah," Gabriela says, lowering her eyes and turning toward the house. I know that's not the answer she was looking for. I'm not sure it's the answer I wanted to give.

Chapter 15

The bone fields of Mictlan and the ever-growing hole yawning in the middle. It seems small from here, but I know it isn't. How far away is it? Dozens of miles? Hundreds? I have no sense of scale. "What the hell even is that thing?"

"Uncertainty," says a voice at my elbow. "Doubt."

"You're not gonna throw me into it again, are you? Because I have had a really shitty night."

"No," Mictlantecuhtli, my other me, says, stepping up to watch the nightmare unfold before us. He looks even less like me than the last time I saw him. Skin stone gray, so thin I can see his heart beating inside his chest. The necklace of eyeballs "That was just to get your attention. Did it work?"

"Fuck you," I say.

"I see it did. Mictlan is dying because of you."

"Not easin' into that one, are ya, pal? Just plough on through and lube be damned. Okay, I'll bite. How?"

"I am more Mictlantecuhtli than I have ever been anything else," he says. "I know this. It's as much a fact as the sun is hot. I know it in my bones." He picks a jawbone from the ground, tosses it casually toward the hole. It sails through the air and I lose sight of it long before it reaches its destination.

"Nice little symbolic punctuation there," I say. "So what? I know that, too. I knew that. I mean, I was . . . Fuck."

"Uncertainty," he says. "Doubt. Are you a piece of me? Am I your progeny? You don't know."

"Do you?" I say.

"No, but that's irrelevant."

"Look at you bein' all cryptic and shit." He's not me, not anymore. I can feel it. Like he said, it's a fact. We were the same once, but we are nothing alike now.

"I really was an insufferable pain in the ass, wasn't I?" he says.

"You still are," I say. "Okay, great. Uncertainty and doubt. I don't know who I am, you don't know who I am. Hurray for us. What does that have to do with that big sucking chest wound out on the horizon?"

"Mictlantecuhtli and Mictecacihuatl define Mictlan. Simple enough. Only you and I are still linked. I know what I am, but you don't. Mictlan can't tell the difference between us. All it knows is that your doubt is my doubt. My doubt is Mictlan's doubt."

"This is why you told me to choose when you threw me into the hole the other night."

"Yes."

"Couldn't have mentioned it then?" I say.

"You wouldn't have listened." Neither of us says anything for a moment. Just as I'm about to ask the question, he gives me the answer. "Mictecacihuatl is good. Worried. Worried about Mictlan. Worried about you. But good."

"Not worried about you?"

"No," he says. "I'm not sure how I feel about that."

"I guess only one of us gets to be the family fuck-up," I say. "Let me make sure I'm clear. I'm killing Mictlan because I haven't chosen who I am?"

"No," he says. "You're not doing anything. It's just happening. Saying you're causing this is like saying you're making your heart beat. It's a function of you, you have the ability to stop it, but you're not making it happen."

"Something horribly tragic and it isn't my fault? Will wonders never cease? Okay. I'm Eric Carter. There, I chose." I look at the hole in the distance. It's continuing to grow. "Yeah, okay, that's a non-starter."

"You have to choose what you are, not who you are."

"Human, necromancer, asshole?"

"Definitely that third one. I can't tell you what you are. We're not the same anymore, and neither of us is who we used to be. What you are is not mine to decide. What's important isn't what you choose, it's that you choose. So long as there's a question, that hole will get bigger. Take too long and all of Mictlan will be swallowed up."

Uncertainty. Doubt. I think back to the other night, yelling at Gabriela that I don't know what I am, hearing Lani's words, "What are you?"

"How much time do I have?" I say. "Finding the right therapist to help with this sort of thing isn't easy, you know."

"You joke because you're terrified."

"No shit. Shouldn't I be? Hell, shouldn't you be?"

"I'm not afraid of anything anymore," he says. "I'm not sure why. I don't know how much time we have."

"Great. You got the sociopathy, I got the tattoos. I think you got the better end of the deal."

"Oh, I know I got the better end of the deal," he says.

Then the fucker throws me into the hole again.

———

I snap awake and immediately my razor's in my hand. I sit up, disoriented, and vertigo pulls me back down. The lights are dim but they're still too bright. I'm not in Mictlan or outside the camp with everybody's eyes burning holes in the back of my head.

"Good morning, sir," Bigsby says, smiling at me from the side of the bed. Right. This is the Werther estate. I came here to get a bead on Werther's soul and then made the mistake of agreeing with Gabriela that I needed to sleep.

So, I came up here and . . .

"Did I pass out in the bathroom?"

"In the shower, sir," he says.

"It's good to know that even back from the dead I'm still on brand." I swing my legs out of the bed and that's about as far as I can get. "Oh, Jesus, everything hurts."

I remember getting to the house, up to my room. Gabriela tried again to get me to agree to check just how jacked up my body is after three fights to the death in less than twenty-four hours. We compromised and I let Bigsby take me upstairs and sew up all the holes and slices I didn't know I had.

From there I remember stepping into the shower. And then I remember Mictlan eating itself because I'm having an existential crisis.

"You got me in bed?"

"I did, sir. I'm sorry, should I have left you in the shower?"

"No. No, this is good. Uh, I don't recall owning pajamas."

"They're part of the wardrobe Miss Amanda commissioned for you. Suits, ties, casual wear, a tuxedo for this evening, and assorted accoutrements are in the closet at the far end of the room."

Wow. A guy could get used to this. Wait. "This evening? I thought the big conclave dinner wasn't until tomorrow."

"Miss Amanda felt that given recent events and the unexpected early arrival of other members of the family the timetable should be moved forward."

Dammit. I need to get out of the estate to see if I can track down

Werther's soul out there. It's not noon yet. I can still do some searching. Maybe I can pinpoint the exact location? At the very least I want to see what the tracker's actually pointing at.

"Okay," I say. "I can work with this. Can you get me out the gates without anyone seeing me?" I'm assuming we're going with the original plan where I don't show up until tonight.

"Unfortunately, sir, the gates are locked, as the conclave has officially started."

"I can't leave?"

"No, sir." So much for that. Clearly, plans have changed.

"Did Amanda tell you anything about what I'm supposed to do?"

"She did not, sir. But she wanted to give you this." He hands me an envelope sealed with wax. I can tell there's a spell on it. Can I trust it? I hand the letter back to Bigsby.

"You open it." If it's a paper charm, it could easily be a trap. Depending on what type, just being in the same room with it when it goes off could still be dangerous, but at least it won't be pointed at me.

"I'm sorry, sir. I'm unable. The seal can only be broken by you."

I haven't even seen most of this family yet and I'm already paranoid. I crack the letter open and the magic locking it dissipates. I'm not on fire or breathing toxic gas or something, so that's a plus.

Eric,

Sorry for the sudden change of plans. The rest of the family has forced me to move the official beginning of the conclave up a day. If you can, please come down for luncheon. I'd like to get all of the surprises out of the way and see who does what when I announce Dad's death and you walk in.

When you're ready, let Bigsby know and he'll have Siobhan meet you outside your room to escort you downstairs. The two of you should meet. I trust her. I probably shouldn't, but I do. She knows what's going on, so you don't need to censor yourself. She'll give you a rundown on who's here.

Thank you for being here. This whole shitshow would be a lot harder without you and Gabriela's help.

—Amanda

Guess I better get ready, then.

Bigsby offers to dress me and no, that's just—no. I kick him out and take a look at what I have to wear. My rain-soaked clothes from last night are nowhere to be seen, which is just as well, since after everything that's happened they stink of blood and sweat and need to be burned.

The clothes are all very . . . colorful. Okay, not so much colorful as not-black. I don't know how formal this luncheon's supposed to be, but the lack of ripped jeans and logo t-shirts from strip clubs tells me it's going to be a little classier than I'm used to.

I get daring and grab a light gray suit. Gray won't hide bloodstains, but it's not like I'm going out on the town with the doors locked. I have to say this thing fits perfectly. It's even cut in a way that I can carry the Sig in a holster at my back and the derringer in an ankle holster without looking like I'm packing.

I step out into the hall. This time it's a proper hall, not a short step to a kitchen. Oak doors, plush runner, wood paneling. There are even framed etchings of ducks and shit on the walls. It looks a little like another house I was trying to escape filled with people trying to kill me. Who knows, maybe I'll get to do it again.

"All right, Bigsby," I say. "What now?"

"Oh, you don't need Bigsby for that, Mister Carter." Tall, light-skinned, black woman. Soft Irish accent. She steps into the hall from a staircase I swear wasn't there a second ago.

"You must be Siobhan," I say. She's wearing a red tunic top with silver edging that goes into a split skirt down to her knees over black leggings and short-heeled boots. Her hair is in long beaded goddess braids, the beads small talismans, most of which I don't recognize, but I can feel the barely perceptible magic coming off them.

"I am. Admiring my outfit?"

"As a matter of fact, yes. You really make it work. Though I'm more interested in your braids." She picks one up and looks at it with a critical eye.

"You noticed the magic?"

"Should I not have?"

"Most people can't, which is how I like it."

"I won't say a word."

"Then let's go down and meet the family."

"I'm looking forward to it like it's a root canal." We head down the stairs arm in arm.

"You'll fit right in. Amanda's asked me to bring you up to speed on things. What do you know?"

"Laughably little," I say. "I know Amanda and Attila. I've met Otto, and Hans and Liam briefly. Oh, and Reinhold."

"I wasn't aware Reinhold was coming."

"He won't be," I say.

"Oh, it's like that, is it? Even more reason Otto is going to love seeing you again."

"If there's one talent I have it's to make any gathering awkward. Hans might be a bit surprised, too. He sent an assassin for me after I kicked him in the nuts and set him on fire."

She fans her face with one hand. "Mister Carter, you're trying to seduce me."

"Is it working?"

"It's an excellent start. What else do you know?"

"Hans has a boy, Tobias, who has no magic. Helga's Otto's and Hans's mother. Attila kicked her out long after he did the others over some spat. Then there's Liam, who I understand came with a wife and a mistress. Oh, and he murdered Amanda's mother."

"Not bad. What holes would you like filled?"

"Let's start with you," I say.

"How forward of you. I don't let just anyone fill my holes, you know."

"I can tell you how I set Hans on fire again."

"No," she says. "That ship has sailed. Now go on, ask the obvious."

"I can't help but notice you don't exactly look—"

"Like a Nazi?" she says. "I am the family's great shame. Our father shared a passionate evening with a black woman in a brothel and I was the product. I wouldn't be here except for one thing."

"You're as powerful as everyone else."

"More so than most. The rest of the family either hates me or ignores me. I'm simply not important enough for them to waste their time."

"Don't you have a stake in all this, too?"

"A stake, yes, but only the one I carved out for myself. Apparently, a racist restriction from the sixteenth century says I can't receive the Great Inheritance. But I have the same restrictions as the rest of them."

"The curse."

"It's more a minor nuisance for me. I haven't seen any of my family besides Attila and Amanda for years, so it's easy to avoid. Helga needs a hot poker shoved up her ass, but the rest of them don't really matter to me."

"I haven't even met everybody and I think I like you more than the rest of them already. What's the problem with Helga?"

We reach the bottom of the stairs and head to one of the many sitting rooms. "There's a bar in this room. Do you mind if we stop for a drink? I'd rather go in with a slight buzz than have to wait for the alcohol to make my family tolerable."

"Best plan I've heard all week." The room is like the rest of the house, movie set Tudor-ish. A bar on one wall is doing its best to look like a British pub, but it feels like it's trying too hard.

Siobhan steps behind the bar, grabs a couple of glasses, and gets to work. She's quick, efficient. Mixing the drinks like a magician shuffling cards.

"Helga," she says, "is trying to be a family matriarch, but none of her people really care, including her own sons. You have to understand that us here are simply the top of the heap. There are thousands of other family members. But none of the rest hold a candle to our power."

"And each of you commands loyalty from a chunk of them. Like serfs."

"Good analogy. We each have followers, for lack of a better term. Most are family, either direct descendants or whoever has married in. But not all. We have a responsibility to each other. We protect them and in turn they—well, I'm really not sure. I don't demand much of my people other than that they not be complete gobshites. I don't really have what you'd call a power base. Most of the people I take care of are the misfit types, low-power talents, folks with no magical ability, that sort of thing. In any kind of fight they'd be useless. So mostly I just try to make sure everyone's got a job and a place to live. I don't know much about what my other siblings do, though I've heard some fucked-up stories."

"And Helga's people don't like her?"

"Helga's people think she's weak," Siobhan says. She pours the drinks from a shaker into the glasses over crushed ice. She slides one over to me, raises her glass toward me as a toast. I don't move.

"Don't leave a lady waiting."

"I'm a little paranoid."

"Of course. Bigsby?" The butler appears in the doorway. "Are either of these drinks poisoned, ensorcelled, or otherwise harmful to anyone?"

"No, ma'am, but from what I recall of the recipe, I believe you may have used a touch too much Grand Marnier."

"Everybody's a critic. Good enough for you?"

"Good enough for me. Thanks, Bigsby. That'll be all." After he disappears I say, "That thing creeps me the fuck out."

"Same," she says. We clink our glasses together. I don't know everything she put into it, but it's good. I flash to the last time I was in a bar, trying to convince Darius to step into a trap. It worked, but it wasn't pleasant.

"I like it," I say. "What is it?"

"Something I thought you might appreciate," she says. "A Corpse Reviver."

"I like your style," I say. "Helga's losing her powerbase. Otto and Hans picking it up?"

"Otto, mostly. Hans is kind of a pussy. Helga could put a stop to Otto trying to undercut her, but I think she realizes she's not the future. Things may have changed the last couple of days, though."

"Because I—" I run my finger across my throat and make a ripping noise.

"Precisely," she says. "And murdered Reinhold. I wouldn't be surprised if she was hoping you'd kill Otto outright. I don't think it occurred to her that he might not stay dead."

"We're a pesky bunch, us dead people. What about Tobias, Hans's kid? I hear he's pretty much the family whipping boy."

"That kid's had it rough. Hans is weak and cruel and he takes his frustrations out on Tobias. Sometimes I want to kidnap him just to get him away from that psychopath."

"Amanda thinks he's here because they're going to try to marry her off."

"I don't doubt it. She's pretty effectively nixed that, though. Provided her girlfriend doesn't get herself killed."

"I wouldn't worry too much about that," I say. "Gabriela can take down any of these fuckers and not break a sweat."

"Known her long?"

"We go back," I say. There's no point in trying to describe our history or relationship. I don't even understand it right now. "Who's left?"

"Jonathan, Otto's slimy lawyer. I'm not sure, but I think he might not be human. Have you noticed that he's hard to, well, notice?"

"Yeah. He's got some sort of camouflage, makes your eyes slide off him. I haven't figured out what he might be, though. Know anything else about him?"

"If it wasn't for him, Otto would be giving handjobs down at the docks for spare change. He's been handling all of Otto's finances for years. Otto's too much of an idiot to do anything himself. As far as I'm aware their relationship is entirely professional."

"I wouldn't be too sure about that," I say. "He definitely plays the sub to Otto. I get the feeling that he tops from the bottom and Otto just hasn't figured it out yet."

"That's an interesting theory," she says. "And an image I really didn't need."

"You're welcome. What about spouses, bodyguards?"

"Ah, well. Except for you and I, everyone came with an entourage, or at least a partner. Those didn't last long."

"How so?"

"There have been"—she does air quotes with her fingers—"'accidents.'"

"I think I qualify as part of Amanda's entourage."

"Not the way she talks about it. She sees you as more of an interested third party. An ally, of course, but not with her. Would you like another drink? There's more here and I'd hate to waste it."

"Shouldn't we be getting to the shindig?" I say.

"Oh, fuck them. This is the most interesting conversation I've had in years."

"Okay, then. Top me up. How come you didn't bring anyone?"

"I don't know anyone I hate enough to subject to my family." She pours the remainder in the shaker into our glasses. "People are going to die this weekend. People have already died this weekend. These fuckers are going to target the weakest links. No one's going to risk bringing someone they really care about here."

"Last question," I say.

"Hit me."

"Why are *you* here?"

"What do you mean?"

"Seriously? We're gonna do it this way?" I should have figured. When your life is a constant game where you have to hide your cards, you're not giving them up easily.

I tick off the points on my fingers. "You haven't been to one of these in decades. You almost universally hate these people. None of them like you. Some of them want you dead. The rest want you to disappear. You can't inherit. All of these psychopaths are acting true to form. But you? No, you're here for a different reason than they are. I'd like to know what it is."

"And if I don't want to tell you?"

"I'll ask Amanda and Gabriela. And if they don't know, you might want to fix that. Because when the shit hits the fan, and we both know it will, you'll have three fewer people at your back."

"It's complicated," she says.

"Tell me something that isn't."

"True. But that's what I told them. I need to see how a couple of things play out tonight. Then I'll tell all three of you. They've agreed to this. How about you?"

"I wonder sometimes if there's ever anything that isn't a pain in the ass in this world," I say. "Fine. If they're okay with it, so am I. For the moment."

"Then let's go join the party," she says. "I hear it's going to be quite the event."

Chapter 16

Lunch is being held in the solarium, or one of them, at least. Maybe it's a sitting room. Or a dining room. The fuck do I know? This place is an architectural nightmare that would give M.C. Escher fits.

Siobhan and I stop in a room just next to it that gives me a decent view of everyone but enough shadows to keep me out of sight. They're all standing or moving about with a predatory awkwardness, like a high school dance for sharks.

"When do I go in?" I say. My job right now is to walk in at the right time and see what happens. I'm like the play in Hamlet wherein I'll catch the conscience of the king. Or more like a bug bomb tossed into the room to see which of the roaches scatter.

"You'll know," she says. "Now if you'll excuse me, I have to go scandalize my siblings." She puts a wide, and oh-so-fake smile on her face and strides into the room. I sit down to watch the festivities unfold.

The other room looks like a set of mismatched chess pieces. On one side there's a queen—Helga, a statuesque blonde woman who looks to be in her mid-thirties—and three kings—her sons Otto and Hans, who look a lot like each other except for the massive cravat Otto is sporting around his neck, and Liam, who looks a lot like Attila, only younger. Two pawns—Otto's lawyer, and Hans's son Tobias—hover nearby. They're all very Aryan.

On the other side stand three queens: Amanda, Gabriela, and Siobhan. And they look every inch their role. These women could lead an army, and at least one has. Siobhan stands out the most, of course. Not because of her skin tone so much as her outfit.

Amanda and Gabriela are wearing fairly conservative blouses, skirts, and flats. Gabriela's hair is up in a bun that hides the purple ends, held together with a couple of hair sticks. Knowing her, they're good for throwing or stabbing and are almost definitely poisoned. The pawn for their side isn't on the board, yet.

"Oh, look," Helga says. "It's the bastard. Have you taken after your whore of a mother turning tricks in back alleys, Siobhan? Or are you doing it for free?" There's a hint of a German accent, barely notice-able.

"It's delightful to see you, Helga," Siobhan says. "You're looking better. Had some work done, I see. Speaking of back alleys, is that where you found your plastic surgeon?"

"Helga," Liam says, upper-crust British, "Siobhan. Please. Being here is hard enough without you two sniping at each other."

"Sniping?" Helga says. "Oh dear, no. She's not worth sniping. I mean, look at her clothes. You look like a hussar. Did you dig up one of your old lovers again?"

"I wouldn't want to make you jealous," Siobhan says. "Seeing as they're all much better preserved than you. But I have to say, dear, your tits are spectacular. Whose are they?"

"Enough," Amanda says, her voice thundering through the room. Everyone's eyes are on her.

"Yes, I agree," Liam says, facing Amanda, who doesn't so much as blink. "Enough of the lies. Where is our brother? We've been here almost two days and he has yet to grace us with his presence."

"My father is dead," Amanda says. She lets the silence drag a bit before she says, "He was murdered the night before last in his study. Someone was able to get through our wards and close enough to kill him."

"Bullshit," Otto says. "If he's dead then you killed him."

"You are the most likely suspect," Liam says. "I take it you've re-ceived the inheritance?"

"I am the most likely suspect, yes," she says. "But I know I didn't do it. It was done by someone who knows the estate, and how to travel through it without being discovered. All of you have been here before."

"You didn't answer my question," Liam says.

"Yes, I've received the inheritance."

The reactions are interesting. Young Tobias looks confused. I won-der if anyone's even told him about any of this. Hans and Otto are trying to look subtle and calculating, but they're doing as good a job as a dog trying not to drool over a steak. Liam looks skeptical, but not terribly upset.

And then there's Helga. I know they were close until they had some sort of falling out. I was ready to discount her as some sort of spider, coldly sitting at the center of her web waiting for the right moment to strike. But she looks genuinely upset.

"Where's the body?" Helga says. Her voice is quiet, but it commands the room despite the quaver in it.

Amanda waves a hand and an image appears in midair of the surgical suite we left Attila's corpse in. The room's been tidied up a bit, and the body's been arranged less haphazardly on the gurney.

"This is horseshit," Hans says. "How do we know this is even true?"

"Bigsby," Amanda says. The butler appears at her side. "Is this the corpse of Attila Werther?"

"Yes, ma'am."

"And who discovered the body?"

"Presumably, I did, ma'am, after which I alerted you and Miz Cortez."

"Bigsby, why do you say presumably?" Liam says.

"When Mister Werther passed, the inheritance, and therefore ownership of the estate, passed to Miss Amanda. My memories directly before and for a few minutes after the transfer are gone. All I can say is that when I regained awareness I was in the study standing next to Master Werther. I do not seem to have moved from the spot between the time I lost awareness and the time I regained it, which was approximately eight minutes."

"That's awfully convenient," Hans says.

"We're going to take the word of a construct?" Otto says. "This is absurd. Take us to the body."

"Bigsby isn't something that can lie," Liam says. "And if you'd try using that melon at the end of your neck to think with rather than for guillotine practice, you'd realize she couldn't have done it. The curse would have killed her."

"By that logic none of us could have," Otto says, pointing at Gabriela. "The Mexican girl is the only one who could."

"Would you like your head cut off again, Otto?" Gabriela says. "I could arrange that."

"She couldn't have done it either," Liam says, clearly fed up. "For the same reason. If she had, Amanda would be dead. We all know how the curse works. None of the restrictions were lifted until the conclave started and that was today."

"We still should see the body," Hans says. "We have a right—"

"The body is being preserved," Liam says. "Would you rather my brother's corpse rot in a morgue drawer?" He turns to Amanda. "Attila was able to use a sort of temporal stasis, that as far as I know none of us have ever been able to master. There's been speculation that it's something that comes with the inheritance. Is that right?"

"It is. I have the room suspended in time."

"Then shut it off," says Hans. "I demand—"

"No," Amanda says.

"I beg your pardon?"

"I said no," Amanda says. Her voice is like cold steel. "In case you haven't fully realized yet, I am now the head of the family. Not only do I have my own powers, which you all know are a match for any of yours, I also have the power from the inheritance itself. If any of you would like to debate this, I would be happy to do so on the lawn where no one else can get hurt. Hans? Otto? Interested?" Silence.

"Why are you preserving him like that?" Helga says. Her eyes haven't left the image this whole time.

"I don't want the body being disturbed. I have a specialist coming in to examine it and the house. With his help I believe we'll be able to find out who the killer is and how it was done."

"What sort of specialist?" Otto says. There's my cue.

"Sorry, I'm late," I say, stepping into the room. "Did I miss anything? Oh, Otto. Looking good. Dig the cravat."

"What is he doing here?" Otto is glaring at Amanda and pointing at me.

"Now don't lose your head," I say. "I'm the specialist."

Everyone is looking at me but Helga, who's still examining the image. When she turns and sees me, her eyes go wide in shock and her wineglass slips from suddenly nerveless fingers to shatter on the floor.

"Ex-excuse me," she says and rushes from the room. Liam looks at me more intensely, and when he sees whatever he's looking for, he gets the same shocked look, but instead of running from the room, he starts laughing.

"Oh, this is just too good," he says. "How did I not see it before? I'll go get Helga. I'm sure she's had a hell of a fright. Is there anything else to discuss, Amanda?"

"Not for me, Uncle," Amanda says. "Anyone?"

Before Otto and Hans can start yelling again Liam says, "Then we will meet you all at dinner tonight. Otto, Hans, go make yourselves useful, or something."

"I demand—" Otto starts, but Liam is on him in a flash, slamming him against the wall with his hand around his throat.

"You won't demand a goddamn thing, you little cumstain," Liam says. "You had your chance and you pissed it away. Now my brother is dead, and given your particular ambitions, you're rather suspect. If it were up to me, I'd simply assume you did it and have you skinned, but it isn't, so I strongly suggest you stay out of your cousin's way. She won't be as forgiving as I."

He drops Otto, who scrambles away, clutching at his throat. I can see a thin line of fresh blood seeping into his cravat.

"Hans," Otto says with a voice like a cheese grater, "we're leaving."

"But—"

"I said, we're leaving." Otto glares at me then marches through the French doors leading outside with Hans and Tobias in tow. Tobias looks back at me, eyes filled with terror. Shit. Hans and Otto are going to take their frustrations out on him, I can tell.

"Can I kill them?" I say once they've finally left the room.

"I call dibs on Otto," Gabriela says. "You killed him once. Now it's my turn. And I want Helga. Bitch thought I was a servant when she got here. Handed me her bags and told me she didn't believe in tipping."

"Yeah, about that," I say. "Why didn't you just kill her right there and then? Where did this newfound restraint come from?"

"I asked her not to," Amanda says. Her energy is spent. She sags and falls into a chair. Jesus, just being in this room with those people must be draining.

"Speaking of Helga," I say. "The fuck was that all about?"

"I have no idea," Amanda says.

"Oh, I do." Siobhan goes to the bar. Does every room in this house have a bar?

"Do I have to guess?" I say.

"No, but you have to wait until I'm done making a cocktail." She pours ice and three or four types of liquor into a shaker and then the whole mess goes into a highball glass. "There. She lived here after World War II, then not long after, Attila kicked her out. Until then the two of them were tight. Everyone her brother knew, she knew. Got close to a couple of them. Very close."

I do a little math. "Shit."

"Oh, no," Gabriela says. "Seriously?"

"What is it?" Amanda says. "What am I missing?"

"My grandfather and Helga were an item," I say. "And since I look exactly like him, she's probably a little surprised."

"Was she any good in the sack?" Siobhan says, sipping her drink.

"You know, I'm starting to like you less and less. Okay, so Gramps was banging Helga. That's one mystery solved. My view of the room wasn't as good as yours. How did everyone react?"

"Liam didn't react much to the news that Attila's dead. But he looked a touch worried when you walked in," Gabriela says. "Maybe he's got something in the works that a necromancer might throw a wrench into."

"Helga seemed genuinely upset," Amanda says.

"I wouldn't go that far," Siobhan says. "Helga manipulates. She's very good at showing feelings that don't exist."

"What's your deal with her, anyway?" I say.

"Besides the fact that she's a lying, manipulative, bigoted, cruel, narcissistic sociopath?"

"Yeah."

"She borrowed a dress one time and never returned it."

"Siobhan," Gabriela says. I know that tone. She's had enough bull-shit for today.

"There's a particular pattern in our family," Siobhan says. "We can't kill each other, so we hurt each other instead. The people we love are always in the crosshairs. Eventually, one of us pulls the trigger."

"Who did you lose?" Amanda says.

"My mother for starters. Helga was right. My mother was a whore. Something our father couldn't abide. Oh, fucking her wasn't the problem, I was the problem. I was raised by her for the first ten years of my life, before my magic manifested. When it did, Dad found out and came to collect me. Said he was going to teach me how to use my magic, how to be strong. Then he slit my mother's throat in front of me. Said it was to show me that you never let anyone know you have a weakness. But he was just a psychopath."

"Jesus," Gabriela says. "Your own father?"

"Well, he couldn't kill me without triggering the curse, could he? One of our ancestors discovered that that includes killing through neglect. But he could hurt me. And so could the rest of them."

"Helga?" Siobhan's eyes go distant as her body tenses.

"Murdered my husband in 1919," she says. "We never had children and she couldn't bear the thought that we might. Can't dirty up the gene pool, you know. He survived the entire war only to be shot in the face by my sister as he stepped off the train." She finishes her drink.

"Be careful, Amanda," she says. "These people are not your friends. I am not your friend. We all use each other one way or another. Even if we don't mean to."

"Bringing us," Gabriela says, "to why you're here."

"You haven't figured it out yet?" Siobhan says. "I thought it was obvious."

And once she says that, it is. "You came to kill Helga," I say.

"The reins holding us back are loosened a bit during a conclave. Normally, we can't even be involved in the planning of a plot or the curse would kill us as soon as our target died."

"And you haven't tried because you can't be the one who actually does the deed," Gabriela says.

"Traps are really popular during a conclave. You just set it, and if it goes off you technically haven't broken the law. Except—" The energy in the room cranks up a few notches. Amanda stands and walks to the bar to face Siobhan. To her credit Siobhan doesn't even blink.

"Lots of things can go wrong with a trap," Amanda says. "If you want to be certain, you need to make sure someone actually sets it off. I think you were trying to find someone else to kill her for you. Is that what you were going to do? Trick one of us into killing her for you? Trick *me* into killing her for you?"

"Yes," Siobhan says. "I don't know who it was I'd work on. Maybe Mister Carter here, who wouldn't need much more than a nudge to kill any of us."

"But I'd be really pissed off at you," I say. "I mean, I would totally do it, but I'd still be pissed off."

"Yes, you don't seem very receptive to being used."

"None of us are," Gabriela says. "You're going to want to watch your step."

"I could tell that the second I walked into the room," Siobhan says. "Admit it or not, but our goals are, if not aligned, at least pointing in the same direction."

"For now," Amanda says. "Whatever you see, whatever you hear, any plans, anything that might tell us what happened to my father, you'll bring to me. Like you said, we're not friends. We can be allies for the moment. But once we're done here, you're never coming back."

"Understood," Siobhan says. "Does anyone fancy a drink?"

The mood pretty much sours at that point, and since none of us want Siobhan around, she takes the hint and leaves. I suggest locking her in a box, but Amanda says she might be useful in an "enemy of my enemy" sort of way. I can't say she's wrong.

"That was fun," I say. I'm slouched in an easy chair, still exhausted. Dream-talking to your other self who tells you you're destroying what used to be your home doesn't really make for restful sleep. "What have you two been up to?"

"Burying bodies, mostly," Gabriela says.

"They're not buried," Amanda says. "They're in stasis. Everyone came with a larger entourage. Hans's staff were killed when they went into his suite and triggered a massive fireball. The only people not hurt were Hans himself and his son."

"How many?"

"Five," Gabriela says. "That time."

"Poison gas in Helga's car. She sent her staff on ahead to the house and by the time they arrived they were all dead. Only she and her secretary were left. Her secretary set off a trap the moment she stepped into Helga's suite."

"We don't know what kind," Gabriela says. "It turned her into some sort of goo. I'm not sure but she might still technically be alive."

"When did anyone have time to lay traps?" I say.

"Who the fuck knows?" Amanda says. "A charm in somebody's pocket, usually. This shit happens every time. Someone tried to take out Otto and that sleazy lawyer of his with a, what was it?"

"Claymore mine," Gabriela says. "Right inside the gates. Not sure if whoever did it was going after Otto specifically, or just whoever walked in."

"Otto came over from Germany with more people," Amanda says. "His son, Reinhold, a couple of valets and bodyguards. You know what happened with Reinhold, and like Helga, Otto sent everyone else in first. Seems to be a habit. Like having their own food-tasters."

"What about Liam? I thought he was bringing over a mistress or a wife or both."

"He didn't. He only came with a bodyguard, who got gassed when he stepped foot in the car to take him to the house."

"Actually, I did bring my wife," Liam says, stepping into the room. "But then I came to my senses and sent her home."

It takes an effort of will to keep the razor from manifesting in my hand, and I can see Gabriela begin to reach over her shoulder to where she would normally carry her machete.

"Uncle Liam," Amanda says. She is sitting ramrod straight, with a smile that looks genuine but which we all know is anything but. She is the consummate hostess. "Is there something I can do for you?"

"I was wondering if I might have a few minutes of your time." He's wearing a different suit than before. I wonder why he changed clothes. If we're lucky, it means he killed one of his siblings and they got too blood-stained. Unlikely, but a guy can hope.

"Of course, Uncle. Bigsby." The butler appears by Amanda's side. "Please show Uncle Liam to the sitting room next door. I'll be along in just a moment."

"Yes, ma'am. If you please, sir." The butler walks out the door, not bothering to see if Liam is following.

"Thank you," Liam says. He looks anything but thankful, his smile strained, the muscles in his neck going taut. He's been dismissed by a woman who's probably a couple hundred years younger than he is. A woman whose mother he murdered. He turns and follows Bigsby out the door. As soon as he's through, the door disappears along with Amanda's smile. That's a pretty clear message.

"You want Eric to kill him?" Gabriela says. Smart way to say it. This way Amanda can tell Gabriela and then Gabriela tells me.

"No," she says.

"Okay, what's the play, then?" I say.

"I go see what fuckstain Liam wants," Amanda says. "I can take Gabriela, but not you. I'll have individual bullshit meetings with these people until after dinner tonight, then we get to have one big bullshit meeting that'll take a few hours."

"Lunch wasn't exactly a food-filled extravaganza," I say. "Maybe grab something to eat before going across the hall to tell Liam to go fuck himself?"

"I would love to," Amanda says. "But I figured this was going to happen once I announced Dad's death. I ate beforehand." She stands up. "Much as I'd like to let him stew for the next few hours, it'll just make the rest of the weekend a bigger pain in the ass."

"How about you?" Gabriela says.

"Well, I can't get out of here, so my plan for tracking your dad's soul outside the estate's a non-starter—"

"Wait," Amanda says. "You need to be outside? I can make that happen. Gimme a second."

Gabriela puts her hand on her shoulder. "You know that's not an option." They share a look.

Amanda gives a terse nod. "The estate can't be unlocked until the conclave is over. Anyone inside is staying inside."

I could have gone out last night, but instead I listened to Gabriela. Probably best not to mention that. "I'm going to take another look at the thread. See if I can find anything else about it." I don't know what the hell else I'd be looking for, but I've got no other ideas.

"If the shit hits the fan," Gabriela says, "let us know."

"If the shit hits the fan, I don't think I'll be in a position to do that."

"Still," Amanda says. "If you need help, Bigsby will be watching. Either he'll help, or if he can't for some reason, he'll notify me. I'll bring the whole house to you."

"Noted."

The door reappears in the room. Amanda smooths out her clothes, puts on a bright smile.

"Hey," I say. "Good luck."

"You too."

Chapter 17

I follow the thread through the mansion. It hasn't moved, but the house has. Corners and hallways from the other night are gone, replaced by walls or whole rooms. The thread continues outside, crossing a paved walkway, into the arboretum and through the other side.

"Mister Carter?"

I turn to see Helga walking toward me. She's wearing a loose cream-colored top, billowy navy trousers, and blue-and-white saddle shoes. Her long blonde hair falls over her shoulders and there's something about the cold blue of her eyes that's very arresting.

I blink and the sensation's gone. I don't sense any magic, but with this crowd, who can tell.

"Miz Werther," I say.

"Helga, please." She puts her hand out and I take it and I see the casino on Catalina Island, a coliseum-like building that's been turned into a museum and exhibit hall but this isn't now it's then with a band playing and people dancing and I hear laughter and—

"Are you all right?" she says.

"Uh, yes," I say, though I'm clearly not. "Sorry. Haven't slept well recently."

"I don't think anyone really sleeps well in this place," she says. "At least I never have. I wanted to apologize for earlier. I knew Robert—it feels strange to think of him as a grandfather. You look very much like when I knew him."

"It must have been quite a surprise," I say. Pressed up against a wall of a hotel room sweating, fucking, screaming. Time doesn't exist and it goes on and on and—

"It was. We didn't communicate much after I went back to Germany. I wonder, did he ever—"

"I wouldn't know," I say. "I'm told I met him, but I don't remember it." Which you'd think I would considering he tried to murder me murdering my grandson fucking monster kill it kill them all burn them to the—

"Are you sure you're all right?" she says. "You look a little pale."

"I'm sorry, I think I must have eaten something that didn't agree with me."

"Of course," she says, something between confusion and concern on her face. "Perhaps we could talk later today."

"Absolutely," I say. I try to not look insane as I turn and head toward the arboretum. I stumble and I know she's watching me. I get inside, heart pounding. Close the door. Catch myself on the knob as my feet give out from under me.

Fucking hell. I want to deny what this is, but I can't. It's bad enough I have Mictlantecuhtli's memories in my head, now I have my grandfather's? Only it's the other way around, isn't it? My memories are in his head.

I feel fractured, unstuck. I know who I am. Then I don't. Then I do and I wonder why I'm not in Mictlast time I saw this place was when Attila built goddammit I need to make this stopwhatthefucIwillkillthatfuckingdjinnwecanbuildaatrapto hererighthereiamiamiiamiam—

Me. I am me. I shove the memories of my grandfather away, confused and afraid. Mictlantecuhtli's are harder, they've been with me longer. They're not memories I can lose, but they are ones I can set aside. But these. Feels like they're hammering on the inside of my skull. I have to focus hard to push through them, and even then I can still feel their echoes.

I gather myself, clear my head as well as I can. Not the time or place to examine this too closely. I'm trying to keep my dissociative episodes down to one per day.

I focus on the thread. I can see it leading from Attila's body straight through the trees and shrubs planted here. I follow a paved path that winds around the plants, deeper into the arboretum. Soon it's less arboretum and more forest. The paved path has turned into a dirt track. And soon I can't even see the walls of the place.

It didn't look like it was this big from the outside, which means fuck-all here. Maybe I should have gone around instead of through. I'm about to turn back when the tree line breaks and the dirt path leads to a small meadow, fairytale sunlight shining down from overhead. Green grass, a little stream cutting through one side. A small cottage right in the middle of it.

There's a scent in the air. Cinnamon? Vanilla? Ginger? I take a closer look at the cottage. It's a fucking gingerbread house.

Amanda said that when Attila remodeled, there would be pieces he'd forget about. One time I was here she warned me that Attila was feeling "whimsical." Turns out that meant turning the estate into a

Willy Wonka fairytale nightmare. Everything was made of candy, and all of it looked deadly. I don't know why he decided to do that, but the fuck do I know? He wants wicked-witch gingerbread houses, who am I to judge.

This must be a holdover from that. The thread doesn't go through the house, it's about thirty feet to the left. But to follow it there's no way to avoid going near the house. And there is no fucking way I am doing that. I don't care if it's a playhouse, a holdover from Attila's "whimsical" days, or made out of real gingerbread.

I back away, then turn around to make sure I'm not backing into anything. The whole place screams trap. I feel a sting on my neck. Great, stinging insects. I put my hand to the spot on my neck and pull out a tiny dart not even half an inch long.

"Motherfu—"

———

"Where is it?" I know that voice. I crack an eye open and though everything's blurred I can see that there are two people in a room with me, my hands are cuffed above my head, and I'm hanging from a hook in the ceiling, my feet just touching the floor.

"It's not here, brother. Maybe he didn't bring it with him."

"He had two guns on him, why wouldn't he bring it, too?" A deeper voice. Otto. That's Otto talking. And the other one is Hans. But what are they looking for?

I close my eyes again. No point in letting them know I'm awake yet. I feel oddly muted. Like I'm in a recording booth with sound-swallowing baffles. I don't have to try a spell to know what's going on. I'm blocked off from the magic. I can't cast, can't draw power. I can't even feel my own energy.

It could be the cuffs. I've run into that sort of thing before. But when it's something on me that's cutting me off, it feels different. Like something's biting into me down to the bone.

This isn't like that at all. This feels more like being smothered. I risk another look around. Otto and Hans are standing over a small table tearing up my suit jacket and shirt looking for something. Hidden pocket, maybe. The Sig, the derringer, and the ghost tracker are on the table. But I don't see the razor there. That must be what they're looking for. I don't know where it would have gone, but I'm glad they can't find it. That would suck in all sorts of new and interesting ways.

There's something else, though. Otto keeps looking around like he's nervous about something. But he's not looking at me.

The room stinks of cinnamon and vanilla, so I'm guessing we're in the wicked-witch hut. One door that looks like a graham cracker, candy glass windows, and walls covered in what I can only assume is fondant. I don't know what the floor is made of, but the floorboards are just painted on.

Furniture has been shoved to the sides of the room, a child-size bed, cast-iron stove, chairs, tables, dresser. This isn't a holdover from Attila being whimsical. I think it's Amanda's playhouse from when she was a girl.

I have to look a little more closely to see the sigils and runes that cover the walls, ceiling, and floor. That's the problem. The room itself has been blocked off. I can't cast any spells in here.

But then, neither can they. They would only have done that if they hadn't had an alternative. Had they been following me through the arboretum and it was an attack of opportunity? That might explain it. No time to do anything but create a makeshift mage prison. Ah, that's why Otto's looking so nervous.

"Hey, guys," I say. My voice is a little slurred from whatever they hit me with and all my muscles feel like lead weights. I've got feeling returning to my legs, but slowly. "Whatcha lookin' for?"

"You're awake," Otto says. No, he sneers. He actually sneers.

"And you're taking a hell of a chance being in a room with no magic," I say. "How long can you hang out here before your head falls off? I can't imagine it feels great without those healing spells working overtime."

For that I get a punch in the gut. I don't throw up, though not for lack of wanting. I haven't actually eaten anything today. So sadly, I've got nothing to puke onto Otto.

"That was a hell of a hit," I say once I get my breath back. "If you'd used that in the pit I might not have cut your head off." Two more punches this time. A second later he adds another for good measure.

"Where is it?" Hans says. "You brought it. I know you did. You'd have been stupid not to. Where did you hide it?"

"The fuck are you even going on about?" Punches five and six.

"The razor," Otto says. "The fucking razor you used on me. I'm going to slice your head off and place it on the front porch of the house for everyone to see."

"Huh. That is weird. Should be in my jacket."

"It's not," Otto says, punctuating his sentence with punch number seven.

"Look, the thing's got a mind of its own. It was in my jacket. Maybe

I dropped it outside. Maybe it decided I wasn't worth hanging around for. I don't know."

"I am going to fucking kill you," Otto says.

"I assumed. But you might want to table that for a few. Speaking of razors, I think you nicked yourself shaving." Confusion in his eyes turns to terror as he realizes what I'm saying. His cravat, a yellow and blue striped number is rapidly turning red. He unties it quickly, giving me a good look at the thick black stitches around his neck. Blood is slowly seeping out between them.

I've seen this sort of work done with hands, but a head's a whole new thing. The stitches aren't holding his head on, not exactly. They're keeping the skin together so that everything underneath can heal. He's got other hardware in there, pins, plates, the usual, but when the magic runs its course all that should be absorbed by the body. Provided there's magic to make that happen.

"Otto, you have to leave," Hans says.

"No," he says. "I'm going to finish this."

"Suit yourself," I say. "I bet your head falls off before mine does."

"Mister Carter," Hans says. "Please. Where is the razor?"

"No idea." Another punch.

"I think he's telling the truth," Hans says.

"No. He has it."

"Brother," Hans says, voice low, "Much as I want to see him die, there are more pressing questions and not a lot of time. I would like to get through this before you suffer any permanent damage."

Otto doesn't like that, but he backs away, making room for Hans to stand in front of me. Though he punches me one more time, because why not? That's nine. I wonder if I can get him up to an even ten. He ties the bloody cravat back around his neck.

"Mister Carter," Hans says. "May I call you Eric?"

"Sure. May I call you Fucknut McGee?"

Hans smiles. It doesn't reach his eyes. "Eric. I think maybe we got off on the wrong foot."

"Which foot would that be?" I say. "The one where you took a swing at me, the one where you sent an assassin after me, or the one where I'm currently hanging from a meat hook?"

"The first two. I'm sorry for that. I was distraught. You had killed my brother, after all. I acted rashly. I'm sure you can understand."

"Kind of surprised you didn't send me a fruit basket, actually." He's trying to be Good Cop. That's a strategy that really only works when you don't know you're already fucked. Points for trying.

"We have a couple of questions," Hans says. "First—"

"Where is our uncle?" Otto blurts out. Hans rolls his eyes, clearly trying to look exasperated for my benefit.

"The dead one or the live one?" I say.

"We know Attila isn't dead," Hans says. "He can't be. We haven't seen a body, and none of us could have killed him before the conclave. You certainly couldn't have done it. That means he's still somewhere here on the estate."

"He is still on the estate," I say. Hans starts to smile. Aha! We're getting somewhere. "Stuck in a time-frozen room dead as a doornail. Sorry to burst your bubble." Otto starts to come at me, but Hans stops him with an upraised hand.

"That's all right. I'll get the truth eventually. Let's move onto the next question. What's the plan?"

"Whose plan?"

"Yours. Attila, Amanda, that Mexican street meat she claims to be betrothed to."

"Oooh. She is not gonna like being called that," I say. "Don't worry. I won't tell her you said that until after I kill you."

"I admire the bravado," Hans says, "misplaced as it is. You know, we've looked into you. Impressive resume if any of it's true. A god? Returning from the dead? Killing a djinn?"

"Don't forget cutting your brother's head off. Not much of a feat, I admit, but I think it bears repeating."

"I'm going to ask again," Hans says. "What's the plan? Is this some elaborate ruse to make us think Amanda's the heir?"

"How about I ask you a question," I say. "Why would she pretend to be the heir? What would that possibly do for Attila or her?"

"She's trying to trick us into murdering her," Otto says.

"Can't say that one was on my bingo card."

"During a conclave many of the restrictions on us are lifted," Hans says. "Particularly when it comes to the head of the family. If Attila is in hiding and Amanda is not really the heir, if someone were to kill her thinking she was, there's a good chance they would also die."

"Amanda is trying to trick one of you into triggering the curse and killing you? By you killing her first? That makes no sense."

"No, it doesn't," he says. "None of this makes sense. But you know the truth. You weren't brought in as some sort of death consultant to get to the bottom of this. You're a part of it. You're a deterrent, a message to the rest of us that Amanda has a deadly enforcer at her back. You aren't good for anything else."

"Oh, I dunno," I say. "I'm pretty good at the Electric Slide. Macrame. Did you know I knit?" Otto pushes Hans out of the way and gives me punch number ten. I win.

"Fuck this," Otto says. He picks something up just out of my vision and then holds it in front of me.

"Is that a vibrator?"

"It's a picana," Hans says. "An electrical prod designed specifically as a torture device. Very popular with the Venezuelans. High voltage, low amperage. It hurts, but usually won't kill and leaves few marks on the body. I've had a lot of success with it."

I've heard of these. It looks like a short stun baton on steroids. Thick handle, couple feet long, a button to deliver the shock and a rheostat to control the voltage. Nasty piece of work.

"Nice. I like the electric blue color. Do they make them in anything else? It'd look pretty cool in red."

Otto answers me by giving me a demonstration. Electricity rips through me, my muscles locking up, threatening to tear themselves apart. It goes on forever like it's never going to stop. And then it does. I can't catch my breath, every muscle screaming in agony.

"Unlike a conventional cattle prod, which can cause a lot of damage in a short amount of time," Hans says, "a picana doesn't usually burn. Unless you apply it long enough. The trick is to keep it in one spot until the room begins to smell like barbecued pork."

"That's a nice bit of trivia," I manage to croak out. "It'll come in handy watching Jeopardy."

"I don't think that's something you'll be doing," Hans says.

"Yeah, probably not. I can't see it going on without Trebek." The next shock feels like it goes on even longer, but what do I know? It's all just one big blur of agony.

"Let's get back to the question," Hans says.

"Were we doing questions? I thought you were just going to fry me until I started to smoke."

"If I didn't still need answers from you," he says. "Tell you what, if you give me what I want, I'll make sure you die quickly."

"You really need to work on your sales technique." My voice is a harsh croak that I can barely hear over the hammering of my own heart.

"Where's Attila?"

"Attila's dead. Amanda's the heir. She's engaged to Gabriela. And no, she's not trying to trick you into killing her." Otto zaps me again and I black out for a second.

"Every time you lie to me, Otto is going to hit you."

"Otto? He hits like a baby." He punches me a few times, like Rocky with a side of beef. "You caught me. I lied. All the babies I've met hit harder than he does." Another punch.

"Otto, please," Hans says. He pinches the bridge of his nose like he's warding off a headache. "Mister Carter, I'm not going to lie to you and say I don't enjoy this. It's rather a hobby of mine, actually. But we are somewhat pressed for time. So, I would appreciate it if you would give us the truth."

"Hans, buddy," I say. My eyes go in and out of focus, stinging from the sweat dripping into them. "You don't know what you're looking for. You want something to make yourselves feel like you have an advantage over everyone else. I get it. This is a power play to bump a piece off the board and put yourselves in position to take out the queen."

"Otto?" Three punches and an extended date with the picana.

"This is getting us nowhere," Otto says. "He doesn't know a thing. Let's just cut his head off and call it a day."

"Speaking of cutting off heads," I say. My voice sounds like grinding gears. There's no saliva left in my mouth.

"Otto, you need to leave," Hans says. "Now. Go fix yourself and meet Mother," Hans says. "I'll join you at dinner. I can break him."

"Are you sure?" Otto looks dubious.

"He's not a threat," Hans says. "And your head's about to fall off. I've got this. Go. I want to try another technique."

"All right." Otto looks at me with an expression almost like pity. "We have another five hours until dinner. He'll drag this out as long as he can. Goodbye, Mister Carter. I can't say I'll miss you."

"Same to you, honeybun. Smooches!" He slams the door on his way out. It sounds like a casket lid closing.

Chapter 18

"Now we can actually get some productive work done," Hans says.

"Somehow I don't think you're talking about interrogation anymore."

"You would be right. All that noise about a plan was for the benefit of my idiot brother, as I'm sure you've already figured out. No, this is just a happy convergence of revenge and a hobby."

"You like frying people with cattle prods?"

He pulls out a leather chef's knife bag from behind me and places it on a table pressed against the far wall. It's held together with straps and buckles, HW embossed in large letters.

"That's some quality workmanship," I say. "You even got it initialed so you know which one is yours at the psycho party."

"You're sounding a bit tired, Mister Carter," Hans says, unrolling the bag and pulling out a short-bladed knife. "I could barely understand you. Maybe this will wake you up a bit."

Every muscle is screaming, my legs are damn near lifeless. Electrocution will do that to you. I try to move my legs, but all I can do is rotate my ankle a bit. Not much I can do but wait and hope he doesn't slice off too much before I can do something about this.

"Feeling awake now?" he says. "I'd hate for you to be unconscious for the rest of this. I don't think I've ever seen so many tattoos on anyone." He runs the blade gently along the borders of my tattoos. "This is going to make skinning you a challenge."

"I always like a good challenge."

"I don't think you'll like this one." He punches the knife into my left pec just below the collar bone and leaves it there. It hurts. A lot. Everything goes black and then snaps back into focus.

"Sorry about that. Didn't mean to knock you out. You had an open patch of skin, you see, and I needed somewhere to put the knife."

"So glad I can be of help."

"At this stage most people would be screaming," he says. "Not cracking jokes. I'm a little disappointed." He turns back to his collection of knives and hovers his hand over each in turn. "Let's see. What to use. Cleaver, Kukri, I do love this Bowie knife."

"Hans," I say, my voice barely a whisper. I've got some feeling returning to my legs and I experiment lifting my knee. Still weak, but it's getting easier. The more I flex the easier it gets.

"Maybe something with more of a serrated edge? A Henckels utility knife, perhaps? An excellent blade for a very reasonable price. No kitchen should be without one."

"Hans," I say again, a little louder. I'm only going to get one shot at this. And if I fuck it up, well, I've died before.

"But I'm not sure that's really—Oh. Oh, yes. I think this one will do." The knife he picks up looks like it's out of a science-fiction movie. Black handle, shaped grip, and a wide serrated blade that curves up to a single point.

"Hans." Louder, but still quiet. But this time it breaks his monologuing.

"You had something to say, Mister Carter? A blade preference, perhaps?" I mumble something, the only clear word being "Attila." "Oh, you want to talk? Of course. We can talk."

He takes a step closer, but it's not close enough. I mumble some more, add "Amanda" to the mix. He gets in close. He's tall, taller than I am, so with me hanging suspended like this we're at eye level.

He grabs my hair and lifts my head. "Did we hurt you so bad that you can't speak? I hardly think so. Go on. Say something."

"I fucked your mom," I say, wrapping my legs tight around him, pulling him closer.

Close enough to bite his nose off.

Hans screams and drops the knife to grab at his nose with both hands. Blood pours between his fingers. He tries to pull away, but my legs are clamped tight. I spit his nose out, swing forward enough to take another bite. This time I get something that gives way a lot more easily than cartilage and flesh and pops like a zit.

His screams are louder, more high pitched. I squeeze more with my legs, getting leverage to lift from my hips. It's agonizing, but it's worth it. A second later I have the cuffs over the hook and I take Hans down to the floor. My chest screams where the knife is stuck, but I don't have time to pay attention to it. I've only got so much energy and it's not going to last much longer.

He finds the skinning knife and takes a swipe. I roll off him before he can stab me with it. He pulls himself up by the bed against the wall as I roll to my feet. I stagger but I don't fall. If Hans were thinking straight, he'd end this by opening the front door that's just a few feet to his right. Just because magic doesn't work in here doesn't mean he couldn't conjure a fireball from outside and roast me while I can't defend myself.

But he's not thinking straight. Hans is scared. Scared people make mistakes. Like leaving themselves wide open. I hit him like a bull, knocking the skinning knife out of his hand and slamming him into the wall hard enough for it to crack. That's not saying much—it is gingerbread, after all.

He kicks, knocking my foot out from under me. I go down to my knee while he runs to his knife bag. He pulls the biggest goddamn Bowie knife I've ever seen out of it, turns to attack me. Instead he gets a face full of the short-bladed paring knife he conveniently left inside my chest. The blade slices across his face and through his popped eyeball, across where his nose used to be and below his lips, splitting them in two.

I knock the Bowie knife out of his hand, punch him a couple times until he goes down.

"Don't," he says, his voice slurred from the split lips, thick with blood from his ruined nose. "I can give you what you want. Anything. I have money. I have power." I pick up the picana. He sees it and starts to whine like a kicked dog.

"Hans, you don't have anything I want," I say. "I'm really sorry about your eyeball. That wasn't on purpose. Your nose was, though."

"Please don't kill me. Please don't kill me. Please don't—" I jam the picana into his remaining eye hard enough to crack bone and sink it deep into his skull. I turn it on. I leave it on. I don't stop until smoke drifts from his eye socket.

"You're right, Hans," I say. "It totally smells like barbeque pork."

———

My shirt and coat are a mess, so I take Hans's. I find the keys to the handcuffs in a pocket and take them off. I'm tempted to leave Hans on the floor where he's still smoking, but it seems a pity to waste that meat hook.

It's fucking agony, but I get my hands under his armpits, haul him up, and slam him down onto the meat hook, which catches him just inside the right shoulder blade. He's lopsided. I decide to let my sense of aesthetics and symmetry suffer and leave him there.

Hans is a bigger guy than I am, so his shirt hangs off my frame like a tent. That's fine. I just need to get back to my room without anyone noticing me. I don't have a Sharpie or my stickers, but they're more affectation than anything else. I use Hans's blood to write I'M HANS DON'T BUG ME on the shirt. When I get outside I'll magic it up. With all the spells these people are throwing around it should disappear in the background noise.

I stagger out of the house and the magic hits me immediately. The power in my tattoos flares to life and I already feel better. Some of them speed up healing, some of them dull pain, some of them help me dodge bullets. None of them are good enough to fix everything.

Blood is seeping from the wound in my chest. Mictlantecuhtli knows spells to heal flesh, muscle, bone, but I'm still working on blood. It takes a few tries, but I'm able to coagulate the blood inside the wound and at the surface, turning it into a thick scab. The burns from the picana hurt more than the stab, but they're hard to see. More like very targeted sunburns. I magic the words on the shirt and, sure enough, even I can barely register it with all the magic in this place.

Getting through the arboretum and into the house is easy enough. Finding my room takes a little longer. The house is a maze of shifting hallways and staircases I almost get lost in and I don't entirely trust my landmarks. I could call Bigsby, but there's something just on the edge of my mind that I haven't quite pieced together yet that stops me.

A little searching and I find my room. It's one of two doors next to each other that don't look like any of the others. Where the rest are all deep oak-paneled doors, these are round-topped monastery doors. The other night there were three, but now the third room's gone.

My door has a traditional Día De Los Muertos calavera carved into it, which is a bit on the nose. Gabriela had the third room, but once the conclave started she must have moved in with Amanda to avoid someone in the family happening upon it. Their door has two crossed brooms over a heart. Really trying to sell that whole lesbian witch motif.

I close the door behind me and grab a field surgery kit from my messenger bag. I wish I'd known this whole blood trick a long time ago. Would have saved me a lot on QuikClot over the years. There's no point in fucking with it, but I tape a 4x4 over the stab wound in case it starts bleeding again. Other than that there's not much I can do. I have some burn cream and that salve I used with my shoulder the other night for the bruising. I keep finding new spots to put it on. A couple I bandage over.

I find the spot in my neck where the dart hit me. It's closed up for the most part, and I don't think I need to bandage it. There's something else, though. Something about the dart and how it got me. Then it hits me. The thought's not fully formed, but I don't think I have to time to pick it apart. I grab my phone and text Amanda.

Turn off Bigsby

A moment later she answers with, *Done. Why?*

Before I can respond there's a knock at my door. I pick up the Sig from the dresser and stand a couple of feet to the side of the door. I aim a little lower than head height. If somebody comes in low, I should still be able to put a round into them.

"Yes?"

"It's Gabriela. Can I come in?" I reach over to the latch and unlock the door.

"Sure. Door's open."

"Or you could open it for me," she says. "Like somebody who isn't expecting this to be a trap, because now I'm wondering if it's a trap for me."

"Wouldn't it be funny if we both shot each other and it turned out we were wrong the whole time?"

"Yeah," she says. "A real knee slapper. So are you going to open the door?"

"Nope."

"For fuck sake," she says and throws the door open. I step back and toward the doorway with the Sig aimed at her head as she steps inside. "Really? Do I need to prove I'm me? Fine. I kicked your ass the first time we met in my hotel."

"I remember doing the ass-kicking," I say. I decock the gun and toss it onto the bed. "Sorry. It's been a day. What are you doing here?" She's wearing blue shorts, a cream-colored top, and tennis shoes. Her hair's pushed up under a hair band. She looks like she's about to go play badminton in the 1930s.

"Jesus, what happened to you?" she says, closing the door behind her.

"Hans and Otto happened." I pick up my phone and respond to Amanda. *Bigsby compromised. Talking to Gabriela*

"And I didn't get an invite to the party?" she says. "Who are you texting?"

"Amanda. There's something fucked up with Bigsby, or the estate, and I'm not sure what it is yet. Otto and Hans caught me in the arboretum outside of, and I shit you not, an actual gingerbread cottage. I think it was a playhouse for Amanda when she was a kid. I mean, the house is full-sized but the furniture's about right for a ten-year-old." I give her the short version. Ambushed, handcuffed, hung from a meat hook. Then fried, stabbed, bit Hans's nose off, torched his brain with his own cattle prod.

"And here I am," I say.

"I don't like this," Gabriela says.

"Not nearly as much as I don't." I look into the full-length mirror next to the closet to see if I missed any spots. There are a couple on my back I can't reach. When did they get to my back?

"Do you think it was planned?"

"Yes and no. I think Hans and Otto were following me looking for an opportunity. Finding the cottage gave it to them. They hit me with a drugged dart and dragged me inside. I don't know for sure, but I got the feeling they prepped the place to nullify magic after they got me in there."

"Once they did, no one would have been able to find you," she says. "Not even Bigsby. But until then—"

"Until then, it'd be like anywhere else on the property. Bigsby's part security system. Supposed to keep guests from killing each other, at least when they're being blatant about it. So, what happened?"

"It either didn't see what was happening, or it ignored what was happening," Gabriela says. "Somebody's gotten control of it."

"Or it's making its own decisions."

"Jesus, that's the last thing we need."

"Either way it's compromised," I say. "Amanda's turned him off."

"She can't keep him off for long, though," Gabriela says. "Part of what's keeping everyone in line is that they're being seen and heard wherever they go. Shut it off—"

"And it's open season. I get it," I say. "So, who's gotten control of it? Hans and Otto would be the obvious choice except for the fact that they're both fucking idiots. I don't think it even occurred to them that they were being watched." I twist, trying to reach the spots on my back with the burn cream. They're really starting to hurt.

"Gimme that," she says. She grabs the jar of cream, her hand on mine, but I don't let go. "What's wrong?" Nothing. Everything.

"You want to know why I've been avoiding you?" I say.

She hesitates. Then, "Yes."

"I hated you," I say. "I was angry, at least." I let go of the jar, turn around, and close my eyes. I don't want to see her face right now, or mine. I don't know if I can say what I need to say if I do.

"I know. I'm sorry. I—"

"Don't be." There's a thought that's been forming in the back of my mind, but it's not quite there yet. "I've been seeing Mictlantecuhtli in my dreams. Or not dreams. You know what I mean."

"How's he doing?"

"Peachy," I say. "I barely recognize him anymore. He's turned into what Mictlantecuhtli is supposed to be. Five years and we still looked human. But in a month's time without me, he's gone full death-god. Gray skin, knobby bones, guts pushing out of his abdomen like it's about to pop. And it's not just the look. We're not the same. I don't think either of us really understands the other. I sure as hell don't understand him."

"What does he want?" She puts some of the salve on a burn I didn't know was there until it lit up when she touched it. I tense. "Sorry."

"All good. He wants me to stop killing Mictlan," I say.

"Come again?" she says. I glance at her in the mirror and look away.

"Uncertainty and doubt," I say. "Mictlan and Mictlantecuhtli are linked. He's confident in his identity. He's very clear who he is, what he is. I'm not. Haven't been since I got here."

"But how is that—You're still linked to Mictlan, too, aren't you?"

"It can't tell us apart. And because the cosmos lacks any subtlety, my doubt has taken the form of a great big sinkhole sucking the whole place down."

"What do you need to do?" She's attended to three burns on my back so far. I am so going to kill Otto for this. Again.

"Figure out who the fuck I am. What I am. Choose it. Be it."

"Kind of a tall order," she says.

"I think it might be easier than I thought," I say. "I've been child-ish. Like the kid who doesn't want to come home from summer camp. There's no way Mictlantecuhtli could be himself with me in him. I'm sorry."

"For what?"

"For acting like a twelve year old," I say. "Bigger picture. If you hadn't pulled me out of there, sure, I wouldn't have this problem right now, but somewhere down the line, a month, a year, an eon, who knows? At some point I wouldn't be a part of Mictlantecuhtli. I'd be a cancer. So, thank you."

She puts her fingers on a spot near my neck, traces along the edge of one of my tattoos. I can feel the magic in it flare as she does.

"Do you still hate me?"

"I never did," I say. "All this time I've been angry and confused. Coming back. The whole shit with Darius. Everything."

"You know that's not why I brought you back, right?" she says. Her finger going down my back is very distracting.

"Yeah."

"And?"

"I don't know. I feel like I'm on fire and numb at the same time. Not myself. I don't know how, but there's something missing."

"Do you think it has to do with what's happening in Mictlan?" she says.

"I do, yeah. Mictlantecuhtli told me the important thing isn't what I choose but that I choose." Talking it out is making things clearer.

"Sounds like one of those things that sounds simple but really isn't," she says. "Like the best way to stay alive is to not die."

"At first it did feel like that. But I think I know what needs to happen. I don't know that it's a choice so much as an acknowledgement. I'm going to have uncertainty and doubt, fears, desires, anger. All the rest of the bullshit. Because what it comes down to, what I've been fighting against, is the fact that I'm human. Even with all of Mictlantecuhtli's memories, whatever left-over power might be in me, I'm still human. So that's what I choose. To be human."

A sudden weight I didn't know was there lifts from my shoulders. It's not relief, or happiness. It's not any kind of emotion. It's a responsibility fulfilled. As clearly as Mictlantecuhtli knows he's the King of the Dead, I know that I'm a human being. That I *choose* to be a human being. Whatever else I am, mage, partial death god, punching bag for Nazis, it all comes down to one thing. I'm human.

And then the pain kicks in.

Chapter 19

Ever see *This Is Spinal Tap?* It's a mockumentary about a rock band, and there's this bit where one of the band members is talking about his amps and how they all go up to eleven. Other guys, see, they only play up to ten. But this band? They play up to eleven.

Everything in my body and soul goes up to eleven. My bruises are throbbing like sledgehammers in drywall, my cuts are tearing me open like I'm being run through with knives, my burns are spewing hot lava. Air is like a belt-sander against my skin.

The only sound I can hear is my own screaming. I can't seem to stop, even though it's ripping my throat inside out. I'm blind from the intensity of the light lasing through my eyes.

I don't know how long it goes on. There's no such thing as time. It just lasts and lasts and lasts. Until it doesn't.

"Breathe, goddammit." A voice I know but can't place. Pressure on my chest I can barely feel, a vain attempt to push air into my lungs.

"You do not fucking get to do this again, you stupid motherfucker," the voice yells. "I pulled your ass out of a fucking god and if you die on me now—Fuck."

Sorry to disappoint, anonymous voice, but I think you're not going to have much of a say in this. Valiant effort. You can probably stop now. Or not. Up to you.

The anonymous voice is closer. It whispers in my ear with a volume that might as well be a scream. "Please don't die. I'm not going to lose you again. I can't lose you again. Please."

A new voice. Higher, sharper. It sounds angrier than the other one, if that's possible. "Oh, you have got to be fucking kidding me. What the hell did you do now, you stupid sonofabitch?"

A brand-new pain lances through me. I feel my lungs twist, shift, creating their own air. Nerves fire, heart beats. My brain is catching up like an old engine that won't turn over. But then something in it changes, too, and it's a fire of electricity. Commands that won't be denied flare through it.

My eyes snap open and I'm alive. "Holy fuck, that hurt." Gabriela

and Amanda are looking down at me. They look more vivid, somehow, more there. I can hear the creak of shifting rooms, people walking around through the house. Slowly, my senses ratchet down to
something almost normal.

"Don't ever fucking do that again," Gabriela says. She thumps my
chest with her fist, again and again. "Do you fucking hear me?"

Amanda grabs her hands. "Keep doing that and he will," she says.
"What the hell happened?"

"I turned into a real boy," I say. I roll over and slowly push myself
up. "Fucking hell that hurt."

"Somebody please tell me what the hell is going on," Amanda says.

"I still had ties to Mictlan that I needed to sever, and I did. How do
my eyes look?"

"Pitch black," Amanda says.

That confirms one thing. Human as I am, I still have bits of Mictlantecuhtli stuck in me, like spinach in teeth. Something tells me I'm
never getting rid of them. I have no idea if that's good or bad. What's
important is that Mictlan is no longer in danger. Not from me, at least.

"How do you feel?" Gabriela says.

"Okay," I say. "I'm okay."

I am. In fact, I feel better than okay. Now that everything is calm-
ing down, I feel more myself than I have since I woke up in that bunker in San Pedro a month ago. Which makes sense. I literally haven't
been myself. Everything was slightly numbed and I didn't even know
it. Now it's all been turned up a couple notches. There is, of course, a
downside.

A whirlwind of emotions comes tearing through me. MacFee's death
a month ago is a punch in the gut all over again. The men and women
whose souls were crushed when I destroyed Darius are screaming
inside my head. The fight with the Baba Yaga, the knowledge that in
that moment I lost a group of people I thought I could help. Who I
thought could help me.

Not to mention what I just heard. Was it real? Did Gabriela say
what I think she said? Real or not, it's hitting some raw spaces in me
that I really don't want to look at right now.

"You don't look okay," she says. "Do you remember anything?"

Plenty. Lots. "Nothing," I say. "Not until I woke up. I was standing
here and then I was on the floor. Thank you, by the way." Gabriela and
Amanda look like they expect me to keel over any second. Fair
enough. I'm not sure I won't.

"Seriously, I'm okay," I say. I hobble over to the closet. I see suits, ties, dress shirts, pants, boxers, a tuxedo, socks, cufflinks all laid out like a department-store display.

"You got any t-shirts in my size?" I say. "I don't want to bleed all over anything fancy."

"Hang on. Yes. Look to your left," Amanda says.

"That's a neat trick," I say, pulling on a black t-shirt and wincing at the effort. No matter how I move, the fabric rubs against the burns like sandpaper. "Part of running the estate?"

"Something like that," she says. "Okay, Mictlan. I have no idea what the hell that's about, but why are you covered in burns?"

"Otto and Hans," Gabriela says. There's not much to tell and she gets Amanda up to speed, with me answering a question or two about the details.

"God fucking dammit," Amanda says. "This is making more sense now. I've told everyone that Bigsby's undergoing some routine maintenance. Not everyone buys it, of course, but nobody's saying anything. I've gone over him as thoroughly as I know how. He's a lot like a computer program, built with magic rather than code."

"Did you find anything?" Gabriela says.

"Yeah," Amanda says. "Somebody changed the spells around his awareness and motivation. They're subtle, but I've been tinkering with Bigsby since I was a kid."

"Awareness and motivation?" I say.

"He couldn't perceive some people. And if he did, he wouldn't help if they were in trouble."

"Can he perceive the absence of people?" I say.

"What do you mean?"

"Does it know Hans is dead?"

Amanda frowns, cocks her head to the side, and closes her eyes. A moment later she opens them and says, "Shit. He wasn't taking into account anyone missing, or anyone new."

"New?" Gabriela says. "Did someone get onto the property?"

"If they did, they're not here, anymore," Amanda says. "I don't know how they would have, but it might explain how somebody got to my dad. Goddammit."

I can see this starting to nosedive into a pity party and we don't have time for one. I change the subject.

"Who couldn't he see?" I say.

"You, Liam, and Helga," she says. "Why, I don't know. You make sense. You're an obstacle and you can be killed without triggering the curse. But I don't understand Liam or Helga."

"Siobhan has an axe to grind with Helga," I say. "I can see her doing that. And she knows Helga and I—Helga and my *grandfather* had a history, so she might think I'd get in her way. But that doesn't explain Liam."

"Or how she was planning on doing it," Amanda says. "She needs someone else to pull the trigger or the curse comes down on her."

"Before we veer too far off the subject, what's your plan with Bigsby?" I say.

"He's fixed. Holes, any I could find, are patched up," Amanda says. "And I've put in more safeguards. If anyone tries to touch those spells, I should know it. If, somehow, they get past that, I've got Bigsby checking himself a million times a second. If his state doesn't perfectly match the previous ten thousand checks he shuts down. But that's not my biggest worry. I don't know how anyone got to him in the first place. The only people who know how he works are me and my dad."

"Somebody figured it out," Gabriela says. "Could Siobhan?"

"I seriously doubt it. Her knack is in plants. I suppose she could have, but I just don't think so."

"We can cross Hans off the list," Gabriela says.

"And Tobias," Amanda says.

"Why Tobias?" I say. "I know he's got no magic, but what if he's got an artifact or a talisman or just happens to know the secret knock to get control of Bigsby?"

"Maybe," Amanda says. "But I don't think so. I've spent a little time with him and he's, I dunno, timid's not the word. Apprehensive?"

"Scared shitless," Gabriela says. "I don't know how he's going to take the news his dad is dead."

"Dance a jig on his grave?" I say.

"No," Gabriela says. "That kid's been beaten into submission. Once he finds out Hans is dead, he's going to latch onto Otto even though he terrifies him. And if Otto goes, any authority figure he can find. I can't see him doing anything like this, even if he was able to."

"That leaves Liam and Helga. No. I'm missing someone. The lawyer. The fuck is his name?"

"Jonathan," Amanda says. "He's definitely playing a game, guys like him always are, but I don't think it's this one. If it was, he wouldn't be the one doing the heavy lifting."

"Fair enough. I like Liam for it."

"I do too," Gabriela says. "But I wouldn't discount Helga or Siobhan. Helga used to live here. She might know things about the estate nobody else does. And Siobhan's still a wild card."

"She says she's here to kill Helga," I say. "But there's no way to prove that."

"We're missing something," Gabriela says. "What if it's not about the inheritance? What if it's about consolidating power? With Hans dead, control of his assets go to Otto?"

"Helga," Amanda says. "But she'll probably give them to Otto, yeah."

"What about Helga?" I say.

Amanda frowns. "I'm not sure. Either to Otto or to Liam. Probably Liam. We've got shit like this codified, so I know there's an answer, but I'd have to look it up. Everything in this family is about succession."

"If everybody here besides you dies, who gets their assets?" Gabriela says.

"I do," Amanda says. "And then we have a shitstorm on our hands. The problem with seats of power is that somebody's got to sit in them. We'd have a mage war started within a couple of days at most. Honestly, it wouldn't be a big one, the heavy hitters in the family are all here, but it'd be pretty brutal."

"This is all great, but it doesn't tell us who's doing any of this," I say. "Let's just fucking kill all of them. Do you want to kill them? I want to kill them."

"I want to kill them," Gabriela says.

"Stop it," Amanda says. "Both of you. That is not a goddamn solution and you fucking know it. This is my shit. Feel free to walk away at any time. But if you don't, then no wholesale slaughter. I'm serious." I know it's not familial attachment that's keeping her from letting Gabriela and I go whole hog on them with knives, so why—Oh.

"They're a buffer," I say.

"Yes," she says. "Those fucking people, those backstabbing mother-fuckers out there, whether they realize it or not, were protecting me and my dad. They're constantly dealing with the rest of our family trying to take them down. If anyone wants to make a run for the throne, they're going to have to go through them first."

"Because none of them would let the inheritance go to anyone else," Gabriela says. "You think of something?"

"Maybe?" I say. "I don't know, yet." Something about what Amanda just said is poking at me, but it's still too vague.

"What do you want to do now?" Gabriela says.

"Act like nothing's happened," Amanda says. "They'll figure out

Hans is dead, at least Otto will, as soon as Eric walks in the door for dinner. But whoever hit Bigsby doesn't necessarily know that they've been found out. Hopefully, they tip their hand and I can be done with this bullshit."

"When do you want me to join the festivities?" I say.

"On time. Cocktails at seven and then dinner at eight."

"I can't promise I won't kill Otto again," I say.

"Can you at least not do it until after dinner?" she says. "It's a family etiquette thing."

"I can see how killing each other over dessert could be a faux pas."

"Speaking of," Gabriela says. "We've only got a couple of hours to get ready, and that's not a lot of time."

"Hair and makeup?" I say.

"Defensive wards and traps," Amanda says. "You might want to consider coming armed."

"Always am."

They leave, but Gabriela stops at the threshold, looks back at me. "Are you sure you're okay?" she says.

"Let's call it intact," I say. "I'll be fine. Just some things I have to sort through I thought I was done with."

"Finish the conversation later?" she says.

"Absolutely." She nods and closes the door behind her. I stagger against the dresser. Everything, and I mean everything, stuck behind my not accepting I was human comes flooding in. A laundry list of regrets, pain, people I've hurt, lives I've destroyed. Deaths in my wake too high to count.

What's really fucked up? I can't think of a single goddamn good thing.

———

The last time I wore a tuxedo I got the shit kicked out of me by an earth mage who was hired muscle for a guy smuggling kids with talent out of the U.S. Human trafficking with a side of magic.

Real piece of work, this guy. He'd take orders from customers, find a kid who fit the bill and have them kidnapped and sent to his mansion in Savannah and then get them on a boat out of the port to points unknown and horrible.

The mom of one of the kidnapped kids heard I was somebody who would do jobs nobody else would touch, mostly because I was stupid, crazy, and have a soft spot for lost causes.

So, smuggler guy, he's a mage, but honestly not that powerful. Only thing he's got to show off is his money. He'd have these Jay Gatsby-level extravaganzas. I manage to score an invite. I get to the party, drink a little, mingle a little, break into his second-floor office, set off a silent alarm.

Yeah, that last bit wasn't really part of the plan. I get worked over hard. Pissed blood for a month. My face was so swollen and purple I looked like an oversized plum.

I come to with smuggler guy and earth mage standing over me. By the way, don't fuck with earth mages if you can help it. They pretty much just know one trick, but that trick is to wallop the shit out of you with half a ton of conjured granite.

They're not happy. They don't even bother asking me questions. They don't care who I am or why I was breaking into the office. It's irrelevant. I'm about to disappear.

They try to bury me in a landfill. Did you know there are a lot of dead things in landfills? Yeah. Who knew?

Anyway, I add their corpses to the already abundant collection, get the kids out, hand over records for a bunch who've already been shipped overseas to the one kid's mom. I get paid. Then I pass out for a week.

I gotta say, I look a hell of a lot better in a tux now than I did then. Because I still have my face and the last one was a rental. But mostly because I still have my face.

Tonight's festivities are drinks, dinner, and then the family, soon-to-be family, and legal representatives go off into a big fancy room and yell at each other about how the Werthers are going to conduct themselves for the next ten years.

I suspect the majority of the yelling is going to be about Attila's death and Amanda's new role as head of the family. There will be at least one attempt to marry her off to Tobias, which Gabriela's fiancée status should cut off pretty quickly.

I wouldn't put it past the lawyer, Jonathan, to pull some obscure family law out of his ass that they'll argue over for two or three hours.

If things start to go sideways, Gabriela will text me, I'll kick my way into the room, and we start killing everybody. I like the simplicity of it. As plans go, it's kind of hard to fuck up.

The trick is going to be getting through drinks and dinner.

It's a different room than the one we were in for lunch, though it seems to sit in the same spot. I take a minute before heading in to listen in to what's happening.

"I'm sure he'll be along soon, Mother," Otto says. "You know Hans. Never on time for anything."

"And that horrid man, what was his name?" Helga.

"You know very well his name. After all, you were almost his grand-mother." Siobhan.

A slap. Holy shit, an actual slap. I thought people only did that in bad eighties television shows. I'm tempted to wait and see if this is the start of something fun, but I should probably get in there.

"Sorry I'm late. Got held up. Siobhan, Helga," I say, greeting them as if I actually give a damn. "Otto, are you all right?" Otto is slack-jawed. He closes his mouth with an audible snap, which of course draws everyone's attention.

The room is large enough that people can spread out but not so large that they could get out of range of a hand grenade. The ones I expect, Liam, Siobhan, Helga, Gabriela, Amanda, a miserable look-ing Tobias, and a difficult-to-focus-on Jonathan.

"Can I get you a cocktail, sir?" Bigsby says, appearing at my elbow. No, you freaky death machine, you may not.

Instead I say, "An old-fashioned."

"Just a moment, sir," he says, and vanishes. Amanda is talking to Jonathan. No, Amanda is being talked at by Jonathan. She somehow manages to look completely engaged, bored, and murderous all at the same time. It's kind of impressive.

Everybody's got an effortless elegance that makes me feel like a clumsy waiter in the lounge car on the Orient Express. Even Otto, who is staring at me through slitted eyes, looks great. Having a head helps.

My eyes reach Gabriela and snag. She's wearing a red, floor-length, one-shoulder dress with a slit up the side and red stilettos. Her hair is gathered in a bun with two hair sticks holding it in place.

"You're gawking," Siobhan says. She's left the conversation with Helga and Otto. I don't know if she was the slapper or the slappee, but everybody's acting like nothing's happened.

"I am not gawking," I say, tearing my eyes away from Gabriela. I take my drink from Bigsby, who's come out of nowhere and then vanishes.

"Uh huh. I noticed Otto shit the proverbial brick when you walked in and Hans didn't," she says. "You like dramatic entrances, don't you?"

"Only when they're funny," I say.

"I don't think he's laughing."

"I am."

"I have come to the conclusion that you are a singularly dangerous person, Mister Carter," Siobhan says. "I just can't tell if the danger is knowing you or merely being near you."

"Could be either one," I say. "It would explain my sex life."

"A pity. Enjoy the evening. I think it's going to be very interesting. You should mingle. I'm sure Otto would love to have a chat."

"I'll get there eventually." She heads off and I start toward Amanda, making a point of keeping Otto in view the whole time. I don't think he'd try anything, but then, he is an idiot.

I don't get very far before Liam slides in front of me. It takes a lot not to whip out the razor and see how fast I can cut his head off.

"Mister Carter," he says. "I was hoping to catch you for a moment."

"You might have to try harder," I say. "I'm a slippery bastard." His laugh is about as genuine as a knockoff Rolex.

"So I'm given to understand. How have you found my family's hospitality? Enrolling you into any schemes?"

"A little attempted murder," I say. "Nothing serious. Hey, I wanted to ask you. You mentioned you'd been out in Vegas not too long ago."

"Ten years ago. After the last conclave," he says, "yes."

"I'm wondering how, when your brother kicked your ass off the continent."

"Ah. Quite simple. We were all given some time to, how did my brother put it? 'Get the fuck out.' I took the opportunity to do some sight-seeing."

"This is after you murdered Amanda's mother," I say.

"Unjustly slandered," Liam says. "I have agonized over her death for years and only wish I could have stopped whoever would do such a horrible thing."

"You don't seem all that shaken up about it now," I say.

"You might not have noticed, but this family's been rocked by tragedy over the last few days," he says. "A man can only grieve so much. I'm sure you understand."

"Your brother's death must have come as a shock." And if you believe that then I've got a bridge in New York for sale.

"It did," he says. "In fact, that's what I wanted to speak with you about. Seeing as you're the specialist, I was wondering if you had any insights into what happened to Attila."

"He's dead," I say. "Beyond that, I'm still looking into it." And I'm looking real hard at you, pal.

"I see. There's quite a bit about necromancy I don't know. I've heard you can sense death."

"When it happens, yeah." Like a twist in my guts, usually so small I don't pay much attention. Get me around enough of them, like when the fire storm turned L.A. to ash, and it's a different story. When Vernon went up the pain was so intense I passed out for about six hours.

"Fascinating. Well, please do let me know if you find anything else?"

"I'll pass that along to Amanda," I say. "Speaking of, if you'll excuse me."

"By all means," he says, stepping aside. "I hope we have an opportunity to talk again soon."

"Count on it." I step past him, every instinct screaming to not let him get behind me. I really wish Amanda would let me kill him.

I come up behind Jonathan, who's so engrossed by the sound of his own voice as he talks at Amanda that he doesn't notice me until I whisper in his ear, "Of all the people here, you're the one I can kill right here, right now, and nobody would bat an eye."

He freezes. "Excuse me," he says. "Thank you, Miz Werther. It was very nice talking to you." He slinks away, and even though there are only a handful of people in here I lose track of him immediately.

"Thank you," Amanda says. "I was almost going to kill him myself."

"I'm sure he'll give you a reason before the evening's out. How are you holding up?"

"Not nearly drunk enough for this shit," she says. "How about you?"

"Trying to shake a memory of gramps and Helga banging each other in a hotel room in San Diego. It's like a fucking earworm. Literally."

Amanda stifles a laugh, covering it by sipping her drink. "Resurrection has some unintended consequences."

"You don't know the half of it. Hey, once the conclave ends, how much time do these yokels have to get out of the country before you sic the dogs on 'em?"

"Dad would give them a week. I'll be giving them a lot less. Why?"

"Something Liam said. He was in Vegas after the last conclave for a bit. My name kept popping up."

"Something I should know?"

"Later. When we're not surrounded by sharks. I was just wondering if he could be telling the truth."

"Certainly possible. How are you doing? You were dead for almost a minute. I was afraid Gabriela was going to shatter your rib cage."

"I'm well enough. Nothing a little Adderall and Oxycontin can't fix. What exactly did you do, anyway?" It was more than shocking my heart or filling my lungs with air.

"I oxygenated your blood. Really more that I turned your blood into oxygenated blood. Slight difference. Created air in your lungs. I restarted your heart by reshaping the atria and ventricles in turn until the blood was flowing and then put it back to normal. I've done it before."

Changed my blood. Created air. Reshaped my heart. I think back to what other magic of hers I've seen. Created pills out of nothing. Or rather, I thought they were conjured. Transmogrification makes more sense. And if that's her knack then she's a hell of a lot more powerful than I realized.

It would be a faux pas to ask if I'm right. A lot of mages don't want anyone to know what theirs is. Understandable. If you know your enemy's strengths, you can figure out their weak spots. If she wants me to know, she'll tell me.

"Appreciate it," I say.

"Don't worry about it," she says.

Bigsby appears in the middle of the room and rings a little chime. "Ladies and gentlemen, dinner will now be served in the dining hall."

"Are you going to actually let it serve us food?" I say.

"I don't see any way around it," she says. "I also think it's not likely he would do anything. Bigsby will announce if there's anything hinky with the food before we eat, and nobody in there isn't going to use their own magic to see if anything's poisoned."

"Good point," I say. "And if it happens to kill any of your relatives it narrows down the field."

"That's what I like about you, Eric. You're such an optimist."

The dining hall has this trick where it feels enormous and cozy at the same time. We're seated at a long table with place settings for five courses. There aren't any centerpieces, giving everyone a perfect view of everyone else. In other words, there's no cover. Something as mundane as a candelabra might not be useful in a gunfight, but it can really make a difference in a mage fight. When you're slinging magic around, everything can be a weapon and everything can be a shield.

I am sitting uncomfortably next to Helga on my right and Liam on my left. Gabriela is across from me with Otto and Siobhan to her left and Tobias to her right. Amanda is at the head of the table. An empty seat is next to Helga.

Some weird etiquette rule that partners don't sit next to each other is what's separating Gabriela and Amanda, but it's the best arrangement under the circumstances. We're both sitting next to the biggest threats so if things go south we can go on the offensive right away.

Otherwise, the seating arrangements look like they're intended to make the guests engage in awkward small talk. Might as well get the awkward train going. I turn to Helga.

"Palm Springs. The Desert Oasis Hotel. Three nights in 1948. You wailed like a banshee." Helga's face drains of all color. She was pretty white to begin with, but this is a shade that would put a clown to shame.

"I don't know what you're talking about," she says, choking out each word. She takes a sip of wine and pulls herself together. "I've never been to Palm Springs."

"No? Huh. How about Catalina?"

"I've heard how that who—how Amanda's fiancé brought you back using Robert's corpse."

"Nice save," Gabriela says. Helga ignores her.

"If you have his memories," Helga says, "then try digging into them a little more and see what you find. There's nothing you can say that will hurt me more than he did."

That, I wasn't expecting. "I'll make a point of it," I say. Now I feel like an asshole. Then I remind myself that she, along with every other one of these fuckers, no matter how human they might act, would love nothing more than to see this room turn into a reenactment of the Red Wedding.

"I would love to hear that tale," Liam says. "She won't tell any of us. I understand it is très embarrassant. If you do dig that particular memory out, please regale us with it."

"Liam," Helga says, "I was so sorry to hear your wife wasn't going to join us. Also surprised you couldn't find some desperate twink to take her place for the long, lonely nights."

"Oh, Helga, dear, I wouldn't want to subject anyone to your shrieking fits in the middle of the night. Are you still seeing your dead husband walking down the halls with a pickaxe in his head? Or have you gotten past that little contretemps?"

"You tread dangerous waters, Uncle," Otto says. He's strung tighter than a bowstring, his knuckles white from grasping the table knife so hard.

"Now that's a story I'd like to hear," Gabriela says.

"Shut your hole, street meat," Otto says. The room goes deathly silent. A beat. Gabriela bursts out laughing.

"Oh my god, you're just so fucking adorable," she says. "And so bad at this game. Helga, honestly, did you teach him nothing?"

"Sadly," Helga says, smile all teeth, "he's a slow learner."

I lean over the table and stage-whisper so everyone can hear, "She's saying you're stupid." If he holds onto that knife any tighter either the metal or his fingers are going to break.

"I understand Hans is quite the protégé," Gabriela says. "A smart boy, that one."

"Speaking of," I say, "where is Hans?"

Huh. Otto's actually bending the metal of his knife. "You—"

Flatware chiming against glass. Amanda standing at the head of the table. She looks regal. Her certainty, her poise. She's in charge and she fucking knows it.

"Before we begin dinner I wanted to take a moment to remember my father. He would be so proud to see you all here. He really loved his family. And I love you, too. Thank you for coming. Thank you for staying. The decisions we make tonight will define the next decade for our family. To my father, and all that he has left behind." Glasses raised, everyone repeating the toast.

"And I would like to propose a toast," Liam says, standing with his glass, "to our new Head of House. May she guide us with wisdom for as long as she lives. Long life!"

I can tell that both of those toasts are massive fuck-yous, but I'm not entirely sure how. I'm missing context and important information.

Bigsby appears at the far end of the table and says, "May I serve the soup course, miss?"

"Thank you, Bigsby." Bowls of what looks like tomato soup appear in front of everyone. "And what is it we're having?"

"Roasted garlic and tomato bisque. There are no poisons, curses, hexes, or magic of any kind currently affecting the soup, the bowls, the cookware, the kitchen, or myself."

Gabriela and I share a glance. Uh-huh. Neither one of us buys that Bigsby is free and clear, but there's not a whole lot we can do about it right now besides accepting that Amanda has the problem under control.

It's kind of a moot point. As Amanda said, everyone is doing their own checks before eating. The room fills with dozens of little spells until we're all satisfied the food won't kill us.

"Thank you, Bigsby," Amanda says. "That will be all."

"Of course, madam." And like all the best butlers, he disappears.

And then the most cliché thing that could happen happens. The lights go out. There's not a shot, but there is a flare of magic. Somebody dies, but it doesn't feel right.

The lights come back on and Liam is face down in his bowl. A thick stream of pink gruel, blood and brain matter mixed, is pouring out his ears, thickening the soup. Helga leaps to her feet, eyes full of fury. She glares at all of us.

"Would it have fucking killed you to wait until after dinner?"

Chapter 20

The accusations kick off right away, flying around like cream pies in a silent movie. Screaming, finger pointing, death threats. "You murdered—" "How dare—" "You won't get—" "You fucking—" And so on.

"Pay me," Gabriela says, putting out her hand. I said nobody would die until the salad. She took the soup course. Neither of us is standing to join the fray. Not like we can do anything about it, and it's kind of fun to watch.

"I don't have my wallet on me."

"I know you're good for it."

Otto loses his cool and launches his soup bowl at Siobhan's head. Of course she stops it midair, soup and all, and slams it back in his face.

Helga, accusing Amanda of murdering Liam, turns around and sees Otto covered in red and screams that her son is dying. I, of course, helpfully point out that he's already died once and she should tack "again" onto the end of that sentence for clarity.

Jonathan's going on about "family law" and no one's listening, though he's making an awful keening noise at the same time, which Siobhan apparently takes exception to because she elbows him in the face and shatters his nose.

Gabriela and I are enjoying the show. I'm not particularly worried that the situation will get out of hand, by which I mean I don't expect the heavy artillery to come out. It's not likely anyone else will die, except maybe Jonathan. And if one of the family gets knocked off by another, that's two we can scratch off our list.

"Can you pass the butter?" Gabriela says, breaking a dinner roll in half. I slide it across to her. She moves her head to the left a couple of inches and a knife sails from behind her through the space where her head had been. I catch the blade in midair with a spell and send it up to stick into the ceiling.

"I'm surprised they didn't last longer," I say. "They seemed to enjoy sniping at each other so much." A basket of rolls sails overhead and I snatch a couple with a spell as it goes by.

"That's because you're an optimist," she says.

"That's me," I say. "Sunshine and unicorns. Didn't get a chance to say this earlier. You look really nice."

"Thanks," she says. "You don't look half bad yourself."

"Give it time." I can't see Tobias anywhere. I peek under the table and he's curled into a ball, his arms wrapped around his knees. He's slowly rocking back and forth. That doesn't look good.

"Hey, kid." Nothing. "Tobias." He looks up at me but there's nobody home. I snap my fingers at him a couple of times. No change. Gabriela pokes her head under the table to see what's going on.

"Oh shit," she says. "Toby? Toby, this is Gabriela. We played cards last night. Do you remember me?" He swivels his head toward her and a little light comes back into his eyes.

"I think he's in the safest place he could be right now," I say.

"Yeah. Hey, Toby? Sit tight, okay? The noise will be over soon. We'll make sure you're okay."

I lift my head from under the table and almost take a spear through my face. I have no idea where anybody got a spear, but then there's a gingerbread house in the arboretum, so the fuck do I know?

"What's the kid's deal, anyway?" I say.

"He's terrified and abused. He doesn't look it, but he's nineteen. I think he's been starved for at least part of his life. Definitely beaten."

"Well, I don't feel so bad about Hans now."

"You felt bad about Hans?"

"Okay, I feel even better about Hans. Sort of an additional rosy glow of satisfaction."

Otto slams Jonathan against the table next to me. He has the lawyer in a headlock, doing a pretty solid job of strangling him. Helga and Siobhan are trading punches, and Amanda has given up and sat back down. She raises her wineglass to us, then downs it in one gulp. It refills on its own.

"How you doing over there?" I say.

"Fantastic," she says. "I honestly thought they'd at least make it to the salad."

"See," I say, "she thought that would happen, too."

"Yeah, but it didn't," Gabriela says. "You still owe me."

"You're taking bets on my family killing each other?" Amanda says, appalled. "And you didn't cut me in? I thought we were friends."

"Speaking of, do you need us to do anything about this?"

"Not unless you want to join the fray. It'll burn itself out in a few minutes."

"No one seems particularly upset that Liam is dead," Gabriela says.

"Nobody liked him," Amanda says. "But he's a good excuse to start whaling on each other. Like all the best families do." She drains her wineglass again, and it fills back up.

"How come my wineglass doesn't do that?" Gabriela says.

"Because I'm special," Amanda says. A shadowy figure appears behind her wielding a sword. It brings the blade down but disappears before it gets anywhere close to her head.

"Spectral killers," I say. "I didn't know anybody did those anymore."

"Jonathan. He doesn't have a lot of imagination. I suppose I should end this." She empties her ever-full glass. "After one more drink."

Otto has lost his grip on Jonathan. I can't see the lawyer anywhere and neither, it seems, can Otto, because Jonathan gets behind him with a beer stein and slams it across the back of his head. It doesn't do what he's expecting, unless he's expecting it to do nothing but piss Otto off.

"Twenty says Otto takes him down," Amanda yells from the head of the table.

"I don't take sucker bets," I say.

"Spoilsport." Otto bounces Jonathan's head off the table and throws him just as Amanda stands up and says, in a voice like thunder, "Enough."

Everyone freezes. Literally freezes. Complete standstill. Even Jonathan stops his Otto-powered trip across the room, hanging in space.

"The fuck is wrong with you people?" Amanda says. "I'm the second youngest person here by decades and you're the ones acting like children." She gets out of her chair and walks around the room.

"Cards on the table," she says. "You're not all dead because I'm not suicidal. Otherwise I'd just fill this whole fucking place with lava and be done with it. I hate you. You hate me. We all hate each other. Hooray for us." She circles the table, looking into the eyes of her remaining family members.

"Take ten seconds and actually think about what just happened. Think about Liam. Think about my father. Do you get it yet? Do you see how bad this is?"

Amanda snaps her fingers and lets them go. Jonathan continues his flight into the wall, bouncing off it and crashing to the floor.

"Young lady—" Helga starts, but stops at the look on Amanda's face.

"I am the head of this house," Amanda says, "and the head of this

family. If you call me 'young lady' again I will throw you into a fucking hole and forget about you. Do you understand me?"

"I—"

"Do you understand me?" The sheer force of Amanda's personality is like a blowtorch burning anything it's pointed at.

"Yes," Helga says, voice tight. Her face is red, from humiliation or
fury I'm not sure. Otto glares at Amanda but looks away as she wins
the staring contest.

"Think," Amanda says. "Somebody either evaded every single one of
us and killed two of the most powerful mages on the continent, or . . ."

Helga's face slides from rage through confusion over to understanding and finally lands on panic. "Oh my god."

"What are you talking about?" Otto says.

"One of us has learned how to murder the rest of us without triggering the curse," Siobhan says, and then adds, "you twat."

"If it was just my father," Amanda says, "we could chalk that up to
a one-time thing. But my father and Liam? No."

"Hans," Helga says. "He's not here. My god, is it Hans?"

"It's not Hans," I say. You can't say that Helga's slow on the uptake
when she's not consumed with rage. Her eyes narrow into slits.

"What did you do to my son?"

"Ask Otto. I used his playbook for most of it. And his cattle prod."

"I—I don't know what you're talking about," Otto says.

"Seriously? Hey, nobody's gonna call you out for trying to kill me.
I bring it out in people. Yes, I killed Hans. The fuck did you think was
gonna happen?"

"Oh, this is good," Siobhan says.

"Where is your brother?" Helga says.

"How should I know?" Otto says.

"He's hanging from a meat hook with a cattle prod rammed through
his eye socket into the back of his brain inside a gingerbread house in
the middle of the arboretum." Which is a combination of words I don't
think anyone's ever said before.

"We will meet in two hours in the study," Amanda says. "We will
finish the business of the conclave and then you will all get the fuck
out of my house. Bigsby, please take them to another dining room and
make sure they get dinner."

"Right away, ma'am," Bigsby says, appearing at Amanda's elbow.

"Now hold on one—" Helga starts, and then she and the rest of the
family are gone.

"That went better than I expected," Amanda says. "Last time an entire wing of the mansion was reduced to rubble and three people were buried for an hour and a half."

"Night's still young," I say. "Shouldn't Bigsby have tried to stop the brawl?"

"I told him not to interfere," Amanda says. "Unless someone went after Toby. He's been through enough. I wanted to see what would happen."

"You didn't send Toby with the rest of them, did you?" Gabriela says.

"God, no. He's back in his room. Hopefully he'll take the Xanax I told Bigsby to give him."

"Good. He's . . . he's not going to be okay after this."

"If I can convince him to stay, we'll work on that," Amanda says. She looks down at Liam's body. The pink slurry that's leaked out of every hole in his head has congealed into a sort of rubbery paste.

"What the hell happened?" she says.

"Well, that's complicated," I say.

"Is this good complicated or bad complicated?" Gabriela says.

"Two people died complicated."

"Come again?"

"When Liam died, I felt it. Only his death didn't feel right. It felt disjointed somehow. I didn't realize what was wrong until just now. It wasn't one death, it was two simultaneous deaths."

"Are you sure it wasn't something else?" Gabriela says. "You notice nobody else is dead."

"Who's the fucking necromancer here? Yes, I'm sure. There was a lot of power going through the room when Liam died. Even with all his defenses, it was a lot to throw into turning his brain into a slushie. I think somebody isn't who they say they are."

"Could it be Liam?"

"I think it's absolutely Liam," I say.

"What do you mean?" Amanda says.

"Liam killed himself," Gabriela says, "didn't he? He sent his soul into someone else, killing them in the process."

"Pretty sure, yeah. I think he might have had some help doing it."

"How so?" Amanda says.

"The other night I ran into Liam after the fight," I say. "He mentioned that he'd been in Vegas a while back and my name kept popping up. It was just after the last conclave."

"Did you do something in Vegas that didn't stay in Vegas?" Gabriela says.

"You ever hear about the Las Vegas Oracle?"

"You're fucking kidding me," Gabriela says. "That thing's real?"

"As a heart attack."

"I'm missing something," Amanda says.

"It's an artifact," Gabriela says. "You've heard of the Oracle of Delphi? This is the same kind of thing. Ask it a question and it'll give you the truth. Like a Magic 8-Ball."

"Jimmy Freeburg," I say.

"Sorry?"

"That's his name."

"I'm not sure which disturbs me more," Gabriela says, "that the Oracle has a name, that it's Jimmy, or that you know it."

"Oh, then you're gonna love this," I say. "So, I'm in Vegas twenty-five, maybe thirty years ago. Connected with a couple who had a medieval spell book to create, surprise, an oracle. Only they can't understand it because it turns out it's a necromancy ritual."

"Don't tell me you created the Las Vegas Oracle," Gabriela says.

"Okay," I say. "I won't tell you I created the Las Vegas Oracle."

"If it were anyone else, I'd call bullshit. But how is it necromancy? I mean, you talk to the dead, but that's not the same thing an oracle's supposed to be able to do."

"It makes sense if the idea is to cut somebody's head off then shove a pissed-off demon that can see into the future into it and trap both souls inside." I give them a second to digest that.

"Anyway," I say, "I wasn't gonna do it, but I kinda screwed something up and then I had to. It got complicated. Lot of backstabbing, double-crosses, shit like that."

"Where does your friend come in?" Amanda says.

"First off, Jimmy and I were never friends. We were roommates. He caught wind of what I was doing. The spray-painted pentagram in the middle of the apartment and the eight-foot-tall smoke monster inside it were kind of a tip-off. I tell him what I need to do, he volunteers."

"He volunteered?" Amanda says. "To have his head cut off."

"He was dying," I say. "Cancer. Less worried about the cancer than what might happen to him after. Grew up Catholic, or something. Figured he was going to Hell." Which is the most surefire way to end up there, by the way.

"And you think Liam talked to him? It?" Amanda says. "Sometimes I hate pronouns."

"If my name came up in Vegas it would have been about that. Or a stripper named Wanda, but probably about that. Maybe Liam went to get some information on the future he could use, I don't really know."

"Is that how the Oracle works?" Amanda says.

"Not quite," I say. "I didn't stick around long enough to see it in action but I've done some digging over the years. It doesn't really see the future so much as it sees all the futures. It can pick the one it wants and make it happen."

"That's terrifying," Gabriela says.

"But not as impressive as it sounds," I say. "From what I understand, it can influence events but not change reality. By, say, telling Liam ten years ago about the soul-ejection spell and letting everything else roll out from that. There are a couple things I don't understand, though."

"Why did Liam tell you?" Gabriela says.

"That's one, yeah. Liam doesn't strike me as somebody who does anything without a reason."

"He's not," Amanda says. "If he told you, he wanted you to know."

"What's the other thing?" Gabriela says.

"What does Jimmy get out of it? The Oracle isn't some fortune telling arcade booth where you pop in a dime and get a prediction. He wants something and I'd be surprised if it didn't have something to do with all this."

"That seems really convoluted," Amanda says. "It sounds like something Liam would do, yeah, but it'd still be easier if he'd just killed me. If I die, he's the next in line."

"Not a lot of this makes sense to me," I say. "We're missing a lot. I think figuring out who else died will fill in some blanks."

"There's no way for you to tell?"

"I'll feel a death," I say, "but I can't necessarily tell who it is and I only have a rough idea where it happened. All I know is that two people died in this room at the same time and neither of them left a ghost."

"Who wasn't acting right?" Gabriela says.

"They all want each other dead," Amanda says. "A brawl isn't out of character."

"Otto," I say. "When Helga asked me what I did to Hans and I punted it over to him he seemed genuinely confused. There was no reason for him to lie about that."

"That did seem a little weird," Gabriela says.

"Or it was just Otto being Otto," Amanda says. "He really is the stupidest person in our family. But I see your point. I say we talk to him."

"How do you want to do it?" I say. "Whether it's really Otto or somebody else in Otto's body, he's not going down without a fight."

"There are mage manacles in the study," Amanda says.

"Odd place for those, don't you think?" I say.

"Don't kinkshame," Gabriela says.

"I'd rather not talk about it if that's okay," Amanda says.

"How do we get Otto in there?" I say.

"Bigsby," Amanda says. "He can't hurt Otto, but he can move him. We'll have to get the manacles on him, though."

"Get him in the study, cut off his ability to cast, ask pointed questions," I say. "I like it. Though I kinda hope it's not him. I was looking forward to killing him again."

"If it turns out that Otto is still Otto, kill him with my blessing." Amanda takes a step toward the door and freezes.

"What's wrong?" Gabriela says.

"I can't feel the house."

"Come again?"

"The house feels like an extension of myself. Like an arm. That's how I control it. It feels numb. It—"

The room explodes into fractals, twisting into a spiral as the walls multiply and doors wink in and out of existence. A wall appears blocking Amanda from Gabriela and me. Gravity shifts. I fly one way, Gabriela the other. I land hard on what looks like a wall, but could just as easily be what was the ceiling.

I roll out of the way of a new dining table that erupts out of my new floor and crashes through a set of French doors that pop out of existence the second it's through. I look up to see Gabriela on the ceiling.

"Are you okay?" Gabriela says. We both duck as a massive chandelier falls sideways between us. As soon as it gets close, the wall shoots away from it, extending into infinity. The chandelier disappears in the darkness.

The room calms down a little after that, though the dishes and flatware float in the air between us as if unsure which way to fall. I move out from under them in case they decide they like my gravity better.

"I'm good. How about you?"

"Nothing broken," she says. She kicks off her shoes. "Fucking heels. Dammit. We should have seen this coming." She's right. Somebody got into Bigsby, the hell made us think they wouldn't do the same to the rest of the estate?

"Yeah, but there's fuck all we can do about that right now. Is it my imagination or have all the doors disappeared?"

"Not your imagination," she says. "And the room's shrinking." She's right. Inch by inch we're getting closer to each other.

"Terrific," I say.

"Can you pull me up to you?" she says. I try a pull spell but it fizzles before I can get any purchase.

"Nothing. You still have that portal ring?" She shows me her left hand with the ring on it.

"We're telling people it's my engagement ring," she says.

"Nice. Okay, they should each be able to open a portal to where the other one is. I'm gonna give it a try." I trigger the ring.

A portal opens in the middle of space in front of me, but it doesn't lead to Gabriela. It's like standing between two mirrors. Portals lead to portals out into infinity. I shut it off.

"No joy," I say. "Can you blow a hole through one of the walls?"

"Going to try. You?"

"I don't really have anything good for that." I find the straight razor in my hand. Pretty sure I didn't pull it out of my pocket. "Or maybe I do. I'm going to see if this thing can do more than chop off heads. Seems to think it will."

"Is it talking to you?"

"Not yet. And it doesn't seem to care whether I kill people with it or shave with it. Just feels kind of . . . clingy."

"That's an improvement."

The Nazi pistol I destroyed when I collapsed a pocket dimension onto Darius was definitely conscious. I started getting images and feelings from it, but it hadn't yet talked to me, which I'd heard would be a bad sign.

"Here's hoping."

I feel a flare of magic and the room shudders, a silent explosion above me as Gabriela's spell goes off. The debris from the wall compacts into a ball and falls with a thud at her feet.

"I got mine," she says. "How'd you make out?"

I press the blade against the wall and push in. It splits the wall like it's soft cheese. I run it all the way in a circle and then use a push spell to shove the piece I've just cut. It falls to a hallway floor on the other side. I poke my head through and look up. Normal hallway ceiling. No sign of the huge hole Gabriela's opened up.

"So far so good. Mine leads to a hallway. Yours?"

"Looks like the arboretum. Can you reach the top edge of mine?" I try, but it's just out of reach. I jump and it's still just out of reach. I wait for it to get a couple inches closer in the shrinking room, and still it's just out of reach.

"Room doesn't want me to," I say.

"Shit." She pulls her cellphone out, of where I have no idea. If she's solved the problem of the lack of pockets in women's clothing, they'll build statues of her. "No signal."

"I guess we'll go our separate ways and hope for the best, then. Did you see anything when the wall came up between us and Amanda?"

"Yeah," she says. "Pool table. As far as I know there's only one in a lounge. Not that that really means anything now."

"Pool table. Got it. Hey, don't die," I say. "I like you."

"I know," she says with a grin and steps through the hole.

I wait until she's all the way through, curious what the house will do with it. As I suspected, the wall reforms, the debris taken out of it flying back into place. No way out but through.

I step into the hallway and, sure enough, when I look behind me the wall is gone, replaced with more hallway. It extends as far as I can see, disappearing into darkness in both directions. There are doors on either side of the hall spaced about ten feet apart with a pair of frosted glass globe lamps between each one.

I try a couple doors. They open fine, but there's nothing behind them. I could try cutting another hole through a wall, but I doubt that's going to get me any closer to Amanda.

"Whoever is doing this," I say, "just know you're an asshole."

"I disagree," Otto says, stepping out of one of the doors to face me. "They've saved me a lot of time."

Chapter 21

Otto looks rough. It wasn't the brawl. He was more than holding his own and when they finished there wasn't a hair out of place. Now he's got a black eye and a limp. His tuxedo jacket is gone, his shirt has a bloody tear in it, and his cravat is askew. I can see some of his stitches through a gap between it and his shirt.

"I see you and the house had words," I say. "Or was it one of your family? Or both?"

"My mother and I had a disagreement," Otto says. I can feel him pulling power into himself. Considering he's already got a lot, whatever he's planning isn't likely to be pleasant for me.

"Yeah? What about?" I draw power from the pool at the same time, less for the power itself than to disguise a spell that should be small enough that he won't notice it. I'm not great at small-scale magic, but he's probably expecting me to throw something big at him so I might as well act the part.

"She thought we should simply leave Amanda be. Said she was sick of us all trying to murder each other." We're already fighting each other to pull in power. With all the magic going around this place I'm not surprised to feel the well running dry.

"Imagine. I can see how you wouldn't be okay with that. Guess old age has made her soft. Not so soft that she didn't kick your ass."

"I let her live," he says, clenching his hands. I've clearly touched a nerve.

"I would hope so. Otherwise your head would have popped off already, and we wouldn't want that to happen a second time."

He forces himself to calm down. "You know, I would have won our fight if you hadn't cheated," he says.

I can't help but laugh. "Bit of a non-sequitur, but I'll run with it. That wasn't cheating. I didn't leave the Pit. And the razor was already there before the fight."

If this is Liam in Otto's body, then this is a trap. Otto I can take no problem. It won't be fun, but I know it's doable. But I have no doubt that Liam could kick seven different shades of shit out me. If it's the first, I fight. If it's the second, I run.

"Before we get started," I say, "you should probably know that Hans was screaming for his life when I killed him. I used that, the fuck is it called? It's like a cattle prod."

"A picana," he says through clenched teeth. Yep, that's Otto. I can feel him drawing power more quickly. Now he's really pissed off. I pump up my own spell just a little and get ready for whatever he's planning.

Which turns out to be a huge lightning storm in the hallway. Clouds rush in overhead hiding the ceiling. Rain pours down like it's coming from a bucket. And then there's the lightning.

It happens so quickly I hardly get my shield up in time, shaping it into a sphere around me. As it is, a flicker of electricity burns through my body and I feel like I've been run through with a hot poker.

Outside the shield, lightning is dancing through the hallway, charring everything into charcoal briquette for twenty feet around me. Otto keeps it going for longer than I thought possible and I can feel my shield weakening. The second it falls, I'm toast. I get ready to slide to the ghost side, but then the storm abates.

I drop my shield, ready to bolt at a moment's notice if it looks like it's going to storm again. If I do, though, the spell I've already got working will fizzle. I don't want to lose it and I don't want to tip my hand.

Otto's not ready to throw anything else at me. Nothing big, at least. We're both exhausted from this round of the fight. He's holding himself up against the wall, while I'm in the middle of a ruin charred black except for the circle around me where the shield stayed up. Jesus fuck, he put a lot into that one.

"Kinda shot your wad there, didn't ya?" I say.

"I did," he says, drawing a gun from a holster at the small of his back. "But so did you."

Shit. I fling open the closest door and duck behind it. Three shots. They go high and through the solid-oak, two-inch-thick door, the bullets punching through just over my head. I try to fire off the spell I've been building, but another shot grazes my arm and I lose my concentration. Fortunately not enough to completely lose the thread, but enough so I need at least a few more seconds. I stand up, flatten myself against the wall. Two more shots right through where I'd been crouching.

"You know, Otto, you may be right. You might have won that fight."

I bolt to the door behind me and throw that open as well. Five shots go through the first door and crack the wood of the second where they hit.

The Sig's back in my room and the derringer would be useless. That's the problem with evening wear, good firepower ruins the lines. Even if I did have them, I'm not sure it'd be an improvement. Just because Otto's using a gun doesn't mean he's completely out of magic. I also don't know how quickly he can recharge.

The spell I'm pulling together, though, should do just fine. He could very well be buying himself time. If he is, then he's buying me time too.

"I'm glad to hear you say that." I can hear him changing clips, footsteps moving closer.

"If you hadn't been kicking the shit out of me," I say, "I never would have had to use the razor. But then again, all I really needed to do was outlast you. Flashy spells like you were throwing can really drain a guy's battery. You should maybe go small next time."

Another shot slams into the door and almost penetrates. A little more and it would have taken my nose off. I almost lose the thread of the spell again but manage to hang onto it. I'm usually a blunt-force-trauma sort of guy. This spell's a lot more scalpel than it is sledge-hammer and it's taking me longer than I'd like to get it together.

Now it's his turn to laugh. "They seemed to work just fine a couple minutes ago. Battles are won through power, Carter. Always power. I wouldn't expect you to understand that. You play with corpses and ghosts. Small magic for a small-minded man."

I move backward to a third door. He gets close enough to start punching rounds through the last one. He's going to figure out I'm not there in a second. He's stupid, but he's not that stupid.

"Sounds like something a guy who reads philosophy and doesn't understand it would say. That might work in the Pit, but this little lover's spat we're having now? I dunno." I can hear him getting closer. If he just comes at me the only chance I have is trying to get the gun or at least knock it out of the way. I might have the razor but he has range. That's never a good bet.

"What could some infantile cantrip do to a battle?" he says. "Are you going to make foam balls disappear in a cup? Pull a rabbit out of a hat?" The final threads of my spell come together. I step out from behind the door.

"I was thinking more like this," I say, and pop his stitches.

They're not what's holding his head on, that's magic, but they are keeping the skin closed, flesh pinched together, all those blood vessels intact.

The wound opens up like a zipper. Blood spurts out from all around his neck like a fountain, meat behind it tearing apart. Blood I can work with. I grab hold of the fountain with the last of my power and pull, drawing the blood directly out of his body to paint the walls on either side of him.

He drops his gun and clutches at his neck, trying to put himself back together, stop the flow. As I pull more blood, the wound rips deeper through the meat of his neck.

My energy's spent. His blood flows to a trickle and he falls to all fours in a puddle soaked into the rug. He can barely hold himself up. He breathes in quick gasps, his body trying to get oxygen to blood that isn't there, the air passing through his torn-open throat as a thin whistle. I pick up the gun.

"You don't have long," I say. "It hurts, I know, what with your head barely hanging on. But pretty soon you'll stop feeling much of anything. After the shit you pulled, I'd love to spend a few minutes and watch you bleed out. I just don't have the time."

I kick his head like a soccer ball and it tears loose from the final scraps of meat holding it on. It bounces a couple of times and rolls down the hall. Huh. I was hoping to get a little more air on it.

I pick up his gun, a compact Glock G19 with half a magazine left. Armed is better than not. Now, how the fuck do I get out of here? Doors as far as the eye can see. I start opening them, looking for non-existent rooms. I stop checking after I lose count. They're all the same. Blank walls behind every one. The hall is dead silent, no sound but my footsteps and the turning of doorknobs.

Fuck it. I pull out the straight razor and put the blade against the blank wall behind a door. No idea if there's anything there, but this is bullshit.

Then I hear the crying. It's muffled, coming from ahead of me. I creep up on it, trying to pinpoint it. It's louder behind one of the doors. I open it to another blank wall, but the sound is definitely coming from behind it.

I press the razor against the wall and start to cut. The crying turns to screaming. I make a quick cut across and push out the small section so I can see on the other side.

It's one of the bedrooms. Tobias is sitting, holding his knees tight like he's trying to squeeze himself into as small a space as possible. I don't see anyone else in there.

"Tobias. It's Eric. We haven't actually met. I'm going to cut the hole bigger so I can get you out of there." Or me in there. Whichever turns out to be a better idea. Just as I'm finishing the cut I hear a crash inside the bedroom. I shove the cut-out section of wall to the floor, razor in one hand, gun in the other.

Gabriela steps through a hole she's blown through the wall across from me. She has her machete in hand, ready to throw, but stops when she sees it's me. It disappears from her hand and she runs over to Tobias.

"Toby? It's Gabriela. You know me. You're safe now." She puts her hand on his shoulder and he shrieks, scrambling away to shove himself into a corner.

"I think maybe we need to give him a minute," I say. He's shaking so hard it looks like he's having a seizure. Gabriela backs away. Soon the screams turn into whimpering.

"We need to get him out of here," she says.

"Got any ideas? I'm fresh out. The hallway out there doesn't end. Where did you come from?"

"I got through the arboretum and stepped into a bedroom. Blasted through a wall into another bedroom. Nothing but fucking bedrooms. Kept going and then I heard Toby. Shit, are you bleeding?"

"What? Oh. No, I've stopped it. Most of this blood isn't even mine. I ran into Otto. I can say for a fact he wasn't Liam."

"That leaves Helga, Siobhan, or Jonathan."

"Or . . ." I nod toward Tobias.

"You're kidding, right? Look at him. He's pissed his pants, for fuck sake. Do you think Liam would do that? It's Helga or Siobhan."

She's got a point. Maybe I'm just being paranoid. I'm still a little jumpy after that fight with Otto. I feel drained and hollowed out, the aftermath of a massive adrenaline spike and pushing through a shit-ton of magic. I can tell I'm not back at full strength.

I could sleep for a week. Which I might do when this whole thing is over. I'm about to sit on the bed, then think better of it. It'd be way too easy to pass out right now. Dammit, I don't have any coke or Adderall on me.

"Fight was that bad?" Gabriela says, looking at my hand. It's shaking. She's probably been here a few times herself.

"Touch and go there for a bit," I say. "But I made sure nobody'll be stitching his head back on."

"Did you notice a big dip in the pool a little while ago?" she says.

"That was us. Scraping the bottom of the barrel. Where the hell does it come from? I mean, this place is all self-contained, right?"

"Have to ask Amanda when we find her."

"Is she okay?" Tobias asks. His voice doesn't have a tremor so much as a minor quake. He stands up, realizes he's pissed himself, and starts crying again.

"Hey now," Gabriela says. She opens what should be the bathroom door. Surprisingly, it actually is. "How about you go get cleaned up? Then we'll all go find Amanda together. Got some clean clothes?"

Tobias nods. He's slow, in a daze, but he manages to get something to change into from the dresser. He steps into the bathroom and looks back at us, right on the edge of another panic attack.

"We'll be right here," I say. "Not going anywhere." He holds our gaze for a moment before nodding and closing the door. A moment later the shower goes on.

Can't blame him for not believing me. Probably count the number of adults in his life who haven't turned out to be abusive monsters on one hand.

"Are you sure this isn't the safest place for him?" I say. "He tags along, we're putting him in the line of fire."

"I know. But we can't leave him here."

"He's going to get even more traumatized if he finds himself in the middle of a fight with his grandmother."

"That could work in our favor," she says. "Do you think Helga will fire on her own grandson?"

"No, but not because she's his grandmother, because she's not going to risk blowing her own head up if he takes a stray shot. She'll be aiming at us extra carefully."

"Let's see what he wants to do," Gabriela says. "Besides, it's a moot point if we can't get out of here. We just start tearing through walls?"

"It would help if we knew which way to—oh, shit, of course." I pull the ghost tracker out of my jacket pocket and flip it open. "I was able to lock onto Attila's soul with this. That'll give us a reference— hang on."

"I think it's broken," she says. The compass needle is swinging between two different points, and the distance gauge is spinning wildly.

"No, I don't think it is," I say. I concentrate on finding Attila and the needle swings to one point. I click the button on the side locking it in place. Distance is still screwed up, but when you can't even trust the gravity, that'd be asking a lot.

"This is Attila," I say. I hit the button and focus on Liam. The needle swings to another point and I hit it again, locking it in place. "This one's got to be Liam. I don't know how this thing works, but when I concentrate on a particular ghost it locks on. Seems to work with Attila's soul, too. The magic Liam's using to inhabit a body must work the same way."

"Uh, Eric," Gabriela says.

I draw the gun when I see where it's pointed, directly at the bathroom door. "Still think he's an innocent kid?"

"That doesn't tell us anything," Gabriela says. "But . . ." Her machete appears in her hand. The shower's still running. If I'm lucky, all I do is embarrass a teenager and cause more life-scarring trauma. Gun at the ready, I reach over and turn the knob.

I feel a huge flare of magic. Tobias screams and the entire bathroom wall blows out, throwing me across the room and slamming me into the far wall. I black out for a second. When I come to, Gabriela is hauling chunks of wall off of me. She's covered in plaster dust. I get some leverage and help push the last of the large pieces off, pain ripping through the right side of my chest and ringing through my head. I think one of my ribs is cracked and I probably have a concussion.

"The fuck happened?"

"Wall blew up," Gabriela says, helping me to my feet.

"Yeah, I caught that bit." I realize she's a little dazed too, and there's blood running down from a cut in her scalp. I stop the bleeding and lead her over to the bed, the only piece of furniture that hasn't been shredded into sawdust. If she hadn't been standing on the other side of it when the wall blew, Gabriela would be just as bad off as me. Neither of us is in very good shape.

"How many fingers?" I hold up my hand with two fingers raised.

"Two," she says. "But they keep wobbling."

Better than it could be but still not great. I can see small cuts on her arms and neck and a splinter about half an inch long embedded in her bicep. I pull that out and clot all the wounds. It's not much, but it's all I can think to do.

"Tobias?"

She shakes her head, which makes her dizzy and a little green so she stops. I limp over to the missing wall and look inside the bathroom. Turns out everything else is missing, too. The floor is a yawning pit I can't see the bottom of, just as the ceiling has been blown out and I can't see a top. The other three walls are gone, revealing bedrooms just like this one. But no Tobias.

"Still think it's Toby?" Gabriela says, limping over to me and grabbing hold of my arm to keep herself steady.

"I don't not think it's Toby," I say. "What the hell is it with you and this kid? You're normally a lot more paranoid than this."

"I—Never mind," she says. "Let's just find a way out of here and get to Amanda."

"How's your head?"

"I've had worse. You?"

"I'm not dead, so yeah, I've had worse. Pretty sure I cracked a rib. Not a big deal. The gouge in my arm from Otto's bullet hurts more." If I don't take huge deep breaths the rib's okay. But the bullet wound feels like it's burning. They always do.

I look around the demolished room for the ghost tracker. I find it under a pile of plaster chunks and part of the door. It's badly dented. When I open it the needle's going even crazier than before.

"So, par for the course, then," she says.

"Normally I'd have at least two more concussions by now," I say, "so I'm ahead of the game. We'll need another way to navigate. Either this thing's busted or the Escher house is causing more problems." Fuck. If this doesn't work I'm not sure how we're going to find the other end of Attila's tether. Maybe I can fix it. I slide it into my pocket.

There's a wrenching noise all around us, like heavy wood reaching a breaking point. We both instinctively crouch, but fuck knows where it's coming from. We'll probably get eaten by some Lovecraftian monstrosity popping up through the floor.

The sound gets louder and louder and then there's a tremendous snap. The room spins, throwing both of us to the floor. It slides away from the pit that used to be the bathroom, the missing wall replaced by one with a window that looks down onto the lawn.

Another wall is flickering, a door appearing and disappearing on repeat. It finally solidifies and is thrown wide open.

I raise a shield around us. I'm too dizzy to shoot straight but I might be able to keep us alive long enough to do something.

"Oh, thank fuck," Amanda says, stepping into the room. "I was hoping you were in here." I drop the shield as she rushes over to us, eyeing the debris, the dust, both of us looking our best. "Where are you hurt?"

"Gabriela's got a concussion." I can see she's struggling to stay conscious. "Maybe worse than I thought. Me, I just got bruises and cuts."

Amanda places her hands gently on either side of Gabriela's head. I can feel a slow build-up of magic that peaks and then drops to nothing.

"How do you feel?"

"Better. Clearer. Thank you."

Amanda pulls Gabriela into a hug and kisses her, Gabriela leaning into it, her hands on the back of Amanda's head, fingers twined in her hair. Okay, then. I'd suggest they get a room, but we're already in one.

Chapter 22

"I thought I'd lost you," Amanda says, pulling away.

"Like I'd let that happen," Gabriela says.

"Speaking of, what did happen?" I say, though I'm not sure which "what" I'm asking about.

"The house went completely insane," she says. "I've only now regained control. I'm putting the rooms back together, but I don't know how long I'll be able to hold it. Liam's fighting me for it."

"What can we do?" I say. "I mean besides find the sonofabitch and kill him."

"You can't kill him," she says.

"I know," I say, "but a boy can dream. Can I beat the shit out of him until he tells us what he did with your dad?"

"That you can absolutely do. I can sense a couple people in the house, but I can't tell who."

"The bathroom swallowed Tobias," I say. "Or something. Either way he's gone."

"And he's really bad off," Gabriela says. "He's going to need a lot of therapy."

"Which one's closest?" I say before we can get derailed onto Tobias.

"Two rooms down," Amanda says. "I'll bring it here." A door appears in what was a blank wall. Gabriela and I press against the wall on either side of the door. I have five rounds left in the gun. If it takes more than five to kill something I've got bigger problems than lack of ammunition.

Gabriela points at herself and then the floor. I give her a thumbs up. She goes low, I go high. The door disappears. We both lean in, ready to kill whoever we have to, but nobody's waiting to ambush us.

Jonathan stands in the middle of the room with his hands in the air. "Please don't kill me," he says.

"Oh, for fuck sake," Gabriela says.

"Jonathan, where are the others?" Amanda says, stepping into the room.

"I don't know," he says. "The house went crazy and I got thrown in here. Look, I know what's going on. I can help you."

"Anybody mind if I kill him?" I say.

"Wait," Amanda says. "What do you mean, you know what's going on?" I lower my gun. But not by much.

"It's Liam. He's not dead. He's soul-jumped into someone else."

"Yeah, we got that already," I say, and go back to aiming at his head.

"Grab him and get him out of here," Amanda says. "I'm losing my grip on the house."

"I know whose body he's in," Jonathan says. "See, it's all about succession. If everyone—" Jonathan's eyes snap wide as a cavalry saber slides through his head. A twist, a yank, and the sword comes free through the top of his skull, ripping through bone and brain in a flash. Jonathan drops, most of the top of his head missing.

I fire off a round as Jonathan hits the floor, but I realize too late that there's not much point. The bullet hits Bigsby in the throat. He pauses a moment, then pulls out a handkerchief and starts to clean the saber.

Gabriela and I both have the same thought and together we grab Amanda and throw her out of the room. Gabriela follows and I start walking backward out the door, firing a couple of shots. They hit the center of Bigsby's forehead, blasting through the back of his skull, but he doesn't seem to notice.

I am really regretting Amanda's whole "make the door disappear" thing right about now. Not that it would help. If Liam's got control of Bigsby, we're screwed. I killed a corrupted one by cutting it up with the razor, but that was luck more than anything else.

"Plan?" I say.

"Gimme a second," Amanda says. Her eyes are closed and she's straining, her magic countered by Liam's own.

"Amanda?" Gabriela says. Bigsby calmly steps over Jonathan's corpse, still polishing the cavalry saber. Gabriela creates a shield to block the doorway, but it keeps flickering. I create a second shield in front of hers, but it's doing the same thing.

"I said give me a second." We're all tapped. There isn't enough magic around for her to draw on. We're not scraping the bottom of the barrel, we're digging a hole underneath it.

Her nose is bleeding and from the red tint at the corners of her eyes it's going to start running down her cheeks in a second. She's going to lose.

Help Gabriela. Help Amanda. I can do one or the other. Simple decision, really. If Amanda loses, we all lose. I stop trying to hold my shield, grab Amanda's hand, and hope I have enough juice to make the difference.

Magic can be shared. One way is to be part of a ritual, each mage taking on some aspect of the spell and adding their power to a collective. It's slow, measured, gradual.

The other way is to slam your magic hard and fast into the other mage's like a high-speed car crash. It's about as pleasant as it sounds.

I can't think of anything else to do. My magic hits hers with the force of a firehose. I shield her as much as I can from the negative effects and take the hit myself instead. Feedback screams at me and it feels like my head is going to explode.

I can feel the spell she's trying to do. It's like watching competitive macrame. She's weaving strands of magic, creating nets and tying knots into parts of the estate's magic while Liam does the same.

The extra boost is all she needs to overwhelm Liam's control of the house. I can hear a wrenching, tearing noise. Somebody's screaming. I think it's me. Or maybe it's all of us. The air pressure builds and builds and then, with a pop like thunder, it's all over. Amanda has the house under control and there's no way Liam is getting it back.

The remains of the power I gave Amanda rush back into me. Vertigo, gravity. Suddenly I'm on the floor. I can hear Amanda throwing up. My vision clears. Still dizzy, but the room we found Jonathan in is a wall and there's no sign of Bigsby.

Gabriela runs over to Amanda to check on her. Looks back at me, anger and worry clear on her face. "You're an idiot," she says.

"That's what I keep telling people," I say. "Am I bleeding?"

"When aren't you?" Gabriela says. She helps Amanda to her feet.

"You okay?" I say.

"Yes? I think? What the hell did you do?"

"Just gave you a jolt. Are we in danger of imminent death?"

"We're good," Amanda says. "I've got the house locked down. I've got Helga, Siobhan, and Tobias in the billiard room. They're not going anywhere."

"Can you tell which one of them is Liam?" I say.

"No. I—I need to take a break. Wash my face. Get myself together."

"Take as much time as you need," Gabriela says.

Amanda stops on her way to the bathroom to help me to my feet. "Thank you," she says. "I guess. That really sucked."

"For you and me both. Let's not do that ever again." She nods, dazed, and goes into the bathroom. The door clicks shut behind her.

I fall onto the bed, arms spread out, completely drained. Gabriela joins me, sitting cross-legged next to me.

"Are you okay?" she says.

"More or less," I say. "I'm worried about her, though. I don't think she's ever done that before. She'll be fine, but the next few hours will probably suck."

"You could have gotten both of you killed."

"She was fine," I say. "I took as much of the feedback as I could. Wouldn't have helped much if I gave her a jolt and couldn't keep the spell up."

"Don't do that again," Gabriela says. "Please."

"Please? You're not the type to say please. Are you—" Gabriela leans down, grabs the back of my head, and pulls me in for a kiss. Without thinking I wrap my arms around her, pulling her body down to mine. She pulls back, the same uncertainty on her face as when we kissed at the Ambassador.

I'm not letting this end the same way. I pull her back down onto me, lean into her. The kiss is harder this time, more urgent. She straddles me, her skin burning against my lips, my hands. Everything is a blur of heat and need and hunger. I pull back on her hair and she tightens her grip around me. She fumbles to unbutton my shirt while I press my teeth against her neck just under her jaw and slide my hand under her dress and up her back.

We don't have enough time. We'll never have enough time. We aren't the kind of people who get to have things like this for long. All we can do is grab it as it comes by and hold on tight because soon enough it'll all be ripped away. Nothing lasts and everything breaks. But right now we're here and for a little while, at least, nothing else matters.

A cough from the bathroom door. Amanda is standing there watching us, a bemused expression on her face.

"Can we go kick the shit out of my uncle now?"

———

We take the long way, stopping at my room so I can grab the Sig and the derringer. Otto's Glock is nice and all, but I've never been a fan of plastic guns.

Amanda doesn't want to take any chances. She's worried that now that the house is stable any change might give Liam a chance to take it back. I don't know how it works so I'll take her word for it.

She slows a bit while we're walking to the billiard room and Gabriela goes a little faster. It takes me a second to realize what's going on. I figure I might as well start the awkward conversation.

"So," I say. "You and Gabriela."

"So," she says back at me. "You and Gabriela."

"The other night I was ready to kill her," I say.

"She told me. How do you feel about her now?"

"I was a little caught off guard. But I liked it. Liked it a lot, actually."

Amanda snorts back a laugh. "I kinda noticed. Should I have not interrupted?"

"Depends on whether you wanted to see a floor show or not," I say. "How about you?"

"I've only known her a month. It's been a really intense month, but it's still only a month. We hooked up after the thing with Darius. I think we were all drained. And she thought you needed some space. One thing led to another and—"

"And now you're getting married?"

She laughs. Her smile eases the lines the tension in her face. "God, no. Marriage. Gah. We're . . . dating? I guess? I really don't know."

"People like us don't get to have normal lives," I say. "Not even normal for mages. Best we can do is grab happiness where we can and not let go. It'll get pried away from us eventually."

"I wish I could say I disagree. I'm not entirely sure how I feel about her. I like her. Obviously. The sex is great. Was that TMI?"

"I accidentally told my ex-girlfriend I was hoping to get back with that I got the car we were in off a guy I'd violently murdered in Texas. As awkward TMI situations go, I think I got you beat."

"Is this gonna be a problem?" Amanda says.

"Not for me," I say. "I don't even know what the hell's going on. How about you?"

"No," she says. "I don't think it will. I don't feel jealous. You?"

"I'm still coming to grips with being alive again. And honestly, I don't think it's up to us anyway."

"When this is all over, the three of us probably need to sit down and have a conversation."

"I think I'd rather have my eyes gouged out."

"I didn't say it was going to be a fun conversation," she says. "Just that we should have it. There are—"

"Political consequences," I say. I think back to the conversation we had back at the Nickel Diner. "If people lost their shit just because I was talking to you and really go nuts when Gabriela and I are just in the same room, they're gonna love this."

"Aren't mage politics fun?" she says.

"Oh, look, we're here," I say as we catch up with Gabriela waiting for us at the door. She looks a little nervous.

"Good talk?" she says.

"We're not telling," Amanda says.

Gabriela takes it in stride. "Do we have a plan?"

"Don't kill anybody," I say. "Just beat them until they're open to answering questions."

"How about we start with the questions," Amanda says. "Anybody makes a move, then we can beat them."

"I vote for the beating," Gabriela says. "I just want to get this over with." She's exhausted. We all are.

"Let's do it," Amanda says. She puts her hand on the door, but instead of opening it, she simply dissolves the entire wall.

Helga leaps up from her seat on a sofa, outrage plain on her face. Siobhan lifts her eyes from the billiard table to see what's happening and takes her shot without looking, knocking the 8-ball into a side pocket. Tobias, as expected, is rocking quietly in the corner with his arms around his legs.

"Has he always been this bad?" I say.

"Not when he first showed up," Gabriela says. "He's gotten worse with everything going on right now."

"How dare you keep us locked up like animals," Helga says, marching up to Amanda as if she's the concierge at a hotel that's not up to her standards.

"I don't think animals get a pool table and a full bar," Siobhan says. "I take it we're under suspicion for something, but I can't imagine it's Liam's murder. None of us liked him."

"He was my brother," Helga says, turning her anger on Siobhan, who simply rolls her eyes and starts to set up a new game.

"Yes, mine too, and you hated him more than anyone else did," Siobhan says.

"Liam wasn't murdered," Amanda says.

"Oh, now this has just gotten interesting," Siobhan says. She puts the pool cue down and hoists herself up to sit cross-legged on the table. "Should we make popcorn?"

"We all saw his body lying facedown in the soup," Helga says.

"Oh, he's dead," I say. "He just wasn't murdered. He committed suicide and shoved his soul into somebody else. They're dead and one of you isn't who you say you are."

"Ooh," Siobhan says. "Exciting."

"This is ridiculous," Helga says. "I demand—"

"Aunt Helga, if you don't shut up, Eric here will put a bullet through your kneecap, because I have asked him not to kill you."

"And I'll have fun doing it, too."

"We're going to find out who's who," Amanda says.

"How do you propose to do that?" Helga says. "Threats and torture?"

"Just a few simple questions," Amanda says. I find myself wishing Letitia were here. Handy when someone can tell if you're lying as soon as you open your mouth. We'd have had this wrapped up hours ago.

"How'd you feel when I cut off your kid's head at the fight?" I say.

There's something bothering me about this whole thing. That's been bothering me since I realized what Liam had done. Then I have it. The Baba Yaga.

"When I heard the next day I was appalled. But I wasn't there. Are you trying to catch me in a lie?"

I walk over to the pool table and pick up one of the balls, weigh it in my hand.

"Yes," I say, though not the way she's thinking. "How about you, Siobhan? Who'd you come here to kill?"

"Helga, of course," she says. "I told you that."

"You what?" Helga says.

"I think this is where you say 'How dare you' again," I say.

"You can't possibly be surprised," Siobhan says. "I've been trying to kill you for decades. And I know half the assassins who've come after me over the years have been yours, so don't deny it."

"Tobias," I say. "Catch." I hurl the billiard ball as hard as I can at the kid's head and add a push spell to it for good measure. If I'm wrong it'll punch through his skull and Amanda and Gabriela are gonna be pissed. The ball stops inches from his face, hanging in mid-air.

"Shit," he says.

When I faced off against the Baba Yaga, I was worried it would hop into one of the normals. A mage will fight, but a normal will crumple like a Coke can in an industrial press. It'd be instantaneous. If Liam had hit any of his other relatives, we would have known.

But if he hit the most vulnerable person in the room, the only one who had no magic, we'd never notice.

I open up on him with the Sig and jump behind the sofa. As expected, he stops all the bullets with a shield. Siobhan flips the
pool table at him, less to crush him and more for cover. Amanda calls
half a dozen iterations of Bigsby to surround him, all armed with cavalry sabers. Before they can so much as move, Liam disintegrates
them.

Gabriela slams her open palm onto the floor, a massive crack tearing through the hardwood and erupting directly beneath Liam. Hands
made of flames reach up through the fissure, but he's too fast. He's
levitating just out of reach.

"Liam?" Helga says. "You sonofabitch."

"Always a pleasure to see you, darling sister. Tell me, were you
distraught when I died?"

"You murdered my grandson," she says. Lightning bursts from her
fingers toward Liam, who sends out tendrils of his own energy. They're
both a match for each other, so who knows how this will end up. I
doubt I'm going to get another shot.

"Don't kill him," Amanda yells, throwing her own spells into the mix.

"Not sure that option's on the table anymore," I say. I run at Liam
and jump. My razor appears in my hand and I slash down when I get
close enough. It hits his defenses, so it doesn't take his arm off, but
leaves a long gash.

Liam howls in pain. He hits me hard with a push spell that throws
me into the wall behind him, and the wood cracks from the force. I
drop to the floor, wind knocked out of me.

He's distracted enough for Helga's attack to get through. He jerks
as the lightning hits him, but a moment later he pushes out, starting
to turn Helga's lightning back on her. She stops casting quickly, before
it can hit.

Thinking she's the greater threat, he ignores me and sends a lance
of green energy at her. She staggers. Her defenses hold, but he has her
pinned down under a barrage of fire. She's too occupied to get back in
the fight.

Gabriela and Amanda are attacking Liam from different angles.
Fire, lightning, wind, a glowing spectral tiger. I need to get them to
teach me that one. He's shunting everything aside. But he's still not
paying any attention to me. I get close enough to take a shot.

I raise the blade and suddenly I'm picked up and flung over to the
side of the room next to Siobhan. I'm pinned to the wall.

"What the fuck, Siobhan?"

"I'm sorry, Eric," she says. "But I can't let you do that. Once Helga's dead, I'll let you go and I'll even help." Of course. Siobhan can't kill her sister, but she can let Liam do it for her.

If Helga goes down, I don't know that all of us combined will be a match for Liam. But with Siobhan and me effectively out of the fight, there's no doubt we're going to lose.

"She dies, you and I hit Liam?"

"That's the deal," she says.

"Gabriela," I yell. She glances at me, sees me pinned against the wall. "Helga." She realizes what I'm saying right away, turns to Helga, and throws a spear of lightning straight through her head. Helga staggers back, sways, and falls over.

"There, she's dead. Happy?" I say.

"Ecstatic." Gabriela's hit on Helga has surprised Liam enough for Siobhan to make a move. She decides that the best weapon to throw at him is me.

I slam into him, knocking him to the floor. I'm about to take a swing with the razor when he shoves his palm against my chest and tries to shove my soul out of my body. The same spell he used on Attila, and similar to the one the psycho baby necromancer at Alice's tried to use on me, only a thousand times more sophisticated. His look of triumph turns to confusion when it doesn't work.

"Oh buddy, did you back the wrong horse." I grab hold of his soul and start pulling. It takes a second for him to realize what's happening. He panics and lashes out, a wave of energy hitting me like a truck and sending me flying toward Gabriela. I stop in midair and float to the floor.

"Gotcha," she says.

"Much obliged." I turn and see Liam running from his corner toward us. More specifically, toward Amanda. I jump for him, snagging his leg and bringing him down just as Gabriela moves to block him.

His fingers touch Gabriela before I can yank him away and I feel and see him do to her what he tried to do to me. I see her soul rocketing away from her body, attached by the glowing thread. Her body falls to the floor, dead.

I slam my head into Liam's face, breaking his nose. "Everyone out," I yell. I follow up the headbutt with a fist, bouncing his skull off the floor. Spells, gunfire, razors he was expecting, but me using his head like a carpet hammer wasn't on the list.

"What—"

"Get us out of here and freeze the room. We have to preserve the body." I'm still pounding Liam's face.

"Don't kill him."

"I'm not," I say. "But he needs to be unconscious." I don't want this sonofabitch in any shape to cast a goddamn thing.

"I'm sending you to the study. The mage manacles are next to the door."

"Manacles. Door. Got it." The room disappears and a study with a brick fireplace and dark wood wainscotting appears around me.

"You fuck," Liam says, voice thick through a busted nose and bloody, broken teeth. "I'll fucking kill—"

"Shut up." I hit him one more time and drag him over to the door where the manacles hang over a coat hook.

The moment I pick them up I can feel their effects. It's like grabbing burning ice, and magic is only barely registering for me. I slap them on his wrists. He screams and goes unconscious.

"Oh, now you pass out. Asshole."

———

Amanda appears a few minutes later. Alone.

"Where's Siobhan?"

"Stuck in a room until I can figure out what to do with her," Amanda says. "I don't like being used. If she hadn't pulled that shit with Helga, Gabriela wouldn't be—" She closes her eyes. "Is she dead?"

"She's in the same state your dad is," I say. "We're going to fix this."

I'm pissed off at Siobhan too, though I can understand why she did what she did. It was the perfect time to take Helga out. Her entire focus was on Liam. Any other time and she'd see an attack coming a mile away. I hate her for it, but I have to respect her for it, too.

"Have you figured out the spell?"

"Not entirely," I say, "but having Liam try to use it on me gave me a better idea of what it is. I can't reverse it until I know more, though."

"Then he'll tell us," Amanda says. She looks at Liam in the corner. One eye already swelling dark and purple, his nose like a ripe tomato, blood crusted on his face. His jaw looks a little out of line.

"Hang on," I say. "I've been thinking about this ever since you brought up how the powerful mages of your family were the only things keeping everyone in check and I think I've figured out what the hell happened here."

"I'm glad somebody knows," Amanda says. She walks over to a shelf and pulls down a decanter of whisky and two glasses. She brings it to a table between two chairs I hadn't noticed before. Christ, if I had to live in this house I'd go nuts. She pours us both a drink.

"Anybody who has the inheritance automatically has a target on their back," I say.

"Yeah, which is why none of this makes any sense," Amanda says. She sits and leans back, her eyes closed. She's beyond exhausted. "If I died the inheritance would go to the next in line, which is Liam. So why all this?"

"Because he'd have the same target on his back. But if all the mages here died, who would it go to?"

"Oh shit. All the really powerful mages in the family are here this weekend. He takes Tobias, we all kill each other, he gets the inheritance and there's nobody powerful enough to take him on."

"It's the only thing that makes any sense to me. I think there's something he either didn't count on or hoped nobody would notice, though. The same magic that makes him free of the curse takes away the protections, too. If you killed him, nothing would happen to you."

She laughs. "Oh, I wish I'd known that sooner," she says. "Not that I think I'd want to take that chance. Okay, maybe a little. Okay, that's the why, but what about the how?"

"How do you mean?"

"You know what Liam's knack is? Architecture. The shit he can do with a building is fucking nuts. He built a lot of this place. How he got control of it so easily."

"I see where you're going with this," I say. "Souls don't really fall under the architecture category. They're more my domain. But that doesn't mean he couldn't have been taught."

"Right," she says. "So who taught him? Your Magic 8-Ball friend?"

"I hope not," I say. I just had a thought, and if I'm right this whole situation just got a lot more complicated.

"Wake him up," I say. "Let's ask him."

Liam comes to, coughs up some blood, spits out a tooth. He looks up at us. "You got me. Bravo," he says. "I'd clap but I can't quite get my hands to work. Is this the study? Delightful. Could I have a drink? I'm parched."

"How about a piranha tank, instead," I say.

"Nicely super-villainish," he says.

"I like the classics," I say. "So, here's where things stand. I know what you did. I know how you did it. The whole kicking the soul out and tethering it to the body thing. My line of work, you pick up a few things about souls. I get it. Smart move. Flat-out killing Toby wasn't cool, but setting it up so you could kill any of your family and not have your head pop? Nicely done."

"Seeing as I'm somewhat indisposed at the moment, magically speaking, I don't see any reason to deny it," he says.

"Couple things, though. One, I can't reverse it."

"And you want me to tell you how?"

"Was kinda hoping, yeah," I say.

"And if I don't?"

"I beat the fuck out of you until you do."

"That's not going to work," he says. "That's the only currency I have in this negotiation. What's the incentive? You can't kill me."

"I can make you wish you were dead," I say.

"Oh, please. Amanda won't let you hurt me. Aren't I right, dear? Good, obedient Amanda. There's a good girl. Listen to your elders."

"I think you're talking about a different Amanda than the one I know," I say. I grab him by the collar, ready to pound on his face some more.

"Wait," Amanda says. "He's right, Eric. I won't let you hurt him."

"There," Liam says. "See? Now Amanda, be a dear and—"

His voice turns into a scream. Bloody bone grows out of his foot, tearing through his shoes like Play-Doh through a sieve. Long calcified tendrils curl and corkscrew back into his foot, up his leg, down into the floor. It looks like curled ribbon on a Christmas present. Very festive.

"I'm the one who's going to hurt you," Amanda says.

"You think this will break me? I won't tell you a goddamn thing," Liam says through clenched teeth.

"You killed my mother," Amanda says, "my father, and my lover. I have wanted to murder you for ten years. But instead, I'm going to hurt you." More shards rip through his leg, curling back onto themselves, encasing it in a bloody bone cage.

Amanda returns to her chair and picks up her glass, swirls it a bit before taking a drink. Liam's screams drop to whimpers, and then he sinks into unconsciousness. Amanda's spell reverses itself and the devastating growths tearing through his body recede until the only signs are tears in his clothing and pooled blood.

Liam jolts awake and immediately starts screaming. That goes on for a few minutes, until he seems to realize that he's not actually hurt anymore.

"You're not getting off that easily," Amanda says. "I can keep you conscious as I strip the skin from your body and turn your bones to glass." I can't imagine how much that must have hurt, but looking at

Liam on the floor shaking, drool running down his chin, I know I really don't want to find out.

Liam mumbles something I can't quite hear. I don't know if this is a trick and he's waiting for me to get close enough that he can bite my nose off, so instead of getting close I kick him and tell him to speak up.

"I don't know," he says, his voice cracking.

"Sorry," I say. "I didn't quite catch that. Amanda, did you hear him?"

"I didn't," she says. "I think he just needs a little more encouragement."

"No, I—" This time his skull grows spikes that rip through his eyeballs from the inside while his teeth drill their way out through his jaw. Blood and skin runs off his skull like wax. He's not even making a sound you could call screaming anymore. And just as quickly the gore is gone.

"You were saying?"

Liam looks up at me with newly restored eyes, and if he doesn't see a pair of goddamn devils in front of him we'll just have to try harder.

"I don't—" He catches Amanda narrowing her eyes at him. "*No.* Please. I'm telling the truth. It didn't tell me how to do that. Just how to cast the spell. Please." Bloody tears run down his cheeks.

"I kinda thought you might not know. That gets me to my next point," I say. "How's Jimmy doing?" Liam stares at me, dumbfounded.

"Who?"

"Jimmy Freeburg," I say. "You probably know him as the Las Vegas Oracle." Wide-eyed recognition on Liam's face. "There we go."

"The Oracle gave you the spell," Amanda says.

"And the plan, yes," he says. "But—how do you know?"

"You told me," I say. "Talking about how my name kept coming up in Vegas?" Then I get it and start laughing. I'm not sure I can stop. "Oh. Oh shit, you didn't know, did you."

"It was part of the payment," Liam says. "To tell you that if I saw you. It told me it wasn't related to this. It lied to me."

"No, he didn't," I say, wiping tears away. "You didn't know that the only thing I ever did in Vegas that people would talk about had to do with Jimmy. It didn't have anything to do with this, but it got me thinking and I drew the connection. He fucked you and you had no idea he was doing it."

But why? Spite? Jimmy—at least living, breathing human Jimmy— was too stupid for spite. The Oracle's a different matter, though. I go through events from the time Liam mentioned Vegas. Sonofabitch.

"My god, what a fucking asshole," I say.

"What?"

"Jimmy. He made all this happen. And he didn't have to do much. All he had to do was knock over the right dominos. Liam went to him and the Oracle gave him what he wanted, a way to knock out the family competition. He omitted a few details, but he told the truth. Then he had Liam drop a hint for me so I'd eventually figure it out."

"My dad? Gabriela? He arranged this?"

"Not all of it," I say. "He didn't have to. Otto was going to come at you anyway. The conclave was going to happen. Except—You said 'if.' To tell me if you saw me. Did he say that exact word?"

"Yes," Liam says. "I—I think so."

Oracles don't deal in 'if.' That suggests Jimmy didn't know whether I'd be here or not. I don't know what it means, but whatever it is, it can't be good.

"Is it important?" Amanda says.

"Maybe. Not sure. What I don't understand is why he—" And then it comes to me. With everything that's happened, Attila, Gabriela, Liam not knowing how to reverse the spell. "He's not done tipping over dominos."

"Sorry," Amanda says.

"You and I are invested," I say. "There's no way in hell we're going to give up until we find a solution for Gabriela and your dad. Liam doesn't have the information we need. So what do we need to do?"

"Find the Oracle," Amanda says.

"He wanted to make sure we would go looking. I don't know why, but for some reason Jimmy wants us to find him. But we'd need a reason to do it. So he gave us a couple of whoppers."

"This is insane," Amanda says. "He could have just called. Sent an email. Not all this shit."

"If he could, I think he would have. There's something that made this a better option, and he knew enough about it to get the ball rolling ten years ago. Whatever he needs, it has to do with you and I specifically."

"I'm going to kill him."

"I don't think you can," I say.

"I'll find a way."

"I can help," Liam says. Amanda doesn't so much as glance at him and his entire body turns inside out, organs rearranging themselves into a horror show. He can't scream with inverted lungs, so he just sort of twitches in place. Just as quickly he's back to normal. This time Amanda lets him pass out.

"What now?" Amanda says.

"I guess we go to Vegas. I hate Vegas."

"I'm sure Vegas feels the same way about you," Amanda says.

That's what I'm afraid of.